FROM AFRICANUS

FROM AFRICANUS

The Roman Empire, the Nika Riots and the Approaching Darkness

A NOVEL

MATTHEW JORDAN STORM

Copyright © 2011 Matthew Jordan Storm

ISBN 13: 9781466479821
ISBN 10: 1466479825

PRINTED IN THE UNITED STATES OF AMERICA

Second Edition

FOR NATALIA,
LOVE OF MY LIFE AND
MY ONE TRUE BELIEVER.

PREFACE

SINCE I FIRST clambered over stones in the Roman Forum as a boy I have been haunted by the image of an ancient light that flickers and fades, struggling to pierce encroaching darkness. The light in my vision represented the Roman Empire and the darkness was the aptly named Dark Ages, spread at the spear point of barbarian hordes until the light extinguished, to be revived centuries later by humanists of the Renaissance.

That story taught to students in the West is woefully incomplete. In fact, since the Middle Ages, Western historians, monarchs and church leaders have deliberately misled us, writing a monumentally important fact out of the history books. This missing history is so important that it is impossible to understand Western Civilization without first understanding this.

Rome did not fall in 476 CE when Romulus Augustulus, the last Roman Emperor of the West abdicated his throne to Odoacer the barbarian warlord.

In fact, Rome survived *one thousand years longer* until 1453 CE, on the banks of the Bosporus, in the ancient city of Byzantium (from which arose the misnomer, "Byzantine Empire"). Scant years before Columbus discovered the New World this Rome fell to the Ottoman Turks, releasing countless sparks of our ancient patrimony from its universities, libraries and monasteries — a priceless bequest that would provide the true catalyst for the Renaissance.

The *Legend of Africanus* trilogy is born of my passion for this neglected Rome to whom we owe an incalculable debt. And amongst the Emperors and Empresses that ruled in Constantinople, the new imperial capital, none deserve more praise than Justinian the Great, the man known as "The Last Roman" and his equally remarkable wife, the Empress Theodora. Justinian was painfully conscious of the "flickering light" referred to above, and he did his utmost to keep the darkness at bay.

Justinian died in 565CE, while the last Caesar, Constantine XI "Palaiologos" would die in 1465, nine hundred years later. Yet Justinian was very much the last Caesar of the ancient world. As this is no scholarly work, I do not speculate as to "why" the Western Roman Empire declined prior to Justinian's ascension, nor do I analyze the world-rending pressures that would forever change Rome after Justinian (I would warmly recommend "Justinian's Flea" by William Rosen for any interested in a brilliant and unconventional analysis of Rome's transition into the Dark Ages).

That said, it is worth repeating a few of the simple reasons why Justinian's life represents such a milestone in world history and why his controversial reign marks the end of the Ancient World. Justinian was the last Roman Emperor to speak Latin as his native tongue. He was the last Caesar to rule over a Roman Empire that included the city of Rome amongst its dominions (thanks to General Flavius Belisarius – another contender for the title of "Last Roman"). And while he lived, Rome remained '*The One*' - after him, she gradually became one amongst many. She would wax and wane over the next nine hundred years and for as long as there was a Caesar on the Bosporus she would influence the world in infinite ways large and small, but never again as she did under Justinian. The list of his accomplishments is vast, but for me these facts seem to dominate all others.

This is the second edition of *From Africanus,* an update that coincides with the publication of Volumes II and III of the series (*Avenging Africanus* and *Immortal Africanus* - both available on Amazon.com. The story of Justinian, Belisarius, Leo and Valentinian has continued to evolve in ways that I couldn't have imagined when I began this trilogy in 2005 and some changes to this first volume were necessary to keep pace. One would think that in a work of historical fiction there is little room for plot twists but I have been surprised by my protagonists - they have kept me on my toes for 10 years!

May they keep you, my readers, equally enchanted.

Most importantly, I hope that *From Africanus* and the books that follow are able to plant a spark of empathy for this forgotten world in your heart.

Matthew Jordan Storm – Miami Beach, Florida
August 2015

"Solomon, I have surpassed thee..."

JUSTINIAN THE GREAT
December 27, 537

TABLE OF CONTENTS

A Note On Places

FOLLOWING ARE SOME of the principle locations in the *Legend of Africanus* series, including their ancient place names along with their current, modern names. Please note (and accept my apologies for my inconsistency) that at times I use the Anglicized version of the original Latin name in these novels despite my best efforts.

Ancient Place	Modern Name	Modern Country
Aspis	Kalibia	Tunisia
Aelia Capitolina	Jerusalem	Israel
Africa		Libya & Tunisia
Antiochia	Antakya	Turkey
Beryus	Beirut	Lebanon
Britannia	Great Britain	UK
Carthage	Tunis	Tunisia
Colonia Claudia Ara Agrippinensium	Cologne	Germany
Constantinople	Istanbul	Turkey
Dara	Oguz	Turkey
Gaul		France
Genava	Geneva	Switzerland

Grasse	Sidi-Khalifa	Tunisia
Hispania		Spain
Isauria	Bozkir - Taurus Mountains	Turkey
Kaput Vada	Ras Kapadia	Tunisia
Lugdunum	Lyons	France
Lutetia Parisiorum	Paris	France
Melites	Malta	Malta
Mosa Trajectum	Maastricht	Netherlands
Neapolis	Naples	Italy
Palmyra		Syria
Panormus	Palermo	Italy
Promontorium Mercurii	Cap Bon	Tunisia
Syracusae	Syracuse	Italy
Thecla	Ma'Loula	Syria*

*This last location that appears in Volume III of this series (Immortal Africanus) deserves an additional footnote. This town in Syria is one of the last places in the world where ancient Aramaic is still spoken by one of the Middle East's oldest Christian communities and it was the location of a terrifying siege during the Syrian Civil War as described in the New York Times on September 10, 2013. The town's history is fascinating and its recent predicament equally tragic - I incorporated Thecla/Ma'Loula into this trilogy as a small tribute to the suffering so recently endured there.

A Note On People

THE VAST MAJORITY of characters in the *Legend of Africanus* series are actual historical personages. Following is a key of some of the principle, historical figures that appear in all three novels for quick reference. In the case of the "barbarians" that appear in subsequent volumes of the series, I thought that this key might be helpful given the similarity in so many of the Germanic names.

Group	Person	Note
Romans	Justinian I (Pietrus Sabbatius)	Roman Emperor (following Justin)
	Theodora	Augusta – Wife of Justinian
	Princess Juliana of the Anicii*	Daughter of Emperor Olybrius, granddaughter of Emperor Valentinian III
	Origenes	Cautious leader of the blue-blooded Senatorial cabal during the Nika Riots
	Hypatius, Pompeius and Probus	Heirs to the Anastasian royal line at outset of Nika (nephews of Emperor Anastasius)
	Narses	Master of the Domestics
	Anthemius of Tralles	Architect/Builder (Santa Sophia)

Procopius	General Belisarius' secretary and last great historian of the ancient world
Tribunian	Legal scholar and author of the Digests
Flavius Belisarius	Magister Militum, Autokrator, and last great Roman General
Antonina	Wife of the great general Belisarius
Mundus	Roman General that served under Belisarius at Dara and was instrumental in quelling Nika Riots, later killed in Dacia
Mundilus	Roman General that served under Belisarius most prominently during war against Goths (first at Dara), serving most honorably in siege at Mediolanum
Bessas	Roman General that served under Belisarius most prominently during war against Goths (first at Dara) and subsequently in Persia
John the Armenian	Roman General that served under Belisarius most prominently, honorably and tragically during Vandal War
John the Sanguinary	Roman General that served under Belisarius in Italy but swore allegiance to Narses

Goths	Constantinus	Roman General that served under Belisarius in Italy and who would betray Belisarius over 'dagger' incident
	Athalaric	Son of Amalasuntha
	Amalasuntha	Goth Queen – Daughter of Theodoric the Great
	Matasuintha	Daughter of Amalasuntha, Wife of Vitiges
	Theodad	Amalasuntha's Cousin, Goth King
	Vitiges	King, husband of Matasuintha, successor to Theodad
	Theodoric the Great	Goth Founding Father
Vandals	Gelimer	Vandal King, great grandson of Gaiseric
	Hilderic	Cousin of Gelimer, King prior to Gelimer, murdered by Gel.
	Gibasmund	Nephew of King Gelimer
	Gaiseric	Vandal King and Founding Father
	Ammatus - Tzazon	Vandal King Gelimer's two brothers

*I have taken a great liberty by including this extraordinary woman in the Legend of Africanus series. A fierce opponent of Justin, and Justinian in his early reign, she likely did not live to see the Nika Riots (though we don't *know for certain she is assumed to have died in 527/528). That said she was so accomplished in her own right, of such a remarkable pedigree and so representative of that blue-blooded Rome that resolutely opposed Justinian and the 'new men' of his cabinet that I could not resist including her herein. I ask the reader to forgive this little fudging of the chronology - it was worth it to have the esteemed Princess' voice in these novels. I trust that she would have appreciated five more years of life so that she might have participated more directly in the momentous events herein that rocked the Roman world and redefined its course for the next nine hundred years.*

A Note On Time

THE PRINCIPLE EVENTS in the *Legend of Africanus* series happened - I stretch, I take liberties common to fiction but this historical chronology is at the heart of the trilogy.

660 BCE - Byzantium founded by the Greeks

660 BCE - Romulus & Remus found Rome

202 BCE - Scipio Africanus defeats Hannibal at Zama

0 CE   - Augustus becomes first Roman Emperor

330 CE   - Byzantium rechristened "New Rome"

345 CE   - Theodosius, last Emperor to rule unified Empire, dies

450 CE   - Roman legions abandon Britannia

455 CE   - Roman legions abandon Gaul

460 CE   - Roman legions abandon Iberia

465 CE   - Roman legions abandon Italy

476 CE   - Augustulus Romulus deposed by Odoacer

483 CE   - Pietrus Sabbatius (Justinian "The Great") born

500 CE   - Justinian arrives in Constantinople

505 CE   - Belisarius born in Germane, Illyria

518 CE   - Emperor Anastasius dies

518 CE   - Justin, uncle to Justinian, crowned Emperor

526 CE   - Belisarius promoted to General

527 CE   - Emperor Justin dies. Emperor Justinian elevated

532 CE   - The Nika Riots erupt in Constantinople

MAPS

1) Justinian's Capital

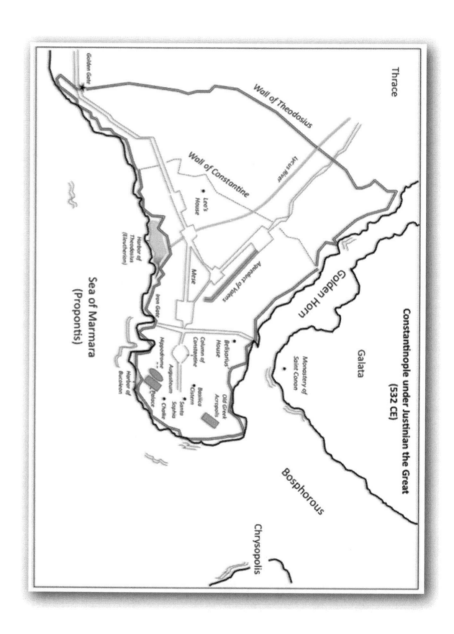

2) JUSTINIAN'S EMPIRE

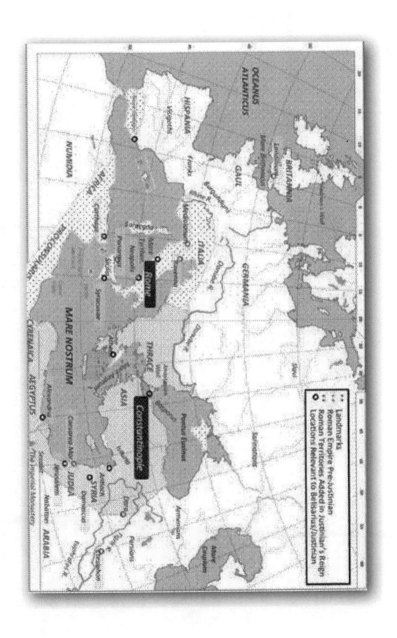

3) BARBARIAN MIGRATIONS

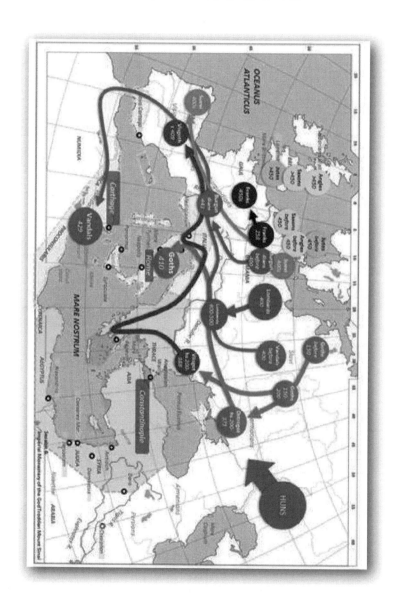

PART I: PROLOGUE – THE WORLD CALLS

...while cleverness is appropriate to rhetoric, and inventiveness to poetry, truth alone is appropriate to history.

- Procopius of Caesarea, Historian and private secretary to General Flavius Belisarius

My Mother's Son

My mother died giving me life. Her last breath was my first.
All that is shining and true in me springs from this. I entered and she exited, all at once, life's brilliance and brutality compressed in one magnificent, apocalyptic moment. I can tell and retell the story, I can find a thousand different adjectives and angles and still the thing eludes description.

What is it about life that makes the simple so profound, so decidedly indescribable? I have grappled with this question for more years than I care to count. Now closer to old than young I am no closer to an answer.

But then, that perhaps, is just what and who I am — profound and simple, blessed with my curses, made cheerful with my weight and ultimately, I pray to every god who is willing to listen, liberated by my fate. That is I, Valentinian Scipio Constans, son of Volerus, humble student of my Uncles, devoted servant of the Emperor Justinian, proud subject of Rome.

So let me start where I began, a tadpole birthed on the shores of the salty Adriatic, in the overgrown fishing village of Volerus. It was a simple place, made important by Roman refugees who had mixed happily with the native Greeks ever since we lost the West.

Volerus is equidistant from Athens and Constantinople but there is nothing cosmopolitan about her. She is and was a country girl, content to sell her wares to the city folk, to stash her money and to live her rambunctious Roman life. Awash in ocean trade, when I was a child she buzzed with her fisherman and sailors, her merchants and tailors. And, of course, she had her rope-makers and amongst them it must be said that my father, Claudius Constans, stood apart.

Lean and gnarled, like a piece of common driftwood, my father had been tested by the elements so many times that he had become one of them, like the wind or the rain. In his youth he must have been a handsome devil but life had rendered him something less and at the same time more. His bronze skin had long ago faded till it was stained in shadows. Sharp roving eyes were set deep into his brow where they measured a thread's width or a man's metal with the same facility. Needless to say there were many in Volerus that couldn't stand the power of that gaze. Accentuating his eyes was a craggy aquiline nose that preceded him wherever he went, testing for integrity.

This is the vision of my father that comes to me now. Claudius in the middle of his workshop, his whip-thin form arched over a cauldron of string, long muscles showing their inner workings. And of course, he would be barking to the sky, just a word or two, clipped and direct.

As you might imagine, Claudius' tongue was just as spare as his body and he never used two words where one sufficed. But don't think for a moment that our relationship suffered because of this. I would like to think that I knew every inch of my father's soul but that knowledge didn't come through conversation. Rather he expressed the deepest parts of him, his unlimited goodness and brusque elegance, through his silences. In all of my travels I have never known anyone else who used those moments between words so profoundly and well.

Like the driftwood that littered our shores there was nothing frail about my father. Life's randomness had left its mark on him but there were few substances on earth more strong, destined to endure.

Spend one day in the Army of Rome and you'll certainly notice that the officers are obsessed with bloodlines. The well-meaning nitwits fancy themselves thoroughbred horses. But if Rome's history has proven anything it's that blood doesn't make the man. If blood were what mattered most there would never have been a Justinian and the world in which we all live would look very different indeed, and this story would not be necessary.

It seems so incredibly obvious and yet, my peers through my years in the army would trip over each other to flaunt their lineage and their father's soft hands. The whole thing would be grotesque if it weren't so damned funny, to prove that this one or that one is a 'true' Roman, cast in the old mold, because of this, that or the other princely attribute.

The simple fact is that our Roman forebears were gruff and crude. They were men of the earth and they were endowed with the wisdom that comes from hammering the same nail, day after day for a lifetime.

When I first entered the army, my preening friends had naturally assumed that my good standing with the General came from a wellspring of blue blood running through my veins. They couldn't be more wrong - how little they knew about him to think that anything other than achievement and honor matter to him! I must admit that when I was a young soldier I took a great and perverse pleasure dispelling this particular myth of my exalted progenitors.

'Yes, my father is the man who wove the rope that holds the sails that carries us across the sea.'

And so he is, and yet, this isn't quite all of it.

I was born into a home filled with loss and with love, so much so that the walls seemed to push outwards with the intensity of it all, showing their cracks with pride no matter how many times my father patched them.

I never met her but I knew my mother as surely as you know yours, she was everywhere, woven into the fabric of our little world by Claudius. He kept my mother with us in a million ways, muddling through her recipes so that I would know her taste, embracing me more than his nature so that I would know her touch, spinning bedtime tales of the old world and the world that might be so that I would know her dreams. And, unwittingly, he kept my mother's spirit with us in the softness behind his eyes, when he drank a glass of wine at the hearth and set himself sad and free.

Many things might be debated but one thing is clear, Flavia Constans was from better stock than my father. She could read and write, she spoke Latin and Greek and she wrote poems, some of which were still painted on the walls of our house in her whimsical script when I was a child.

I never thought much about the forces that brought them together when I was a child - the sinister concepts of blood and breeding never entered my calculations then. What I did notice, however, was the fiercely possessive way Flavia's friends remembered her. According to virtually all her acquaintances my mother understood them like no other. They spoke of her as if she was their sister, mother, daughter or confessor. She was special to each of them.

Astounding. How could one thin, fragile life spread so much color, how could such delicate wings fly so far? When life's eternal mysteries are pondered around the watch fires at night this is the one that perplexes me most, how my mother the gentle butterfly could have unearthed the secrets of the grocer, the fishmonger, the washerwoman and the constable. She didn't have their life experiences; she didn't hear the words of fear and love they whispered in the dark of night. And yet, she knew them enough to make them feel understood, appreciated, worthy.

With her innate grace my mother, your grandmother, achieved the closest thing to immortality that I have ever seen. Flavia Constans possessed a glorious life force, flawed and divine in the manner of the old gods of Olympus or even Jesus the Carpenter before the Church decided to sanitize him.

I never embraced her and I never had the chance to hold her warm hand. I couldn't even bid her farewell. But I was nurtured in her womb, I breathed her breath and shared her blood. When I need to comfort myself I think of this.

You, my children, will never experience such loss at a young age. I am proud to be your father and grateful that your mother and I are with you, involved in all that is big and small in your world. But my Caecilia, Simeona and Matthaeus, though you are large in character (surely as a result of your remarkable mother), you are yet small.

I record these words so that you may know more about the world-changing events that preceded your births, and the legendary Romans that your father had the privilege to know, including the great Belisarius.

◆ ◆ ◆

A ferocious summer squall hit Volerus one week before my eighth birthday. Rain sound and thunderclaps preceded her and just as the sun rose the storm hit like a Hun, ripping through town and into the hinterland beyond.

At the height of the deluge, strangers' voices echoed outside the house. Visitors always piqued my curiosity and visitors that ventured out on a day like that were doubly interesting. I flew to the door, banged it open, and flashed the two drenched men my most dazzling smile. But they were too busy shaking the rain from their tunics and eyeing each other suspiciously to notice me, the little squirrel, at their feet.

And so my tutors had arrived.

In time I would call them my Uncles.

They stayed with us for the next eleven years.

Most children are used to the attention of a mother and father. But in my case I had a father and two adopted uncles. Once or twice I've heard from an acquaintance that this arrangement *'didn't sound so very odd'* but they have no idea. It was odd. In fact, it was so beyond odd that it was precious and wonderful in a way that I still can't properly describe.

Let me try to explain.

To me, Leo, Claudius and Zeno were stone, wood and fire. Aristotle had his four elements that made the world go round but in my life there were these three, fundamental, pieces. And though I might fancy myself my own man now, they are the three elements that continue to define me.

Leo's immovable stone.

Claudius' enduring driftwood.

Zeno's sputtering fire.

When Zeno walked into our house he pressed a small marble globe into my hand and bowed to me as if I were the Emperor himself. I decided on the spot that he'd be my favorite unless Leo could do better. But when Leo stepped inside the only thing he brought was his cool atmosphere – he didn't attempt to charm me. He had arrived and that was enough.

Though he spent more than ten years under our roof I knew the least about Leo. Of course that would change, everything would change in the years that followed but in Volerus, Leo remained an enigma.

Delicate as a ceiling timber, he moved with a sense of immense power kept barely in check. There were no soft surfaces on Leo. Mind you, he wasn't massive and he wasn't overtly threatening but I found him positively terrifying. It was no single thing but the combination of him, the cold fire of his eyes, the way his limbs swung in the practice yard, his habit of tossing a sword and spear as if they were nothing more than straw.

What few friends I had stopped coming around after Leo arrived but I couldn't blame them. After all, this was a man who had killed. My little boy's brain knew it with certainty. That knowledge mortified and fascinated me and when I lied awake in bed at night I wondered if I would be like him one day.

On the surface, Leo's job was the simpler of the two. He was to teach me to defend myself with brute force. But from the beginning he bristled at that description.

"Boy, it's that kind of thinking that gets the fools killed young."

There would always be someone faster, stronger and more ruthless on a battlefield. Survival was about cultivating the '*blend of attributes*' as he called it, the intelligence to know when to employ arms and how.

"Subtle maneuvers and shrewd negotiations, that's where the battle starts and true champions end it there with a little luck. Don't get me wrong, when it can't be avoided you'll fight but that's no brute force thing. Only brutes employ brute force and they tend not to live long. It's the blend of attributes boy, brawn tempered by a brain. That's what's kept me alive for more years than I deserve."

And according to Leo that would keep me alive as well.

I was a sheltered boy and it had never occurred to me that 'staying alive' might require work someday. That revelation marked the end of an era, the end of the child that had been.

The training that began then would last from my eighth birthday to my eighteenth and it moved to the rhythm of half days. Mornings were spent with Zeno, lunch with my father and afternoons with Leo, that was the pattern set at the very start.

Leo's half day unfolded in the practice yard. Hours passed deliberately, stretching, swinging weapons, squatting in the dust as he drew diagrams and described great generals and their tactics. We repeated the same exact routine day after day, year after year. It took some time before I understood that this was exactly Leo's point, he was turning me into a disciplined man and that was Leo, clear as day.

But Zeno, Zeno was a very different story. There was nothing clear about my Philosopher Uncle and that's why it was so easy for a young boy to love him. I don't want you to think that I played favorites. Of course I felt affection for Leo, he was as much a part of my life as my father or Zeno, but there was always a distance between us. Zeno, however, was different, a special case.

Our Empire is littered with blowhards. I've met a million more in my travels and I know this for a fact – Zeno was cut from a different cloth. In fact the only man that I have met with comparable intellect and wit was Procopius the Historian. Had Zeno resisted the lure of alcohol in excess and kept his political opinions in check he might have achieved comparable success but Zeno was not one to resist his demons.

All professors study the same dead men and their same dead wisdom - Zeno was no different there. But he never made the smallest attempt to render that wisdom impartially. Instead, he absorbed, interpreted and colored everything that he touched with his own imperfections, his own humanity and that was his flaw. Mind you, the man understood his flaws and instead of working to correct them he called them 'virtues' and embraced them like old friends.

Zeno was looking for a partner in crime, not a disciple, and he always sought to make our afternoons more entertaining. To my absolute delight we spent the bulk of our time in between formal lessons on my true love, the heroes of Rome's past, and no one I have ever met before or since could spin a tale about heroes like Zeno.

There were so many giants to choose from. Augustus, Caesar, Titus, Pompeii, Antony, Vespasian, Hadrian and Constantine, all of the familiar names filled our afternoons as Zeno bellowed their legends to me, to the sky, to the sailors that drank with him then scattered about the harbor to sleep it off.

Zeno's stories didn't lack for color and frankly I had no idea what was fact and what was fiction. He said things that might have had a lesser man crucified but he did it with an authority and volume that somehow worked for him. Who knows, all I know is that he captivated me with those stories and no story, no hero was more captivating than Scipio Africanus but for some reason, Zeno saved him for last.

I didn't hear the name of 'Africanus' until the tenth year of my apprenticeship. We had just stepped out of the tavern into the bone chilling, briny air of the harbor.

"Africanus god damnit!"

Zeno slapped me on the back so hard my teeth almost popped out.

"Scipio Africanus was a man Valentinian listen to me you cur, Scipio Africanus was a man. You take all your heroes, great men all of them, and they aren't an inch of Africanus. Scipio Africanus was a man."

I remember the rest vividly, everything he said, everything about that day. We sat on the hull of an overturned fishing boat, there were dozens of them scattered about the harbor. Each was painted in a different pastel. The sea smell competed with fish scent but the breeze made it bearable, even pleasant. Sunshine had dissipated the winter damp and my raw hands were just starting to loosen as I flicked shells with my fingers. Gulls scavenged around us but there wasn't much for them, the fishermen were a meticulous lot. We sat there a few moments, taking it in and I pretended not to notice the deep draught Zeno took from his discrete flask. Then, as the last fisherman hauled his boat onto the cobbles, turned it over and placed it against its neighbors, Zeno launched into his story.

"Valentinian, listen to me very, very carefully."

His sweet wine breath filled my nostrils and I listened.

"In the days of the high Republic, long before Sulla, before Julius Caesar and Augustus and the Emperors, the Senate ruled but it had become a sad shadow of its former self. Senators still spoke noble words but there was nothing noble about those old beasts. They were craven, they gorged and indulged and lived shallow lives. Yet, despite their depravity, the Republic flourished. In a few generations Rome had been transformed from a feeble city-state in Alexander's day to a true Mediterranean power.

"I've told you many times that human nature is dark and that good fortune invites envy – that is precisely what happened to Rome. Though the Italian tribes couldn't oppose her, she had other bitter rivals in the Mediterranean including Persia, Macedonia, Egypt and the *Punici* in Carthage. Mind you, they were all fearsome enemies but it was Carthage that sent Rome her scourge, in 218 BC, and his name was Hannibal Barca.

"Hannibal was more than a man. He was more than a warrior. He was a fire-breathing beast, a demon, a gentleman and one of the greatest generals the world has ever known.

"From mountains that kissed the sky, he swept down into Italy upon elephants that he had brought across the Mediterranean in ships, by foot through Gaul, to the Alps and through mountain passes full of ice and evil to the banks of the River Ticinus where the Roman Army made its stand. The Legions were led by Publius Cornelius Scipio *'the Elder'*, a decent man, true to the old values and to the older battle plans. And so he split his troops in two lines, cavalry behind and infantry in front with their long spears dug into the ground.

"When Hannibal made the bluff he ran the elephants ahead of his cavalry and smashed through the Romans whose horses were driven mad with fear. Only a handful of dismounted riders remained after that first rush. They circled their general as the main enemy force advanced.

"Scipio had a son by the same name who watched the battle unfolding from a nearby hilltop. His father had placed him there in the care of his private bodyguard. When Scipio the Younger understood his father's plight, he ordered the centurions to attack.

"The squad leader told Scipio that orders were orders, that the boy was just a boy and that he, a distinguished soldier, would not move. *Life is cruel but the smart man knows to cut his losses'* he told the boy.

Legend says that Scipio offered him a crisp salute. The centurion saluted right back and was still saluting when the boy drew his sword and hurled himself down the hill to save his father.

"Shamed into action, the centurion and his dozen companions followed the boy into battle, plunging into the Carthaginian flank. Their small attack was so unexpected, so disjointed and loud that it caused the enemy to panic. Perplexed by the tumult, Hannibal called the retreat. Rome had definitively lost the battle but Scipio had won his first engagement, and saved his father's life in the bargain.

"Weeks later, the Roman Senate awarded the boy one of its highest honors, the Medal of Valor. Young Scipio took the Senate floor, bowed graciously and spoke a few simple words that shook them to the core.

'I thank you and I decline the honor because I did no more than any of you would have done to save his father.' That's what he said and that's the first time that history noticed him."

A gull had been circling Zeno's feet and at that moment, it offered my tutor a cautious peck, breaking his rhythm. Zeno shushed him away, took a sip from his flask and continued.

"So years passed and the war between Rome and the *Punici* moved from Italy to Iberia. Iberia was a short trip from Africa and it made a perfect staging ground - close enough to strike at Rome, far enough for our enemy to organize unmolested.

"The Roman Army spent three frustrating years chasing the elusive *Punici* across Iberia, unable to defeat an enemy that they couldn't see. But if they could lure Carthage's army out into the open, if they could fight their fight, surely they'd prevail. That is what they engineered in the Baetis Valley. And it resulted in an unmitigated, monumental disaster for Rome - one of the greatest in our history. In one terrible stroke, Hasdrubal Barca, Hannibal's brother, crushed the Legions and killed their commanders, Scipio the Elder and his brother, Gnaeus Scipio. Rome's entire western frontier had been ripped wide open.

"On the Capitoline Hill, a panicked Senate couldn't find an experienced officer to take command. No one wanted to be responsible for Rome's inevitable defeat until young Scipio stepped forward. He was barely seventeen when Hannibal first defeated his father at Ticinus and twenty-seven on the day his father died in Iberia. By the time he left for Iberia he had been observing his mortal enemies, the *Punici*, for a third of his life.

"Scipio arrived in Iberia and avoided battle for two years while he trained the legions in wild tactics that he had been dreaming of since he first met Hannibal. Once satisfied that his troops were ready, Scipio began to methodically pick apart Carthage's war machine, eventually chasing his enemy back across the Straits of Gibraltar to Africa.

"Though Hasdrubal had been defeated, the problem of Hannibal remained. Hidden in the wilds of Southern Italy, Hannibal terrorized the countryside and prepared to strike at the capital. Scipio could have attacked him in Italy but native Italians would have suffered most, caught between the warring giants. So Scipio decided that the best way to remove Hannibal was to strike at what his enemy held most dear. And so the General retired to Sicily to plan his assault on Carthage in 205 BC. Mind you, he went by himself because the Roman Senate refused to give him permission to bring his own army. They told him the threat was in Italy, not in Africa."

By this time Zeno and I had meandered back home from the harbor. Claudius was stooped over his desk when we walked in but his prickly ears caught the subject matter. The smile he offered us both was tight and Zeno took the cue.

"Valentinian, I'd say that's enough for the day. Tomorrow we'll pick up where we left off."

With a bow, Zeno left the workshop and my father and I sat down to supper. Most days the four of us ate together, but on this night my father made it clear that he wanted me to himself.

Not until we finished our meal and retired to the workshop fireplace did Claudius open his mouth.

"My boy, it's time we talked."

New Threads

C LAUDIUS TURNED HIS back to me and held his hands out before the fire. At times his silences spoke clearly and at times they were deliberately opaque and so it was that night. There were no signals to be read.

The young fire crackled, he cleared his throat and turned to face me. For a moment I imagined a tear in his dark eyes but when I looked again it was gone. He cleared his throat a second time.

"Valentinian, you're practically eighteen years old now and this conversation is overdue. Your mother and I discussed this day. We had a plan. I just didn't expect eighteen to come so soon. Part of me thought you would stay little forever."

A faint smile touched his lips and he planted both his hands on my shoulders. He meant to soothe me but that terrified me even more. My heart thrummed so loudly I could barely hear him speak.

"I know you love your heroes and its good you get to know Scipio. Because where his story ends, yours begins. So listen boy, this is what your mother wanted you to know."

I had no idea what my father was talking about and the entire thing, the mention of my mother and my father's demeanor had me transfixed, desperate to know more. And on this one, rare night, my father was determined to talk.

"Everyone in Palermo turned out to meet Scipio as his light ships approached. Sicilians had devoured invaders for millennia and they would devour him too in their lazy way. Scipio was just the latest curiosity, a little army, a little man. The universe packed itself onto that wharf and watched him. And deep in that sea of sharks, no one watched Scipio more carefully than Apollonia.

"She must have been like your mother, delicate and feminine, sharp and strong. So sharp that Apollonia had been the right hand to Sicily's most brazen merchant since she was a girl. That man was also her father and though he never married Apollonia's mother he loved Apollonia first and foremost. Because, as the father observed, not only was she beautiful like her mother but she was ferocious like him, the best of them both.

"Daddy's little girl and preferred thug strode into the General's field tent just one day later. Scipio was interviewing wheat suppliers and her father's Egyptian wheat was the most expensive of them all. But it wasn't a question of price, she explained, a true leader had to consider quality as well. Scipio prolonged the argument to keep her near.

"The passion between them was instantaneous, it was all consuming. And I know that immovable, transcendent thing my boy. I had it with your mother."

My father had never spoken so many words consecutively in my life. And I was so intoxicated with it all that I couldn't see where it was leading.

"When the winds changed, blowing out of the north, it was time for Scipio's fleet to leave for Africa. And Apollonia did all she could in those final weeks to speed his departure. She barely slept, spending all of her time down on the docks as she personally supervised delivery of the foodstuffs that would sustain Scipio's army.

But when the last bale of hay swung onto his flagship she pulled him aside and made her final request, her only request.

'Take me with you,' she said. 'I won't ask a single thing more, but take me with you.'

"The General held her face tenderly and told her that he could never take her into harm's way. He was going into battle with the greatest enemy Rome had ever known. He might not make it back alive and he wouldn't take that risk with her.

"And so the fleet sailed, slipping across the horizon with the fate of the Republic strapped to its decks. Apollonia stood alone and watched them blow away, knowing that she was with child - the General would not know of his abandoned child until he found her hidden note in his saddlebag months later in the throes of war. By then it was too late, the die had been cast, the history had been written.

"The story of Scipio's triumph is well known and I'll let Zeno complete the details, he lives for those things. But I'll tell you that after many battles Hannibal fell to Scipio at Zama and Carthage fell soon after, ridding the Mediterranean of Rome's last rival until the Vandals would occupy that same city so many centuries later.

Scipio's duty to the Republic didn't end at Zama. He stayed in Carthage for a year to make certain that Rome's old enemy could keep its dignity in defeat. Then he returned to Rome where he was feted as a savior and given a surname after the land of his triumph. From that day forward he would forever be known as *Publius Cornelius Scipio Africanus*.

"When he returned to Sicily three years later to find Apollonia he found an empty home. The local prefect told Scipio that her father had died and that Apollonia, her husband and child had moved to Neapolis. *And child.* She had married, he couldn't blame her but there it was nonetheless. He had lost her, and the child, *his child*, forever. Though he would carry the grief from that loss with him to his grave, he had no choice but to let them go.

"Back in Rome, popular sentiment had turned against the Senate and the capital was rife with talk that Rome needed a strong man, a noble man to clean what the Senators had sullied. The people made their choice clear when Scipio returned from Carthage, he was wildly popular and deservedly so - he had saved the Republic from defeat. But he was no dictator. Soon after learning about Apollonia, Scipio Africanus renounced his commission in front of a suspicious Senate and retired to his country home where he eventually died.

"The General left instructions in his will that his valet was bound to execute. And so, days after Scipio's death, the valet galloped straight to Neapolis with a small chest and a scrap of parchment, in search of Apollonia.

"He found her lovingly cared for in her son's home, a stately affair commanding the heights of the town. Apollonia received him on her terrace overlooking the bay, rung with bougainvillea, where she passed her days gazing at the sea. Like a lioness surrounded by her pride of grandchildren, she was advanced in years but she was still a handsome woman.

"Scipio's man placed the chest at her feet and the sealed parchment in her hands. She saw the seal and immediately understood. Speaking in a soft voice that stilled the children, she whispered *'tell me please, I know, he is gone.'*

"The valet relayed the single message that the General had carried in his heart for so long."

'My master thought of you very much in his final days. He sent you his everlasting affection and profound wish that you should accept his gifts in

the name of the love that you shared, that he carried with him to his grave. With your consent he would like your child, his child, to carry his name. Finally, he wished that you might enjoy the blessings of the gods and that your family should forever walk the land, forever persevere.'

My father leaned in close to me and stared at my eyes, waiting to speak until he knew he had my attention.

"As your family has persevered my boy, for many centuries. That child was the first of your line. The blood of Scipio and Apollonia ran in your mother's veins and now it runs in yours."

◆ ◆ ◆

My head spun and for an endless time my dry mouth produced nothing but silence.

Leaving me to struggle, Claudius plucked two spades from his workshop before marching me into the garden. At the line of lemon trees he handed me a spade and began to dig. For what seemed an eternity we excavated a trench between the last two trees in the line. The dark earth, nearly frozen with mid-winter frost, scattered reluctantly about.

Upon his command we switched to our hands, brushing aside the hardscrabble dirt to reveal a tightly wound leather satchel. Claudius plucked it from the pit and with great care he placed the satchel's contents at my feet.

The small chest that sat before me was an exotic thing, carved from wood that glowed honey in the night. It was sealed so firmly that my first clumsy attempt to force it open failed. With a nod from my father I continued probing the outside, trailing my fingers across the top, then lightly down the sides. Finally, along its belly I came upon a rough, barely discernible nub. I pressed it but nothing happened. I pushed it to the side and still nothing.

Finally, in a fit of frustration I twisted and it gave, spinning under my fingertips. With a snap the top of the box swung open and released a breath.

The world about me disappeared.

Three soft skins sat within - each covered something compact and hard. I took the first in hand, pulled a bronze tablet from its wrapping and held it up to the starlight. The winter stars gave me just enough light to make out the inscription. With my father's encouragement I read out loud.

> For Apollonia, my first and only love, mother of my child, never have I forgotten you. Please accept these gifts. May your brood take strength and solace from them. May they flourish and forever live. And may they remember this flawed man kindly. You are all and everything that I shall miss in this world.
> Publius Cornelius Scipio "Africanus"

The second package held another tablet, similar to the first but less even around the edges.

> To my child, so that you may know from whence you came. The man they call "Africanus" was your father and is much in you. He was the greatest of warriors, the greatest of statesmen, utterly human but ultimately above us all. And yet, to me, he was quite simply life itself. Know this and walk with confidence in this world but eschew pride. Many remember him fondly. Many fear him still and it shall always be so. Keep your secrets close my son and you shall indeed live long.
> Your Adoring Mother, Apollonia

It was a message from a mother to a son that had lived centuries before, but at that moment it seemed as if the words had been written especially for me. I was overwhelmed with a sense of my mother. Tears stung my face as Claudius whispered to me.

"One last piece Valentinian, there is one last piece."

And so there was. Placing Apollonia's tablet to the side I extracted the chest's final secret, a medallion of brilliant gold. It too had an inscription.

To Publius Cornelius Scipio the Younger, hereafter known as Africanus, on the occasion of his Triumph, by decree of the Consul, with the consent of the Senate.

It was real but could not be *real*. Scipio, Apollonia, their love, the proof of it all lay in my garden but how could I know that its connection to me was also real? From the beginning I doubted.

My father cackled softly, a sound that I had never heard before or since from his lips, followed by a tortured exhale.

"That's the truth of the matter, there is your answer. Yes, his blood runs in your veins. Now tell me, do you have any more doubts?"

Of course I had a thousand questions. Of course I had a million doubts. But I couldn't ask, I couldn't press, I didn't speak. And so that stunning moment, filled with infinite possibilities, passed abruptly when Claudius leapt to his feet.

"Good. Come then. Take your patrimony and follow me."

In front of the fire I separated the small gold medallion from the rest.

My father watched me and nodded.

"It's all yours boy, do with it what you want."

With the cord that had bound it I replaced it in its satchel and hung it around my neck, under my tunic. I remember that it felt warm there, comforting, a piece of me already.

I thought that the drama was over until I saw the pain in Claudius' eyes

"My boy, now that you know about your past we need to talk about your future." Claudius looked at me but didn't see me - I could feel him far away. I wanted to approach him, to embrace him, to reassure him, to feel reassured. His raised hand warned me to stay in place.

"Valentinian Scipio Constans."

His gnarled hands clenched as he continued.

"You are everything good in my world. Everything that is right. Everything that your mother and I wished for and much more my boy, you are your own man."

His next words reached me from many leagues away, through cotton and pitch, and they changed everything forever.

"But you are too much for this place.

"Your fate calls you away.

"You will not be a rope maker's whelp and this rope maker won't be your anchor. And so I decided. You and Leo will leave Volerus this morning for Constantinople. He has many friends there and that's where you belong. In the Empire's heart you'll find opportunity, real opportunity and the chance to do something great. That is what your mother would want Valentinian. That is how it has to be."

The world froze, my heart froze but somehow I spoke. I chose not to leave, my place was with him. I had no interest in Constantinople, in greatness, in destiny.

My father looked at me and his face drew taut. I felt activity in the house. Leo appeared somewhere in the room, looked at us both then exited. I finished talking, screaming, crying and waited for a response.

Claudius took three slow steps backwards. Standing in front of the vat where his life's work stewed, he placed his hands on the rim and gripped, bleeding his knuckles white.

"Leo has packed what you'll need and he's waiting for you outside. The sun has risen. Don't hesitate. Go now."

And so it would be. I could do nothing but obey. Perhaps I should have taken that moment to show more strength but I didn't. I think that I managed a stiff bow. My father placed a gentle kiss on my cheek and then its companion with equal tenderness.

"Just remember me son, remember your father who loves you, remember me."

PART II: Nova Roma

Besides the city's other blessings the sea is set most beautifully all about it, forming curving bays, contracting into narrow straits, and spreading into a great open sea; and thus it makes the city exceptionally beautiful, and offers the quiet shelter of harbors to navigators, thereby abundantly providing the city with the necessities of life and making it rich in all useful things.

- Procopius of Caesarea, Historian and private secretary to General Flavius Belisarius on Nova Roma

Travelled Companion

I HAD KNOWN LEO for half my life but I saw him for the first time on the *Via Egnatia*, the principle land route to Constantinople that cut through Thrace. He was not yet forty years old, though as his chiseled frame loped along the Hebrus River it seemed to carry more than one lifetime. Travelers on the highway couldn't have known him but all acknowledged him, moving aside, giving us a clear path ahead.

Leo was Isaurian, one of a wild breed from deep in the Taurus mountain range. Since time began, history's great powers sought to control Isauria and its mountain passes connecting Europe to Asia. The Hittites and Phoenicians, the Spartans and Athenians, the Macedonians and Persians all came to Isauria expecting a quick victory and all left bloodied and bruised. As Leo explained, the problem with most invaders was that they looked to subjugate and move on. But when the Romans came they sought to civilize and integrate. They thought in centuries, not in quick victories. That shrewdness won them their empire and they won Isauria as well.

Rome controlled her territory but they could never entirely control her people - to their credit they didn't try. So the Isaurians remained high in their mountain redoubts for centuries more, until one of them became Emperor of Rome. It was this man, the Emperor Zeno, who called a thousand of his countrymen down from the clouds, to Constantinople. There he organized them into a new military service dedicated to protecting him, the Excubitors.

Leo had served in the Excubitors, with distinction.

My tight-lipped uncle had shared the barest particulars of his life over the years. As he and I marched out of Volerus I reviewed what little I knew. Leo had arrived in Constantinople as a young man and he sold his arm to the Empire as his father had before him. After some years in the army on the Asian borderlands, Leo was accepted in the Excubitors. He made his name there as a brave fighter, incorruptible and on occasion incorrigible. His peers respected him, his enemies feared him and Caesar knew his name. There was much to be proud of but something still escaped him. He had missing pieces - he could feel them. He just didn't know what they were.

When the Emperor Anastasius died something changed for Leo. The Excubitors, and Constantinople itself, lost its hold on him. He tendered his resignation, closed his home and bid farewell to the few people that mattered. I would soon learn that only one had *truly* mattered and the truth of their relationship chased Leo from Constantinople and drew him back again with me in tow.

Leo left the capital behind after the Emperor died on a brilliant July morning. He exited the city through the Iron Gate and boarded the Bosporus ferry to Chalcedon, beginning his great meander.

First he traveled south through Antioch, across the Persian border and west to Jerusalem where he spent several months, fascinated by its many, rabid faithful. Mounting his horse again he moved north and west along the Mediterranean to the edge of the Vandal kingdom, built on the old site of Carthage. The barbarian Vandals called themselves vassals of Rome but in truth they operated independently in ancient Roman lands. Leo found them to be an oddly noble people and he spent months amongst them. From Africa he caught a pirate transport across the sea to Gaul where he encountered many pockets of old Rome in that great country, like small lights in growing darkness. It inspired him, *'life ends and life continues'*, he explained to me, determined that I too learn the lesson. In northern Gaul a flat-bottomed ferry carried him to Britannia where he fought with the renowned Arturius, son of a Roman knight that had refused to leave the island when the legions were called home. Arturius and his men of the *'round table'* as they were known in Britannia, battled the Celts, Picts and Jutes to protect the Roman world that Caesar had deserted. Leo was happy there in the company of those noble men that sought to keep home alive for the Left Behind. Yet something called him home. After a year in Britannia he began his slow return trip to Constantinople with a heavy heart.

Finally, nearly four years since he left Constantinople, Leo reached the very gates of Volerus. He could smell the capital on the clothing of westbound travelers but he still wasn't ready to go home. So he stepped off the Via Egnatia, entering the town and making straight for Volerus' garrison. He asked the soldiers on duty if they knew of anyone in town that was looking for a day laborer. They introduced him to my father, who occasionally hired men to help in his workshop. After a shake of hands and a short conversation, the two retired to a local tavern for more intimate discussions.

There, over a simple meal, Claudius offered Leo a job, to mentor his boy. The concept took Leo by surprise and he told my father as much.

"I'm absolutely the last man on earth who should be tutoring your son. I don't know the first thing about children and I had no formal education myself. I just know a thing or two about swords, shields and such things, no more."

According to Leo my father sat up in his seat as if he had just returned to the table from a long journey. He looked for Leo's eyes then slapped the table with the flat of his palm.

"Commander," my father answered, "that's exactly why I won't take no for an answer."

◆ ◆ ◆

Silence and sun are all I remember from our first two days on the road from Volerus to Constantinople, some ten years after Leo first arrived in my home. We must have seen other people, we must have shared words but I don't remember them.

But, then, on the third night, we entered Selymbria.

It was so cold my bones clacked as we walked our horses around and up the ancient hill.

Long before Byzantium was born, long before Troy and Athens, Selymbria sat proudly on that rock overlooking the Propontis Sea. Of course I knew her story, her magic, but I was too tired, too sick with emotion to feel anything that night. All I could do was put one foot in front of the other, following Leo, resenting him all the while.

At the hill's peak we reached the city gate. It swarmed with night guardsmen but Leo didn't slow and neither did I. He just flashed a curt salute before plunging down the darkest of dark alleys.

My head spun. I had a million things to say but I couldn't muster the spit. I needed to sleep, to cry, to eat, and to turn back the clock to a time when my home was still *my home* but all I could do was to stumble on. And then, with a final twist in the alley, the light poured forth.

A brute emerged from the stable. With a few gruff words he took our reins and we pushed our way into the adjacent tavern. Smoke hung low inside and strangers rumbled, studying us out of the corners of their eyes. They didn't look kind.

But I was so bewildered and so angry at the world that I barely noticed. If my father had been there maybe I could have confronted him but all I had was Leo. It seemed logical at the time. My uncle, my mentor had become my tormentor and as he bit into his cold fowl I neared the breaking point.

'Leo. Explain this thing to me. Help me understand what I did so I can fix it, so that I can get my life back.'

He drained his cup and placed it gingerly on the table.

"Valentinian, this has nothing to do with what you did or who you are my boy, quite the contrary. This has everything to do with who you might be. Understand, I know your father well, I know him better than most, but he only told me so much. Just be patient, Valentinian, be patient and eat your food."

That's when I lost control. With all my restraint worn away I roared at him and dug my nails into the table.

'THIS MAKES NO SENSE!'

It took me a moment to realize that I was shouting, making heads turn across the room. And the worst was yet to come.

'If that's true then how could he send me to Constantinople? Damn it Leo, you're speaking in riddles and I don't have time for riddles. Why are you lying to me?'

Leo stood up and moved his chair around the table until it touched my side and sat down deliberately. Then with visible restraint he leaned in so close to me that I could feel his breath on my cheek.

"Valentinian, close your mouth before you say something else that you'll regret. Now, if you would listen to me *calmly* I will calmly explain as best I can."

He took the goblet in front of him, pressed it into my hands and urged me to drink. I obliged him with a gulp then refilled my cup as he spoke.

"My boy, I spent a good part of my life in Volerus because your father is a decent man and because I was touched by his devotion to you. Mind you, I've lived amongst Emperors and princes and I've seen parents do things to children that made my blood boil. Children placed on pedestals when they soil their pants. Children stroked gently when they should have the back of the hand. But when I walked into your father's house I saw something different. In you, your father saw the realization of an ideal, the consummation of his love for your mother."

When Leo invoked my mother I winced.

"I see your eyebrows twitch. How could I possibly talk about your mother - what right do I have? Someday you'll understand the excruciating subtlety that comes with age, the damned sensitivity that makes me wiser than I want to be. So I didn't know your mother, Flavia, but I understood your parents' love. And I understood that it was this love that sustained Claudius so that he might fulfill *his part of the bargain.*"

Leo had slate grey, frigid eyes and at that moment they locked on me. A muscle flicked along his jaw.

"You want more? Two weeks ago your father came to me. He asked me about your progress and I told him what he already knew, there wasn't much more I could do for you in Volerus. Then the conversation turned. Claudius knew that I wanted to go home and he shocked me by suggesting that I leave sooner rather than later and that you go with me. We spoke through the night. Before we parted, shortly before daybreak, your father made me swear three oaths: to not reveal what we discussed, to take you with me to Constantinople and to care for you as if you were my son.

"And you, Valentinian, are a damned fool. How can it be that you still haven't figured it out? Your mother died for you and your father lives for you. If you can't see that then you don't deserve either of them."

— 36 —

For a skin of wine the stable manager let us sleep in a loft above the horses. Leo threw a wool blanket across us both but there was no kindness there. The horses' manure perfumed the frigid air while my mind whipped and tumbled. Everything was wrong. Nothing was right. I knew Leo could never forgive me. I didn't think life would ever be the same.

Leo's tough hands shook me awake at dawn. The horses were already saddled and waiting outside. We stepped into the same streets but they were different by day. Wind still blew but it didn't cut. And the sun came from below, reflecting off the Propontis, shining straight up the mountain, warming me to the core.

Selymbria.

The name was pure magic, rolling from the tongue, evoking Zeus and thunderbolts. As we meandered I remembered loving the idea of Selymbria as a child, and the sound of the word as I repeated the name over and again, loving the abstraction.

But there was nothing abstract about this enduring rock. The city was marked by a hill that shot five hundred feet into the sky from the flat Thracian plain. A citadel crowned that hill long before the Athenians had an acropolis, built by local tribes. Many thousand years ago ancient hunters had stood on that peak and stared out over the sea. The Thracians were an inland race but from the base of that hill they began to explore the waters of the Propontis. In the 8th century BC, refugees from Megara, traveling with the Byzas that became king, pushed the Thracians off their hilltop. And so the Greek Selymbria was born, sister city to Byzantium.

I had always wanted to walk those streets. And there I was, living a childhood dream.

Leo caught it all and the smile spread to his face. Then, with a chuckle he cuffed me so hard I almost fell off my horse. He laughed harder and I joined him, relief flooding my body. Maybe I hadn't lost my friend after all.

Later that day, after lunch on horseback, our march slowed as we approached the Anastasian Wall, on the edge of the rough Thracian hinterland. Leo explained that before the Anastasian Wall was built, the rich farmlands around the capital were constantly harassed by barbarian raiders. The Emperor Anastasias decided that Constantinople needed an additional line of defense. He started construction on this wall, modeled after Hadrian's Wall in Britannia, during the last years of his reign.

"I must tell you, it made me proud to work for the man that called this thing from the earth. Walls can separate and they can civilize, when done properly."

It had been a quiet stretch since Selymbria but Leo was talking again. Anastasias' wall stretched a full fifty kilometers from the Black Sea to the Propontis. The basic principle was to slow down invading forces and to give the legions time to rally. We trotted beneath the Wall and into a long, sloping valley. Dismounted and walking our horses to avoid trampling the merchants and pilgrims we emerged slowly from the valley. The first colors of sunset warmed the sky. Leo called over his shoulder.

"Look up from your shoes now boy because there it is, the center of the world."

And so the journey was over. And so the journey had finally begun.

Across the bluff, spanning the horizon, stood the massive Theodosian Walls, the capital's second and principle line of defense. Carved out of a stone more pure than ivory, cut with exquisite precision and rung with sharp battlements, the Wall meant to endure.

And behind the Wall, the Maiden stood.

GOLDEN GATE

S HE WAS A saint and a harlot, chastity and tender seduction embodied. Many miles and years distant I must admit that I do not
miss her a whit! But on the day I met her, the child I was thought
that she shined alone for me, washed with a thousand colors from
the sinking sun, noble head held straight, arms thrown skyward,
shoulders tapered and proud.

Byzantium. Constantinople. *Nova Roma.*

Leo encouraged us forward and we moved, slower now because
we weren't alone. My love had other suitors that I resented a bit,
the tide of Romans that swelled around us as we rolled towards her
Golden Gate.

Zeno had told me the story of the Gate many years before. After
smashing the Bulgars, deep in the northwestern forests, the
Emperor Theodosius commissioned a triumphal arch to celebrate
his victory in 388 AD. For years it stood in the middle of the
plain, solitary and proud. Then a new ring of walls enveloped
Theodosius' Arch and it became the city's great Imperial entrance.

I had never seen anything like the Gate's solid gold doors before
or since. Melted into coin, they could have bought an Empire. All
around me people bowed their heads to avoid the sunlight that reflected off those doors but I couldn't look away. My fingers trailed
along the battlements' skin as we passed and I felt just what I expected, faint but palpable, the pulse of the city.

Constantinople's central boulevard, the *Mêse*, greeted us on the other side with a roar. Bodies raced everywhere, pushing us from behind, obstructing us in front, and jostling on every side. And everyone spoke at once while the air vibrated with energy. They chirped, roared, cajoled and bullied in Latin, Greek, Persian and barbarian polyglot, singing the song of the capital.

The song was foreign but the city smell was a familiar blend of spice and milk, blood and incense. Somewhere in that mix I caught a hint of salty Bosporus breath. We couldn't see it yet but Leo told me that the water lay just beyond the line of hills that dominated the city center. Those hills sparkled, lit by the capital's basilicas that glistened like a thousand small suns. As I admired them from a distance Leo rumbled by my side.

"To judge by the crosses you'd think that everyone here worshipped at the same altar with a smile on their perfectly pious faces."

He used his powerful arms to clear a way through the crowd before returning to his theme.

"But the world isn't that simple boy. It has never been that simple."

He dropped back so that we walked side by side.

"There are a million souls living here, more than every other city in the world put together. Those souls pray and war, love and covet in this perversely divine place. Now, they aren't all saints and they aren't all sinners but they are all alive, boy, this city is a living thing. That one thing is sure. So pick your eyes up and pay attention, this paradox is your new home."

We entered the Forum of Theodosius, famous for its butchers and columns with peacock eyes carved up and down their length. Those eyes must have served some benign purpose but I couldn't think of one as my horse and I mucked about in the blood that ran freely across the paving stones. The thick-necked butchers were busy murdering heifers and sows so that the city could eat. My stomach turned with all the hacking and defiling, I was born in and of the sea and survived on sea creatures. Never had I seen anything like that carnage. The dying brutes all around me moaned and I fought the urge to slay the butchers in retribution. I couldn't leave the place fast enough, practically retching on myself as my horse and I scrambled back onto the Mêse. So I thought, from the pure gold of the Gate to the liquid crimson of the Forum, this was Constantinople.

Traffic grew more dense and aggressive as we climbed. Pilgrims, farmers and long distance travelers swept towards us from the West. They flowed with measured pace, looking for the public houses and taverns where they would find warm company for the night. From the East ran the hard-edged merchants, barely pausing to raise their heads as they wove through the traffic. Several bumped me as they rumbled along but no one touched Leo. I moved closer to him to take advantage of his effect.

We caught sight of the Aqueduct of Valens on the last leg of its journey from the dark Bulgarian forests. Cool liquid rushed overhead, plunging headlong into the Imperial Quarter. I assumed that we were going to follow it and I started to imagine my first sight of the Palace. Would I see the Emperor? Would it all be as magnificent as I imagined?

That's when Leo slipped off the Mêse and I spurred my horse so I wouldn't lose him. He disappeared around a corner, already many paces from me without bothering to look back. His head was in another place.

Simple, straight-backed homes crowded the narrow street, gleaming beneath white washed plaster. I had never been there but there was something familiar about it all, the horse smell, the immaculate homes.

When I turned the corner I saw Leo dismounted, bent on one knee in front of a home whose wash was not quite as white. From his satchel he removed a small roll of leather that he deliberately unwound. Slowly, gingerly his fingers emerged with a long iron key that he eyed a moment before slipping it soundlessly into the lock. Palm pressed against the center, a brush of fingers, a snap of the mechanism and the doors swung open. Leo led his horse inside.

I crossed the threshold a moment later and stopped to let my eyes adjust. As the black interior faded to charcoal I saw my mentor standing in the room's center, taking deep breaths that whistled through the exposed wood beams above.

"My home.

"Part of me didn't expect to find it standing but here it is. And the strangest thing, the most unexpected thing, is that I smell the future here. I expected the past, you know, I dreaded the past..."

LION'S DEN

WHEN WE REACHED the second story, Leo left me in the disorienting dark at the top of the stairs.

I had no idea what to expect from his home. Leo was a nomad and a warrior — those creatures didn't belong to any place. So you can imagine my surprise when he struck a flint and the room stepped out of the shadows.

Fire burned in two bronze bowls in the far corners, one emblazoned with Medusa's head, the other with a Minotaur. Slender marble pedestals scattered about the room, supporting a collection of singular glass bottles. Glowing in shades of azure and sea green, they opened their long throats to the ceiling, singing silence.

"My boy, you see something of home, do you?"

Indeed I did. Splashed across the wall were frescos of thick lemon trees in full blossom, painted with care down to the light breeze that ruffled the leaves. The similarity to our Volerus garden left me speechless. Leo spared me the need to talk, placing a hand on my shoulder.

"It's remarkable, I know, I felt the same when I entered your home."

At that moment I noticed the strangest thing about the house — it was still warm with a human touch. Someone had tended to that place, some caring heart had dusted and arranged. Like so many things the explanation is obvious in retrospect but at the moment I didn't pry, I was simply happy to be there, anywhere I could sit.

It had been an infinitely long day and I think that everything caught up to me all at once. Leo must have sensed it because he pushed me onto a low divan and pressed a cup into my hand. The wine we had bought on our way into the city filled my nostrils and my head lightened, detaching a moment from my heavy limbs. Beside me Leo took his own cup and slumped into a heavy boned chair, fit for a barbarian king.

"To the Gods my boy, may they continue to treat us kindly."

I took a deep draught and felt it. My head started to sag but Leo called me to attention.

"One more toast boy, to the City. Take a sip and listen just a moment more."

His eyes filled with energy.

"You're in ancient Byzantium now. She is mistress and master, holy and profane; she is a city known the world over and at once unknowable. Byzas the Greek founded her over a thousand years ago when he wrested these lands from the tribes of Thrace. But even before Byzas there were people here, tough ambitious folk. Needless to say, Byzantium was ancient when the Republic of Rome was young. Her location made her virtually invincible and it gave her fleet access to the Bosporus, Black Sea and the Aegean. She plied them all with daring, gathering the world's riches to her harbor.

"And when the Emperor Marcus Aurelius saw that harbor he decided it would be his. The old emperors had that way about them, see a piece of the world that appeals and take it in the name of Rome. So he took Byzantium to glorify the Empire and the Empire promptly forgot about her, letting her fade into obscurity.

Two quiet centuries passed. Then Constantine the Great rediscovered her and made Byzantium the center of the world.

"Constantine had already moved the Empire's capital from Rome to Mediolanum where he could be closer to the frontier. But he knew the Empire's future - her challenges and her opportunities lied in Asia. So he gathered his generals, his architects and engineers and marched east in search of a new home. He stopped in Troy first, then Selymbria and seriously considered both to replace old Rome. Then a retainer pointed him to Byzantium.

"The Emperor stood on this peninsula and stared across the Bosporus into Asia. Then he plucked a wooden staff and began walking, trailing it along the ground to trace the periphery of the isthmus. *'Mark this line, all of you. You'll build a wall along it and inside, we'll create a New Rome.'* And so Constantinople was born."

My eyes must have closed. I felt Leo drape his cloak about me. The torches winked, a deep sleep took me and on my first night in Constantinople I dreamt of Scipio Africanus.

NEW ROME

ARLY THE NEXT morning we joined Mêse traffic.
Leo's long strides were infectious and I pushed to keep up but
he was too fast, so fast that when the collision happened I was a
dozen steps behind.

Charging forward, Leo smashed headlong into a group of soldiers that had just cut across the Mêse, slicing blithely through the
pedestrians. The resulting impact sent one soldier straight onto his
back while the second was swept off his feet into a comrade's arms.
The remaining six must have imagined that the attack was deliberate because they rushed forward and seized Leo.

"If you knew discipline this wouldn't have happened," he lec-
tured. Then, turning to the soldier who had peeled himself off the
street he added, "my apologies young man but it would be better
for us all if you observed the road ahead instead of your sandals."

The tall oaks that circled Leo drew closer, tightening their grip.

I was pondering desperate measures when the onlookers parted
to let two soldiers charge into the center of the ring. Behind the
guardsmen followed their commander, cut from bronze, bull neck
thrust forward and his right hand raised before him as if to brush
away the nuisance.

"What the devil is this about," he bellowed.

I couldn't lift a finger to help. All I could do was watch. Slowly,
the iron circle unwound to reveal Leo, standing straight, unfazed

by his scowling companions. The Captain of the Guard stared a second then shouted loud enough for the entire city to hear.

"BY THE GRACE OF JUPITER AND JESUS YOU ARE ALIVE! Leo the Brave lives. This is truly a day for celebration. Never in my life did I expect to see you again."

Hours later, Leo, Captain Basil and I lingered over lunch in a military mess hall built in Constantine's day. It looked like the inside of a prison but I didn't care, everything was sunshine to me. We had just gone from near apocalypse to a joyous reunion and for a moment everything seemed right with the world.

A half-dozen long tables stretched in the center of the hall, filled with Basil's night guard, indulging in bold tales and wine before returning home. Round tables were set in the shadows to accommodate more intimate parties and we sat at one of them, drinking from heavy alabaster goblets, leaning in close to be heard above the din.

"You were never one for telling tales, my dear Leo. I know bricks that talk more about themselves than you do. Gone for over fourteen years by my count with not a word from you. When you finally return I hear that you've been hiding in a village, just a stone's throw away. The legendary Cantecuzen stuck in Volerus? No offense but I've been to Volerus and I wouldn't send my dog there. And to top it all off, you say that you're a tutor now? That's how I know you're lying, you might be brilliant with a sword but what man in their right mind would hire you to tutor a child?"

Basil's deep laugh brought a deeper grimace to Leo's face. Leo tried to interrupt but there was no stopping his old friend.

"All jesting aside, Valentinian, you find yourself in fine company, this much I can assure you. Leo and I entered the Imperial service together a lifetime ago and from the start I counted myself fortunate to walk in his footsteps. He'll deny it but I wouldn't have my current command if it weren't for him."

Catching Leo's burning stare, Basil unconsciously brushed the table in front of him with his brawny arm. Then softening his voice, he flashed his crooked smile at me.

"So, enough of the past, let me tell you both about our fine capital. This isn't Anastasius' city anymore, may he rest in peace. It's Justinian's city now, his treasury, his army, his Empire and he is using his chance at the helm to change the world in his image. Cut from the old Roman purple he is, stubborn as a mule and brilliant to boot. But my mother always told me to beware of the brilliant ones and for good reason. The dunces tend not to dream quite as big and those big ambitions are the ones that cause all the trouble.

"But this is an ambitious one, without a doubt. In fact, according to the gossips he is consumed with the biggest dream of them all – *Restoration*."

Leo's face tensed, drawing a smile from the Captain.

"Ah Leo, I knew you wouldn't be able to resist. So sip that wine, listen for a moment and judge for yourself. These are the facts as far as I can tell.

"Three years ago Justinian took a young, unknown officer and gave him command of the Eastern legions, comprising some one hundred thousand men at arms. The officer's name was Belisarius. One day he barely had enough whiskers to shave and the next day Belisarius was Rome's most important general. Mind you, I loved the sheer lunacy of the move but not many of the Army's old-timers agreed with me. They tried to invent more than one 'accident' for Belisarius, in the bath and on the hunt, but they couldn't touch him. His success and decency have bred a loyalty amongst his troops that make him virtually impervious to knives in the back.

"The man is improbably competent. He managed to skim a few thousand men out of that half-assed army he inherited and to convince them that they could win battles decisively, as if they were the old Romans and not the new breed that we've become. Then he took them out into the field where they have done just that, they have triumphed. First they crushed the Persians at Dara and then at Callinicum they showed a shrewdness and subtlety that our armies haven't had for years. And finally, even you small town mice must know, in the wake of these battles Justinian negotiated the 'Endless Peace' with the Persian King Khosru. This final stroke of genius gets us to the heart of the matter.

"First, peace with Persia frees a large part of our army for other uses. Second, and most importantly, the Emperor has a general that he trusts."

Leo drew his mouth tight and carefully unclenched the fists that he held under the table.

"Dear Basil, I'm pleased to hear that our Emperor has some backbone but I have no special interest anymore in military matters. That's all in my past my friend, I'm just a simple civilian now interested in his simple civilian life."

Basil leaned across the table, so close that I spotted the grey sprinkled in his beard and deep creases at the corners of his eyes.

"Leo, you aren't listening to me. This conflict with Persia offers just a hint of what lies ahead. This isn't about politics. This is about the soul of Rome. Will we reclaim our birthright or will we be content with what's left? Is Rome the One or is Rome one amongst many? Those are the questions at hand and they are big questions my friend, the very biggest of questions."

Leo harrumphed and Basil continued unperturbed.

"The facts obviously haven't done it for you so listen to a bit more gossip. The Emperor is a Thracian and Thracians think

West, they don't think East, they're just a different breed. How long has it been since our armies left Italy, Gaul, Iberia, Germania and Britannia – sixty years or so? Well I know for a fact that every Thracian, man woman and child has been dreaming about Rome's return for that long. Your young Valentinian is a Thracian and he can't help but nod his head, look at him, he knows it's true."

I *was* unconsciously nodding my head when Basil called me out. My face flushed and I was starting to feel the wine, thinking about what my father always - *'you can judge a man by the friends he keeps'*. I believe that's true and the more I listened to Basil the more Leo rose in my estimation. Basil flashed me a smile as he continued.

"Thracians live just across the Adriatic from Italy, they can practically row there in a boat and they can smell it on the breeze. They're all born obsessed with the idea of recovering Italy and Justinian is no different, he's got the same fixation. But at the risk of stating the obvious, unlike most Thracians, Justinian has the power to make those dreams a reality.

"Now, contrary to what some say, the Emperor is no simpleton and he's not obsessed with conquest for conquest's sake. I suspect that Justinian will resort to waging war because he's already negotiated as much healing as he can. Let me explain. You, my friend, are an out of town pagan so you probably don't know this, but Justinian just ended a feud between two of the most powerful and pompous asses in the world. I'm talking of course about the Pope in Rome and our Patriarch here in Constantinople. For decades they and their predecessors have debated who exactly Jesus of Nazareth would love more if, in fact, he were still here. That debate, while highly amusing, was a mighty distraction that split the Church. And we both know that the Church is the most important force in the Empire after the Emperor himself.

"So the two old bats are talking again thanks to the time, gold and political capital that Justinian spent and if you ask me he spent it well. Now the Emperor can count on the Pope, the only civilized voice left in Italy. And to summarize this very long introduction, I am convinced that Italy is precisely where we're headed. Justinian will hit the West and he will move on Rome first. Rome is the linchpin and then the rest of our Lost Lands will fall into our hands. It's only a question of time and tactics."

Basil swallowed a deep draught and looked about the hall to satisfy himself that no one listened. But even then he stretched to draw closer, pressing his ample stomach against the table planks. Our three heads converged over the wine, bread crusts and beef carcass. That is when he shared the last piece, the crucial piece – the rumors of conspiracy.

"Listen now. Not everyone is in love with this idea of restoration and not everyone is keen to see Justinian succeed. There are many that still resent our Emperor. They don't care for his taxes on the nobles any more than they like his reorganized army or his popular appeal. And there is another thing, more subtle and more powerful. Not everyone thinks that we should try to resurrect the past. There is a large movement, a growing movement amongst the aristocrats - people like that Anicii princess - aimed at keeping the Emperor focused on the East. These people like the status quo, their endless Asian estates, the safety and comfort of this smaller and more homogenous Rome. No barbarian hordes, no endless expansion, just their own little islands of prosperity and tranquility. I suspect that they are capable of many things in their quest to preserve what they have. They might even go so far as to openly oppose an Emperor."

Leo pushed his chair away from the table and glared at Basil while I hung on every word.

"I see your skeptical look and that's fine, you don't need to pay attention to me today but I'm telling you, some powerful forces are gathering that oppose Justinian. Loyalties will be tested everywhere, even in the army. We will all have to choose sides."

Basil reached out and wrapped his fingers around Leo's forearm.

"Leo. When you left this city it was a different place, it belonged to the Emperor Anastasius and you served him with distinction. But that day, and that age, has passed. Listen to me, pay attention to what I say."

Basil went silent. Leo growled, pressed his fingers into the table. "Constantinople. I'm back, back in the cauldron. Basil I missed you but I didn't miss this, these spicy concoctions of whispers and wives' tales. But don't get me wrong, you still tell a good story and if I were a younger man my blood would be racing. Hell, my blood did race back then and you know it because you were right there beside me. We went to war for much less, ready to sacrifice everything for much, much less."

Leo paused a moment and eyed me before continuing.

"So let's leave the gossip where it belongs, at least for tonight. And let's raise our cups and thank the gods that we met you on our first day here. As usual you've been a generous and kind host, Basil, and I missed you."

Basil watched his friend and fell silent, relaxing deep into his chair with hands joined behind his head. I found myself doing the same with more than a hint of wine in my veins. My mind wandered, retracing the road we'd traveled over the last few days, back to Volerus and my father. I wondered what he would say about me, about this place, this conversation and the new orbit we had entered. Perhaps that's exactly why he sent me away. It was a radical thought that didn't shake me, it felt almost right. I had begun to understand.

While I struggled with the newness of this world Leo resisted its familiarity. Sitting in a room that belonged to another life, across the table from an actor in the drama that he had cherished in his youth, he mulled over the significance of this chance meeting that set the past on his left arm and the future on his right.

Basil called a soldier to our table with a carafe of wine. When he got closer I recognized him as the young man who had collided with Leo earlier that day.

"Be quick Mellius, and don't spill a drop. You have an old friend here waiting for you."

The Mellius in question was a fair-skinned youth with a shock of red hair that moved even when its owner stood still as he did then, hovering over the table. He cleared his throat so we'd notice him but I was already staring. There was something compelling about him, something distinctive.

Basil lifted his chin in Mellius' direction, bidding him to speak. Mellius saluted Basil like his life depended on it then turned to face Leo.

"Sir, I'd like to offer my apologies for what happened today. Sir, it has been an honor to meet you. Please forgive my clumsiness, sir."

Hearing the apology, realizing that it was meant for him, Leo spoke without raising his eyes.

"Young man, you don't need my forgiveness, you just need a little more luck. A soldier can have the best intentions in the world, as you clearly do, but sometimes it all boils down to luck."

Mellius arched his eyebrows and started to respond but Basil shooed him away. The young man hesitated, there was something more that he wanted to say. But he evidently decided that the moment wasn't right because he saluted again and returned to his companions. Another burst of noise surged from the cadets' table just as Basil refilled our cups.

"Leo, it appears that my men are somewhat taken with you. So much for your cherished obscurity. Some deeds, it seems, can't be erased by ten years."

Leo grimaced in response and stood from the table.

"Think what you will Basil but don't over-think, sometimes things are exactly what they seem."

With a parting grunt he excused himself and marched across the hall. Basil's men increased their volume then, with Leo's name rising above the din. I was as tantalized with the mystery of Leo as anyone in that room and I couldn't help but ask Basil.

'What is it that everyone around me seems to know about Leo that I don't?'

Basil grabbed his seat bottom and shuffled towards me.

"That's a fine question, Valentinian, and you asked the right man. You see, I consider myself an expert judge of character and the proof is that I'm still alive. Now, I know that you're a fine young lad because if you weren't, Leo wouldn't treat you like a son."

With this declaration I told Basil that Leo was no father to me. He was a mentor, a tutor and a friend, not a father. I've always been oversensitive on the subject of parents, mine are off limits, sacred to me. Basil's exuberance faded into something softer.

"My boy, don't take offense, I'm simply honoring the man who honors you with his devotion. As for your desire to know the 'truth', I know it through and through but I'm afraid that I can't say much, only Leo can do that. Yet this I will tell you. He's a fine, honorable soul. He is a strong man whose honor and devotion make him stronger still. An ordinary soldier might be defined by the lives he takes in the course of duty but Leo defined his service with lives saved, a general, an Emperor and the man you see before you amongst them.

"As you can imagine, there are many in Constantinople who were sorry to see him go and many of those will welcome him back with open arms. But understand that time doesn't stand still for anyone, especially not for heroes. So, as he walks back to us I leave you with this thought. Constantinople is a beautiful place and it's a treacherous place. Should you or Leo ever need my help, I am your man. Just remember that."

City at Rest

After a rough embrace outside, Basil took his leave of us. The winter chill nipped as we watched him stroll away to his warm chimney. Leo forced a smile, I could always recognize the mask he wore to hide his deep thoughts.

"My boy, the moon is full, the night is young and if you can keep up I'd suggest that we take the long way home."

He didn't wait for an answer before continuing.

"Zeno relishes story time. It has never been my thing but the night, and this place, deserves some explanation. Let's pick up where we left off last night with the Emperor Constantine. Now, any half-wit could tell you that Rome's eighty-four Caesars have been a mixed lot, as varied in their vices as in their merits. That said, they have been a remarkable collection of characters and many distinguished themselves. Amongst those, a few have been truly *great* and in my opinion Constantine was amongst the few.

"He was a fierce warrior and a thinking man. He was a vision-ary, an inspired tactician and one driven son of a bitch who would let nothing, no man and no god stand between him and what he was put on this earth to do - salvage the Empire. It's been almost two hundred years since he died but Constantine's force lingers. Spend more time here and you'll learn to see his traces. After all, this re-ally was his place, this little spit of land he named after himself and made the capital of the world."

It was long past the hour when most families said their good-nights but we had never been most families. Hearth fires burned throughout the city and the familiar smell made me think of my father's workroom. But I couldn't have been further from the stirring string that night. Shivering, half drunk and less bewildered then I should have been, I hopped along, following my mentor as he flew up the Mêse and spun his tale.

Leo threw bits of history at me over his shoulder as we climbed. Rome's engineers had built terraces into Constantinople's hills to provide for its defense and to expand the level spaces. I had never been to the old Rome but I couldn't imagine anything grander than what I saw. Fortresses, palaces, forums and basilicas crowded streets that covered the city like veins. Everything was big, huge, larger than the largest. And everything was pristine. Even in the near dark I saw a world carved in marble, glistening brighter than the stars that just emerged to light the sky.

We met Constantine's original wall, the one he traced with a stick, buried deep within the city. Even though it no longer protected her from the outside world it still marked Constantinople's heart. I brushed my arm along it, picking up dust, appreciating the touch and smell of permanence.

Leo arrived at the gate that he was looking for and he elbowed me through before him. On this side of the inner wall his voice dropped from its normal bark to something approaching a whisper.

"Despite what they say, Constantine was no brute. Look carefully at his subtle gestures and you'll see his genius."

Like my father, Leo rarely strung together more than three sentences at a time. But he hadn't stopped expounding since we left the tavern. He talked and the Mêse unwound before us, around, up, higher and closer.

"You'll meet many true believers here, jackasses, humble folk and the vast muddle in between and most view Constantine like he is Jesus Christ's second cousin. Well I know the damn truth of the matter and I want you to know as well. There's no being safe in this world unless you know the truth.

"Old Rome had the creation myth of Romulus and Remus and the gods of Olympus to protect her. But by Constantine's day the old gods were weak as the Empire. For most Romans, Jupiter, Zeus and the rest of them were just quaint relics. And as faith left them, Romans filled their emptiness with vice. They sent mercenaries to hold the frontiers while they indulged themselves in filthy rites, in perversions of the flesh and the soul. You can just imagine the chaos in an Empire with a failing heart, with rulers who failed their people, with people who failed their gods, each other and their ancestors. And everyone searched in vain for meaning and purpose, hoping for something or someone to protect them from the barbarians at the gate.

"We were under attack from so many tribes, and in so many different places at once that the Senate promoted four legitimate Roman Emperors to rule simultaneously. They were Licentius, Diocletian, Maxentius and Constantine's father, Constantine Clorus. History calls that arrangement *the Tetrarchy* but I call it plain stupidity. The thought was that four mediocre souls could do what one mediocre soul couldn't was fool's logic.

"And Constantine was no fool. The day his father died, Constantine's own soldiers lifted him on their shields and declared him one of the four Emperors. Despite what the historians say you can imagine he didn't object. This was his chance to save Rome. But to save her he would need complete control and then he would need a dose of magic.

"It took him ten years to establish that control. First he defeated his brother in law and fellow emperor, Maxentius, in Rome on the

Milvian Bridge. Diocletian retired, never to be heard from again.
Then Constantine's last rival, Licentius, fled into Asia where he
eluded Constantine for a time but it didn't matter, he was a spent
force.

"And then it was just a question of magic.

"New cults, foreign gods and obscure portents had always fascinated Constantine. For many years he had followed the cult of
Mithras and later he was enchanted by Helios, the Sun God from
Egypt. Both espoused the concept of a single deity in stark contrast to Rome's official polytheism. Then Constantine stumbled
on the new Cult of Christ that borrowed heavily from Mithras
and Helios. Amongst the ferocious Christian faithful, the warrior
emperor recognized forces that could save an Empire. Devotion,
austerity, and unquestioning commitment marked its believers.
But to harness that devotion he would have to take the Empire
to the brink. He would alienate millions. He would lose the old
guard and the patrician pagans and he would elevate an under-
class, turning the outsiders into the ultimate insiders. It was a
supreme gambit, but Constantine decided that the Romans had
nothing to lose.

"Shortly before moving the capital from Rome to Constantinople,
the *Nova Roma,* Constantine declared that the faith of Christ would
be the faith of Rome, one Empire under one God. The people
would strive for salvation in Christ and the Emperor, would be the
principle disciple of the Almighty. The old pagans would be toler-
ated but that was it, the Emperor would never again embrace the
old gods.

"Within a generation Jupiter and Zeus disappeared into the shadows from which Christianity had just emerged, just as Constantine
had predicted.

"For certain my boy you already know most of this but you needed to hear it again, to place this grand experiment in some context. This is a city of faith but I tell you as one of a dying breed that what Constantine did wasn't born of his spirit but of his brain. He was a tactician above all else whose single objective, that which he would use all means to achieve, was the preservation of Rome.

"People might call this blasphemous conjecture but I'm just telling the truth. In fact, I have incontrovertible proof and it comes from Constantine himself. The man who guaranteed Christianity's place in history, more than Christ himself, wasn't baptized until he lay on his deathbed over thirty years after he forced the religion on the Empire, allowing himself to sin until the very end. Therein lies the lesson I want you to commit to memory – it is the substance and not the form of the thing that wins battles.

"And with that I present you with The Colossus himself. Look around you boy because *this* is the city that Constantine built."

We stood at the edge of a dip between two hills, facing down a broad street lined with wide paving stones. Everything radiated the moon's cool light.

I slapped my arms around my body to brace against the chill and my nerves, for some reason, were back. So I stood there, on top of a marble mountain, blowing life back into my hands. It was winter after all and without the sun there was no relief from the raw Bosporus wind. My ankles twitched with an uncontrollable urge to run precisely as Leo's hand fell on my shoulder.

"Up boy, look up."

I looked up.

The column wasn't big – it was titanic, as broad and tall as a full-grown oak. Tilting my head, I finally caught sight of the giant at its peak. Staring out across the city, a twenty-foot tall marble

Constantine stood with his head in the heavens, a broad sword in his left hand and in his right, an orb of brilliant gold.

"That is the man my boy, that is *the* man."

◆ ◆ ◆

That night I dreamt of war.

Vast armies massed in Asia and flooded westward. Kingdoms rose and fell. Fools triumphed and heroes died. Through it all I ran naked with a sword in my hand. And all the while the sun grew darker, menacing the battlefields, tempting the vultures.

The horror of the night still gripped me when my eyes flicked open. I was bathed in sweat, lying in the middle of Leo's great room, laboring for breath.

My after-dream was so deep that I barely noticed the intruder at first. Then I did see, just a shade before it was more, a menace backlit by the morning, advancing, threatening.

It must have been part of the dream, there was no other explanation. And if I were sleeping there was no need to react so I watched. The dark shape hovered, filling in the space between me and Leo.

And then the silence stopped.

"For years I waited for you, tending your home with care and comforting everyone you left behind. I assured them that you still loved us wherever you might be. I soothed your mother and scolded her for doubting that you were alive even though I doubted it myself. And when she couldn't stand the heartbreak any longer I buried her and shed the only tears that fell on her grave.

"On dark days when I thought that I couldn't take it anymore I looked for your face amongst the Mêse nomads, wanting to scream your name. Maybe, just maybe I'd attract the pity of someone with news of you. I did all of this and I felt all of this and how do you thank me? Now I know that Antonina was right! Only an ill-mannered beast could creep back into the world without a sound, without a single thought of me, without the decency to let a fool know that she doesn't need to grieve any longer."

The fool in question was a woman indeed, irate, convulsed with a laughter that shook the tears free from her handsome face, framed with long strawberry curls run through with silver.

Leo was off his feet before her first tear struck the floor, embracing her with both arms so fiercely that her toes no longer touched, whispering '*forgive me, forgive me, forgive me*' as they spun in a pirouette.

◆ ◆ ◆

"My boy, I introduce you to Julia. She is all of the goodness that I've ever known, concentrated in a form even more lovely than she was when I, the fool, left Constantinople."

I bowed. Leo rambled nervously.

"Julia, I introduce you to Valentinian, my pupil and friend, the only good reason I had for extending my absence."

Minutes later we sipped on wine and shared dry beef and bread. Julia and Leo chattered about the events of their separated lives while I watched, quietly amazed. There were traces of the man I knew but they mixed with a boyish charm I could never have imagined. The old warrior was gentle and gallant, jumping from his seat with the smallest hint from Julia, fetching her salt from a hidden store, grasping her hand from time to time to hold it gently.

Julia radiated warmth that captivated me at once. But as I looked closer I saw melancholy behind those vibrant green eyes, the luster that comes from an old spirit. I couldn't explain the feeling because she was clearly a beautiful young woman but there it was, something else.

"Alive not dead. In Constantinople and no longer in the wilds. You've been resurrected Leo and to be honest with you, part of me wants to kill you again. Of course I'm happy, how couldn't I be happy to see you, but knowing that you were so close for so long..."

The wine-colored scar rippled on Leo's jaw. Thick hands strangled his knees as he picked up the thread in his sparse way, briefly recounting the journey that led him from Constantinople through the territories of Old Rome and back again. More than a decade of life took fifteen minutes in the telling. It wasn't until his wandering brought him to Volerus that he slowed down, describing the day he met Claudius, 'an exceptional man, great in his goodness, my true friend' and how he was convinced to become my mentor.

"We both thought that wisdom came from the accumulation of small experiences, not from a few encounters with the epic and the grand. I think that's why he hired me. And that's where I've been, teaching Valentinian those little things that I know."

Julia looked at Leo with such care that I averted my eyes when she spoke.

"I'm certain that you succeeded. I always knew that you had a father's patience and generosity buried somewhere within."

A cloud crossed her face then as she smoothed her hair, looking away.

"And I don't doubt Leo that you have a father's firm hand. Tell me Valentinian, is he also patient and gentle or is he all discipline with you?"

I took my cue from her.

"My Lady, it's like the old story about the Bulgarian bear. He's a jolly enough fellow but he's still a bear. Even when he shows you love he leaves some scratches so that's how it's been with us. But I'm not complaining, I've survived and I'm better off for it I promise you. With a little pain and a little suffering I've survived."

Leo's face fell and he stood, ostensibly to clear the table. Noting his pout, Julia poked a finger into Leo's side.

"How dare you? I'm the only one here allowed to look long, cross or forlorn. Just because I choose not to exercise it doesn't give you permission to act like a child. Trust me when I tell you that you better be on your best behavior with me, Leo Cantecuzen. And frankly you are an old bear, one that I am inexpressibly happy to see."

The boy in Leo returned as he whisked scraps to the pantry.

After he left I explained to Julia that I had known Leo for more than half my life yet I had never seen him act as he did in her presence.

Julia brushed the hair from her face with the back of her hand, long tapered fingers trailing across her forehead.

"Valentinian, you're not alone. I've known him forever but I still don't understand him. I wonder if he understands himself and the things that give him shape and form."

She held her hands together a moment then released them.

"Part of me wants to believe that he's a changed man, that he found his answers. But I don't know. I've been convinced in the past. And I've been disappointed in the past."

A hint wrinkled then unwrinkled her brow. She pressed her smile and continued.

"So I decided long ago to take him as he was, with all his flaws because we all have them Valentinian. Though I must admit that after all these years, and in your presence, his flaws don't seem quite so damning. Amazing how time can soften sharp edges."

As I listened I began to wonder about the two of them, Leo and Julia. More than once over the years Leo had referred in passing to a certain 'cousin' that lived in the capital, the only memory that brought a hint of affection to his voice. On a whim I asked Julia if she might be this cousin. She tried to hide it from me but I saw her face fall.

"Oh no, he's no cousin of mine. At least he isn't my blood though he has been my family for many years, forever really. We both grew up in the same village and our parents were dear friends. Leo was older than me so I obviously knew him but not well, what young boy cares about little girls? But all of this changed when my parents died and Leo's family took us in."

Leo interjected from the doorway.

"And you're as precocious now as you were with pigtails. What stories are you telling Valentinian?"

Julia stood and turned to Leo.

"Oh please, your reputation is safe with me. I'm hoping that you aren't that self-absorbed man anymore but I must admit that I'm not convinced. So convince me, I give you one more chance to convince me so use it wisely, Bulgarian Bear. Valentinian, you have been an unqualified delight and to you I warmly issue this invitation. I would like you to please bring the old bear with you to my sister's wedding. After a solitary life she finally met an honorable man, a young general named Belisarius. But from the look on your face it seems that you know him already."

Leo countered with a wave of his hand.

"No, I don't know the man though I've heard of his exploits. It would be our pleasure to attend if you're sure that we wouldn't be intruding."

"Nonsense, first of all, and second of all, I invited Valentinian, you are his companion. And third of all, more always makes a party merrier. That's exactly why I'm bringing my son who you will both have a chance to meet."

Leo's face darkened as Julia swept her belongings into a blue satchel of heavy Ancyra wool.

"But we aren't done here Julia, I have so many questions to ask. What about this son of yours?"

Julia paused on the top step and whispered through pale lips.

"Time doesn't stand still for anyone. Much has changed and you must know that you aren't the only one that has endured. But you'll know more when you know my son, more than you deserve to know. And with that I say goodbye. Valentinian, enjoy Constantinople and listen closely to Leo. She is a city with many faces that you best learn well."

Down the stairs she went with Leo calling after her "but when is the celebration?" Julia's harried voice echoed through the stairwell.

"Today, dusk, at Chora" followed by the clap of the street door slamming shut.

Silence descended, falling heavily.

BLUE AND GREEN

UTTER TRANQUILITY IN her presence and turmoil when she left. That was Leo, rumbling in Julia's afterglow with nothing more for him, nothing more there, just the prickle of her perfume for comfort.

Needless to say that didn't suffice. In the two minutes we were alone Leo went from gentle lamb to wounded leopard. Mind you this uncle wasn't prone to moody – Zeno was the mercurial one – but when Leo went moody he went in force. As a child I would just watch it happen and suffer the consequences, but as a young man I knew a trick or two. The next time he paced by me I hijacked his momentum, 'it's only a few hours to dusk Leo, why not leave early and take a good walk, give me a chance to see more of the city by daylight'. And he agreed, plucking me by the tunic, sweeping us both downstairs, back into the street.

A different Constantinople waited for us, another animal completely. I went to sleep the night before thinking of the city as slow, expansive and majestic. Today she was immediate and raw. Plastered with incense, manure and blood – each step immersed us deeper in the concoction. And each step took its infuriating time. The charming lane that connected Leo's home to the city roiled with beggars, merchants and tourists, making it impossible to move. I would have lost my patience if Leo hadn't lost it first. Though he didn't exactly swat people aside his size and energy cleared the way just as surely.

We hustled along, winding towards the Mêse and my head swam, twisting with the city. Oxen moaned while solemn bells clanged believers to prayer. And on the street corner a harlot leered, her plump breasts pushing mechanically into traffic. As we strolled by she stabbed a finger towards Leo's arm but couldn't catch him.

Fascinated. I stared at her and she stared back at me, spitting her contempt. My god, my gods where was I? We broke onto the wide Mêse, flowing like the river Styx and I thought of Julia's admonition. It had just begun to make sense. *'Learn her well'* she had said of the city and she was right, I should and I would. Amidst the tumult I focused on her advice and it began to center me, giving me a sense of purpose amongst the flotsam and jetsam.

Next to me, ahead of me, Leo was another story. As fast as I went he remained two steps beyond, pounding his feet into the pavement, fixated on Julia. It was something in her eyes that worried him, a fire that flared when he mentioned her boy. As a mother she was naturally proud and he sensed that pride but there was something else in the muddle that concerned him.

Like my father, Leo could surprise on those rare occasions when he opened up and he did then as we rubbed shoulders, shimmying into the city's finer quarters.

"She was just a speck when I met her, a wisp with corn silk hair that completely hid her face. I don't think she could see a thing and it's just as well, she and her sister Antonina had just watched both parents die."

Tenderness returned to him as he described that day. The girls' parents were murdered in a raid and Leo's mother literally plucked them from the burning remains of their home. The elder girl, Antonina, left at once for Constantinople but Julia stayed behind, spending her days in the small vegetable garden out back, preferring her doll's company. The light seemed to coalesce about her.

Leo was a man at twelve - Isaurians were born men. And most able-bodied adult males, including Leo's father, aspired to serve in the Emperor's bodyguard. During his father's long absence in the capital Leo was responsible for the house. With the orphan Julia his responsibilities increased, but as he described it, that was the natural order of things. Eventually his father saved enough money to bring them all to Constantinople and when Leo reached the capital he didn't unpack, he just marched to the nearest army barracks and enlisted anonymously. He didn't use his father's name or connections to secure one of the plum jobs in the city. And so, predictably, within a week he was stationed on the Hungarian border as a raw infantry recruit.

With Leo gone, Julia the adopted daughter focused on the only constant in her world, her adopted parents. They settled down to a new life in the capital with a degree of comfort that they had never known. The three, Julia his mother and father filled that home, Leo's home, with warmth and when he received letters from the front he felt their happiness.

For a time it eased his guilt.

Then, three years later, deep in the Armenian badlands, news reached Leo that his father had been mortally wounded. An assassin made an attempt on the Emperor's life and Alexander Cantecuzen had been stabbed in the attack. *'The Emperor lives'*, they said, *'but your father...'*

Leo rushed to Constantinople but he was too late. Alexander received a hero's funeral that the Emperor himself attended. Afterwards, Leo considered returning to the frontier but his mother asked him to stay. She needed him.

The Excubitors immediately accepted his application and before Alexander's sword had a chance to tarnish Leo strapped it to his side and began walking his patrols. He was the youngest man on the detail but people deferred to him. Maybe it was because he looked like his father, maybe it was because he had always been old. By the time the Emperor died nine years later, Leo commanded the Excubitors.

Leo went quiet after we passed the Column of Constantine - looking even more imposing by daylight - and ascended the rise that brought us to the very edge of the Augusteum. I watched his clear eyes glaze as we stared across the vast expanse of public gardens filled with a well-dressed throng that took in the sun. The principle buildings of empire surrounded us. With a start Leo recognized our position.

"So here we stand in the heart of Constantine's city, a short walk from the four centers of power that wink at us now in all their glory. They are, in order of importance, the Palace, the Church of the Holy Wisdom, the Senate and the Hippodrome.

"The Palace lies ahead and to your right and needs little explanation. It is home to the Emperor, still the most powerful man on earth though in these days more than one barbarian vies for the title."

I followed Leo's outstretched arm to the Palace compound on the hill. It was not one structure but many. The first buildings stood at the hill's crest and the rest followed its gentle slope towards the Bosporus. Its gate, the Chälke, consisted of an enormous arch, crested with bronze, flanked by twelve columns of alternating marble and porphyry. They glinted permanence in the sun.

"Boy. Focus – this isn't the moment for daydreams. You may recall that that when we stood here last night we could just barely make out the Church of the Holy Wisdom."

The church was three times taller than Constantine's Column. Perfectly round, it was bordered by a colonnade in the manner of the old pagan temples. A brilliant dome floated above and at its center rested a cross of solid gold.

"The cornerstone was set by Constantine a few months after arriving in Byzantium. It is home to the Patriarch, peer to the Pope in Rome and competitor for all of the influence and riches of Christendom. While there might be some debate as to the Patriarch's ultimate standing in the Church, in this city there is no question about the weight of his opinion. Study his home my boy, you may or may not believe in Christ but do not doubt that the Patriarch holds the power of life and death over his flock."

Pointing east across the square, Leo picked out the Senate House from its peers.

"Now, today the Senate is just a shadow of what it used to be. But even so, the Senators' wealth and ancient privileges makes them a force to be reckoned with. Look carefully at their home. The proximity of the Senate House to the Palace tells us something about its place in Constantinople's hierarchy and something more about Constantine's feelings for them. By keeping them close he accomplished two objectives, he soothed their deflated egos while keeping them under his thumb. The old dog was never one for subtlety. Enough with the Senators, they are relics from another time, their Temple is a mausoleum.

"Finally, touching the Palace, we have the Hippodrome."

Leo directed my attention to the stadium where it lay south of the Senate, nestled against the western edge of the Palace. Its three vaulting stories were clad in crisp marble that glistened with the sun. Arches stretched around it at street level with three larger than the rest on the western, eastern and southernmost points. Only the three principle entrances opened directly into the arena.

The next two stories were wrapped in many hundred columns that wound about the structure. The Coliseum in Rome couldn't possibly be any more spectacular than this.

"Its neighbors might be fancy but you can see the Hippodrome couldn't care less, it has the self-assurance of a true peasant. And this is a peasant's place.

"The masses need an escape my boy, a means of letting the emotions drain peacefully. And despite what the freaks say Christ isn't our only salvation and becoming a monk on a mountaintop is not a legitimate alternative to life. Though you probably know that we Romans choose this route in droves, Constantinople has more monasteries than the rest of the civilized world combined. That said, they could build a thousand more and it still wouldn't soothe the beasts amongst us. No, the common man needs an outlet and in this peculiar capital that outlet is provided by the Blues and the Greens. Those are the colors of the two teams of charioteers and their partisans that fill the stands. After the Emperor, the Church and the Nobles there are the Blues and Greens – that is what defines this place. But you could argue that the Blues and Greens have more weight than some of the others on the list.

"The People have always had weight. The Emperors harnessed that power to steal the Republic from under the Senator's noses. You see the Tyrants understood better than the old blue bloods that common men make this world go round.

"So, when the Hippodrome's partisans shout louder than they should, Caesar understands that the force they waste might otherwise have been directed at him. The Games are a tool and the Emperors have always used them wisely. Nothing shocking there, this has always been the case though as I said, in recent times, these sporting groups have taken form and structure beyond the track. They're well organized now, involving themselves in civic functions, policing their neighborhoods, providing for the poor, holding local councils where the citizens air grievances.

"From what I understand this Emperor is partial to the Blues whereas the old Emperor Anastasius was a Green through and through. Not certain what that means, but there it is."

I remember spinning slowly on my heel while Leo spoke, taking in the epicenter of our Empire. Clapping my arms about my body to fight the cold, I asked Leo which team he preferred.

"Boy, I don't belong to any damn team of partisans. I don't follow anything or anyone blindly and I don't don colors to make myself different from some or the same as others. That's a fool's game. Study, absorb and try to learn from everything then choose the bits and pieces in life that are right for you. But whatever you do, walk your own path. That has always been my philosophy. And while I can't force anything on you I hope that you'll believe the same in time. But come now, Chora isn't far and it's time we get going if we are going to make this ceremony."

The mild afternoon had turned bitter. Our breath puffed as Leo led me across the Augusteum and back through the Wall of Constantine. We Thracians are native Latin speakers but much of Constantinople's residents spoke Greek then as their mother tongue. Leo spoke both, and explained to me that Chora meant 'outside the walls' in Greek and when the church was first built it was considered to be in the country. The city had now grown around it but it still retained that charm and the small neighborhood square it occupied looked like a traveler from another time. Leo hurried up Chora's short steps and banged through a side door. I dashed after him, into the darkness.

◆ ◆ ◆

Chora swallowed us whole.

There was no air inside, just incense. Somewhere in the soup a wedding party lurked but we couldn't hear them, not a soul breathed, not a beam groaned. All I could hear was the whisk of my feet on the flagstones.

We were late but I wasn't surprised, Leo never willingly entered a church. And once inside he tried to disappear, tip toeing like a burglar through the House of God. I couldn't help but laugh when I looked at him.

"Damn it boy, you know that I believe in the old gods and I'm proud of what I am. But I'm no fool and I know that this Christ character doesn't look kindly upon my sort. So yes, I walk softly in his presence. Now shut your mouth and follow me, let's be done with this."

I did as I was told. We clung to Chora's outer wall and instead of passing directly into the central nave we snuck into a side chapel. Painted emperors and empresses watched us skitter down a narrow passage. Our heads practically touched at the temples as we poked our noses around a doorframe and into the nave.

The bride and groom had their backs to us. Both wore traditional white togas but Antonina's was tailored for a different effect. She was all curves, glistening skin and rose oil that overcame the incense and practically overcame me. He was timber straight with broad shoulders and arms pressed to his sides as if his life depended upon it.

Just beyond them rumbled the man who officiated that day and he was no simple priest. He was the Patriarch of Constantinople, a man who spoke to the Pope as an equal and to the Emperor as a friend. But Christ was the last thing that came to my mind as I watched his plump hands rise in benediction. The movement wasn't graceful, his arms swung like a prize fighter's and when they stopped high above, his holy flesh continued to vibrate. The rich smoke moved about him, rippling to the far reaches of the room as he plunged his thumb into the bowl of sacred oil, scattering drops across the marble. With respect for the substance he removed his plump digit, pressed it to Belisarius' forehead, then to Antonina's before making the sign of the cross.

The ceremony had reached its climax.

Belisarius bowed his head but appeared more astute than contrite. He acknowledged the holy man with diffidence but not submission. In my young eyes the General was raw power incarnate.

You are too young to have known him in his prime, but I tell you that many made the mistake of underestimating him upon a cursory glance - he looked normal enough after all. But if you were patient you'd begin to see the details I saw in Chora. He was his wife's height but his bearing carried him to the ceiling. Everyone else in that room looked winter peach but not Belisarius. His skin was so dark with southern sun that he would have disappeared in a shadow had he not been bathed in light beaming from the colored glass above.

Without warning Leo jabbed his elbow into my ribs. Fortunately I had the presence of mind not to yelp. When I looked at him for an explanation he waved his head to the left of the room and whispered to me.

"Do you see them? There is Julia and that must be her son. What a blasted coincidence is that?"

It took some searching but I found Julia in a simple dress, pale pink, cinched at the waist with a silver rope, pressed against the far wall. Next to her was Mellius, the young soldier that had collided with Leo the day before, standing rod straight in his uniform.

It was an odd coincidence to be sure. But Julia herself is what interested me most at that moment for reasons of my own. I stared at her through the crowd and wondered if she looked like the mother I never knew. Not in the specifics of course, there was no chance of that, but maybe the effect was the same, the mix of quiet pride and the beauty she carried so lightly.

"Man and wife, you are."

The Patriarch pronounced his magic words and that was it, the thing was over. I was standing on my toes to get a sight of the new couple when Leo grabbed my wrist and hustled us out the door.

That's where Julia and Mellius found us, hiding awkwardly on the steps. She approached us with a warm smile and open arms. By her side her completely composed son gave no indication of emotion.

"Leo Cantecuzen, why have you always acted so strangely around holy men? You know that everyone there could see you lurking in the shadows."

Leo thrust his hand forward and clasped Mellius' forearm.

"It's good to meet you again, soldier, though I can't say the circumstances are more pleasant. Now, as far as your question goes, dear Julia, strange places bring out my strange behavior and there is nothing stranger than a Christian church. So how would we all like to go somewhere else, anywhere else, promptly?"

The corner of Mellius' mouth turned up. I couldn't tell if it was a grimace or half smile.

"Then I suppose you two gentlemen will be joining us for the celebration after all. My mother was right and I was wrong."

That's when I understood that this boy, he was barely more than a boy after all, disapproved of us. Part of me wanted to confront him but a quick look at Leo convinced me otherwise. My mentor was a study in tranquility. He just smiled his tight smile and I decided to follow his lead, trying to look uncomplicated and reassuring, above it all.

But that's not how I felt. Despite my best efforts there was no defining Mellius and it bothered me. I grew up in a simple world and my playmates were readily labeled. There was the brute, there was the fop, there was the scholar and they all played true to type. But Mellius just didn't conform. He had pieces I recognized but the way those parts were assembled…

Without another word Mellius took his mother's arm and off they went, strolling through the city center as if no one else, nothing else existed. For the mother there was just her son, for the son there was just his mother. And for the briefest of moments I envied them.

We passed through parts of the city that I hadn't seen before but I barely noticed. Instead, I eavesdropped on the conversation between Mellius and Julia. Again, it was his tone that caught me by surprise. I looked at him and saw a waif, whip thin, almost fragile. But when he spoke I heard a young lion.

'Yes, mother, it irritates me. Once again we turn our world upside down for her.'

'Mellius. It's her wedding day and we are the only family she has. I understand that you have passionate feelings but would you begrudge my sister even this?'

Mellius looked over his shoulder and saw us close but he evidently didn't care.

'It might sound horrible but from the bottom of my heart I do. I do begrudge her even this, why should she have the comfort of our presence? Where has she been for us all of these years? When my grandmother died where was this aunt of mine? When my father left, where was she? Did she rush to your side, to offer you comfort, to dry your tears, to bring you hope? Has my aunt ever been there to share our joys and sorrows? I know that she's your sister and I know that you can't say these things but you have to feel them sometimes.'

'My son, I can't make you love your aunt though I do know that she loves you, she loves us both though it pains her to show it. You're too young to understand that she's not the person that she wants to be, she is the product of the life she was given. And now, finally, a good man has found her and loves her dearly. Don't you see the beauty in that? Can you find it in your heart to give your Aunt this one moment?'

Mellius rubbed the uneven stubble on his face.

'Mother, you don't need to ask me, you know I'll behave myself. There's just one last thing I want to say. You and Antonina have both lived difficult lives and you have both experienced loss. But there is one gaping difference between you.

'Antonina wears her trials as a badge on her chest. She nurtures them and keeps them close. She flaunts them as a sign of her divine right to do as she would please. Deep down inside she believes that Life owes her something truly grand.

'You, my mother, do not walk this way.

'You have always taught me that one cannot know the beauty in life without knowing life's pain. You have taught me that no one is entitled to anything, no matter how mighty. We are what we do, what we give and what we create. Finally, you have always taught me that sunshine is sweetest when it peeks through the deepest, darkest clouds, and that is the difference between the two of you.'

Julia smiled fiercely.

'You are your father's boy after all. I don't hear a peep from you for days and when you speak it is always straight to the heart of the matter.'

The furrow in Mellius' brow deepened as he spoke.

'I am only my mother's son. How could I belong to someone that I never knew?'

Julia turned away from him then. She saw us trailing some paces behind and stared for a long moment. I could feel heat on my face where her eyes touched but she didn't say a word. Instead she waved her long fingers, fluttering them down the street, pulling my attention.

The street itself was really just a square with two mansions on each side, eight in all. They seemed to float like galleons, shimmering like only the priceless and unattainable can. In the center of the square was an Egyptian obelisk, sitting in a pool of water that swirled with the spirits.

"More privileged places might exist but this street has always charmed me most. As a little girl I would steal moments here, dreaming wild dreams."

Julia stopped walking. We had reached our destination.

Belisarius' home stood before us, unique amongst its rich fellows. The neighbors were taller than the trees and heavy stone walls that surrounded them. But the General's home had no protective wall, just mature elms that shared glimpses of the home beyond. And in the center of the tree line there was a single gate, firmly shut, that must have been part of a wall long ago. The whole concept of the General living in plain sight of friends, enemies and all, struck me as crazy. In retrospect, I wouldn't be surprised if Belisarius himself had the wall removed. He was not one to hide.

So we approached the gate that could have stopped a marauding army instead of simply walking around it through the trees. Julia grabbed the door strike and swung it against the wood.

Almost at once we heard a shuffling and then a distant voice from the other side.

"Forgive me forgive me I meant to leave it open."

The voice grew louder as the courtyard pebbles protested. Julia turned and flashed us that brilliant, comforting smile again as the door opened.

Beyond it stood the silhouette of a man whose broad shoulders dipped almost imperceptibly as he beckoned us over the threshold. Julia pushed us through.

THRESHOLDS

"**M**Y FRIENDS, I am Belisarius, and I welcome you to the monstrosity they call my home."

Two hands of leather and sand thrust themselves into our midst, grabbing us by the forearms as if we were old comrades. I was instantly captivated.

"Lovely Julia, you bring more joy to us on an already joyous day. And Corporal Mellius, I'm pleased that you could steal a few minutes from your regiment. Now, please come in, come all of you, Antonina is waiting."

The General didn't wait for a response before turning back towards the house. Stepping like a leopard, he picked his way through the courtyard's long grass and weeds that defied the cobbles. The four of us skipped behind, straight to the home's imposing entrance. Its bones were still handsome despite years of neglect.

When Belisarius reached for the heavy front door it burst open and a flash of grey hair and tangled robes ricocheted off him and fell to the floor.

"Oh my, gentle master, forgive me. I didn't hear the knock until late and I came as fast as I could forgive me."

Petronius, Antonina's valet, rose to his knees and begged for forgiveness.

"And that was evidently quite fast, good Petronius and yet, I think that we are having a communication problem. I told you that I've seen to my own needs my entire life and that is how I plan to keep things. Now, go tell your mistress that the guests have arrived and that we'll be along shortly."

Without another word Petronius disappeared into the house and we followed him. Just as Leo and I passed over the threshold Belisarius caught his arm.

"Leo Cantecuzen, it's an honor to have you in my home. I know what you did for the Emperor Anastasius. This isn't the time to talk of these things but I want you to know that I could use your talent on my staff. But later, we'll have time to talk later."

Before Leo could respond, Belisarius moved on to address us all in the center of the home's grand foyer. In contrast to the outside, the home's interior was in pristine condition and as bare as a vault.

"Julia, welcome to your sister's home. To be honest, I'd feel more comfortable in a field tent but it gives her joy and so, here we are."

Leo took stock of the hollow palace and began to look skittish. The General noticed.

"Now, you are the last guests to arrive. Ah, Leo, I see that grimace and I can tell that you are an antisocial wretch like me - all the better. But you needn't worry. We only invited three more strays to this thing. And with a little luck we'll find them somewhere in this cavern. Please, follow me."

With Belisarius in the lead we slipped through a series of chambers that were barren but for a profusion of white roses scattered along the floor. Julia walked by Belisarius' side, holding his arm, chirping in a low voice that broke with occasional laughter. Leo and I followed a few paces behind, absorbing the stark oddness of that place. Mellius trailed in his mother's footsteps but not quite with her, not quite with us.

And the shadows swallowed our footfalls.

After a series of wrong turns that were quickly retracted, Belisarius approached a set of austere wooden doors. His hand lingered on the rough-hewn oak and for that moment he cut a lonely figure. He must have found the conviction he sought because the moment passed and he thrust the doors open.

A wash of light splashed from the room, across our faces.

My eyes adjusted to the glare to find Antonina standing in the exact center of the room that was itself an exact circle, speaking with two older men and a woman. The backs of these latter three were to me but Antonina faced us as we entered.

I wouldn't have called her beautiful but Antonina was striking, even a fool could see that, her regular features, her light and color. Later, on closer inspection, I saw that skin was not quite smooth, it had been powdered and colored but her face still impressed. My father always said that a bride is beautiful by definition, warts and all.

"Come in please. Come in and share this delicious event with me, with my husband. Come in and let the celebration begin."

After offering her warm cheek to Julia, Antonina shifted her attention to me and Leo. She took Leo's hands into hers and smiled broadly.

"My almost brother, what a delight it is to have you in our lives again. You bring the past with you, most constant Leo, and it warms my heart."

Leo responded, barely tempering a blunt response to the subtle sarcasm.

"Antonina, I would rather think of myself as the future than the past but today I won't argue with you. May this day and this marriage bring you all the happiness that you deserve."

From the look of her she wasn't entirely pleased with the comment. There was energy between them, a prickly thing. I watched Antonina as she scrutinized my mentor, probing the man for weaknesses. Now I don't know who Leo was when they last met but I knew this uncle of mine as well as any and knew she wouldn't find a thing. Leo never gave an adversary enough rope to hang him with and when he pressed his lips to Antonina's hand he did so gallantly. But from his response I saw what category he placed Antonina in and I must say I watched her even more carefully afterwards.

With one delicately plucked eyebrow raised till it almost touched her hairline she turned her attention to me. If I could have disappeared I would have in a heartbeat. I had never been to such an event and I had never seen such a ferocious creature up close. Placing one hand on either side of my face, she effused like only predators can.

"What a fine young man you are Valentinian. Now tell me what father would send such a youth off to the capital in the hands of this old scoundrel?"

As I wracked my brain in search of a suitable response, Antonina fluttered past me as the other guests approached.

The first was Leontius, the Imperial Surgeon. From a distance his rich beard reminded me of Zeno's. The whiskers weren't nearly as wild but they made him instantly likeable. The Surgeon stepped towards Belisarius and grasped him by the forearm before greeting Leo with smart, burbled words. I might have heard something revealing if I hadn't caught sight of the Surgeon's daughter trailing in his wake.

Layla.

Cappadocia is littered with salt flats. And when spring rains flood those crystal beds the water turns a piercing blue unlike anything else on earth. That was the color of her eyes. Tapered long at the corners, touched with charcoal, they turned languidly towards me and stopped me dead.

Though I lacked experience, I wasn't an insecure boy. Then I saw her and realized at once that I was nothing and she was everything. You could have told me that she was Cleopatra's own blood and it wouldn't have surprised me. In her exquisite features and bearing she was every bit worthy of that ancient queen. Layla was an *Upper Nile* Egyptian and the air shimmered about her just as it did around fire, repelled by and attracted to the source. Though winter lurked outside, she glowed like fresh-set bronze and when she inclined her head towards me I couldn't help but bow deeply.

Not even Antonina's well-fed torches out-shined my Layla. *Mine.* I felt immediately possessive of her, before she uttered her first word.

Her power was such.

My weakness was such.

Exchanging quiet words with the General, she stood as straight as a rail but still emoted grace. I couldn't tear my eyes away from her, I would have stared until the sun rose and set and rose again if Leo hadn't pinched the back of my neck between thumb and fore-finger, directing my attention elsewhere.

A large man, with a life force so strong I could feel it as a physical thing, stood directly before me. Then I realized his toes literally touched mine he stood so close, leaning towards me till I could smell the food on his breath. He said something, he must have repeated a question.

Leo saved me from what I might have said by mustering his own inappropriate, if genuine, response.

"By the gods..."

The Patriarch of Constantinople laughed when he threw one impossibly heavy arm around me and one around Leo. Then, with a jerk, he pulled us both into his chest with a bull's finesse.

◆ ◆ ◆

"In God's name, I beg of you not to stand on ceremony. I was a parish priest once and that's how you should think of me. It is in this least affected and most human of capacities that I celebrate the marriage of my friends."

Of all of the stupendous things I had encountered in my short life, the sight of the Patriarch up close, round like a cask of wine, ruddy as a sailor and soft like an apple blossom was far and away the most breathtaking. This was no parish priest, this was the Patriarch, one of the most important men in the Empire. And he stood inches away from me, leaning his head back so that his nose might sample what the chef had to offer.

A broad smile followed.

"Pheasant and beef. Fruit and wine. My nose tells me that dinner has been served. Come my children, let us start this fine marriage on the right note."

With that he led us through the nearest door and into a small adjoining courtyard. The night was crisp but it couldn't penetrate that courtyard, open to the sky. Winter stars blessed the proceedings while two roaring chimneys kept us warm. A square table dominated the courtyard and a great silver urn sat in its center. Its high polish reflected fire along the walls in orange tendrils, giving the courtyard a feeling not quite of this earth.

Dinner fluttered in upon a stream of servants, carrying an aroma so rich it made my nose itch. Petronius fussed with the plates while Antonina swept us aside in favor of the Patriarch. Our newest friend tiptoed around like a dancer before delicately wedging himself into a chair that made a valiant effort not to complain.

Once his eminence was seated the bride turned her attention to the rest of us.

Since that day I have met Empresses and I have met barbarian queens. But I have never known a woman with Antonina's qualities. Though I must admit I didn't understand her attraction at first. Back then I still possessed the young man's notion that perfection in a wife meant beautiful, demure and docile. Now, with the benefit of years I know that some men might be happy with those flavors in isolation but not I. As I have told my son many times, a man should aspire to a partner, an inspirer, an equal in the enterprise. In hindsight I can understand the General's choice.

Antonina had a leader's strength, a tactician's wit and a warrior's courage. She directed her husband like a foot soldier and he hopped to, beaming proudly in her direction. And though I hadn't met the emotion myself I could tell Belisarius was truly in love.

Belisarius. The General of all generals. The *Magister Militum per Orientem*.

I was in his home, celebrating his wedding and I clearly didn't belong. My father was the Rope Maker, not the Prince and not the Senator. I should have been catching fish in the shallows but here I was, obviously misplaced, mismatched, mistaken. Again, I fought the urge to run just as Julia caught my eyes. She motioned me to the empty seat on her left as her own son occupied the seat to her right. Safety of a sort. I crossed the courtyard in a grateful bound and slipped into place at her elbow.

Only one guest was left standing and that was Leo. Julia and I both laughed as we watched him sit down gingerly at the Patriarch's side. What a sight! It was as if Hercules and Christ had met on the road and popped into a tavern for a quick dinner together.

Julia, her son Mellius and I sat across from Leontius, Layla and Leo. Layla and I faced each other, placed at the two ends farthest from the newlyweds. I couldn't help but gawk at her, I had gone beyond staring, now I was just transfixed in a way only young men of a certain age can be.

She must have felt my eyes because at that very moment her nose crinkled in profile.

Mellius watched Layla as well and I couldn't blame him, it was hard not to. He might have been a charming fellow, but at that moment my first thought was that I had a rival. In the off chance that Layla was aware of me I tried to look noble.

"What a blessed evening. What a blessed couple. And what a true pleasure it is for me to be here, raising my cup to celebrate these two faithful servants of God and Empire." The Patriarch took a deep draught from his cup and bared his purple teeth.

"Now, what none of you know, including you Antonina, is that if it weren't for General Belisarius I wouldn't be alive to witness this day. Flavius Belisarius, you had asked me not to speak of this thing but surely, amongst dear friends, on your wedding day, I can say this much.

"Nearly ten years ago, before I was chosen by Emperor and God as Patriarch, I was the proud priest of Chora parish. To celebrate the birth of Christ that year I journeyed to Jerusalem, to walk those storied streets and to get a feel for the man that was the Son of God. Sometimes we get so bogged down in doctrinal nonsense that we lose sight of the basics like the fact that Christ was, in fact, a man.

"There are many in the Church that would burn me at the stake if they heard me say it but thanks to my elevation, they can do no such thing. You have no idea how I could bore you with the endless debates that split me and my equally plump brethren. Was Christ divine or mortal? What exactly is the Holy Ghost? Is the bread at mass really flesh, is the wine truly blood? And the reality is that none of it matters, all that matters is the central message, respect, humility, kindness, and good deeds. We are a young organization. One would hope that we weren't so damned bureaucratic but one day we'll get it right, I have faith you see.

"But that's enough of that, on with my story.

"So there I was, absolutely delighted in Jerusalem amongst the fanatics. Everyone there believes fervently in something and no two men believe the exact same thing. They all stink to high heaven and they froth with an intensity they've cultivated for centuries, what a place! Just imagine, an entire city filled with prophets and holy men, women, children and cats, endless cats. And the food was unimaginable, laced with such spices, blended in such delicious concoctions. Suffice it to say that I had a truly great time there but eventually I had to return to my flock.

"Oh dear, this toast is running long, bad habits from the pulpit are the enemy of brevity. Cutting to the chase now, against my friends' objections I decided to take the land route home through Damascus instead of jumping on a chartered ship. My stomach, you see, is not happy on the sea.

"So I willfully ignored my overcautious friends and started out by land with a small group of pilgrims that were simply too poor to afford sea passage. And I thought, what better way for a god-fearing man to return from Jerusalem than in that little caravan. What an ass I was! The road was alive with bandits but they didn't take us at once. No, they watched us patiently for days before making their move. We were just hours away from the Syrian frontier when they pounced, Persian raiders, charming, greedy and quite violent.

"Things did not look good for any of my little party and least of all for your Patriarch. The brigands took one look at me and evidently thought I might have some value as a hostage. They were mistaken of course, I had no money on my person and I refused to send word to Constantinople for help. I tell you all that I would have died in their hands had it not been for General Belisarius who held the Roman frontier that I so desperately wanted to cross. Through shrewd negotiating he managed an exchange of Persian hostages for this one humble priest. Not a single drop of blood was spilled and thanks to him I live. And for this act of kindness I shall be forever grateful.

"Now my stomach rumbles so much that my legs shake. So let us toast this *divine* couple. May you live long together my children, may you know the sublime love born of devotion and may you not forget that He is the thread that binds you together."

I had never seen or heard anything remotely like the Patriarch. He was a plump, subversive seed planted in the heart of the Church. I'd never look at him, or any priest for that matter, quite the same though I must say that I have not met his equal since.

After he took his seat the table broke into different conversations that rushed and bubbled in small torrents. Julia tapped her goblet against mine and Petronius raced to keep cups full. The food was spectacular. Boar roasted with apricots and apples, pheasant filled with spiced beef and juniper berries, huge loaves of steaming bread and every fruit known to man, grapes, apples, cherries and more. I can barely remember the dishes but I remember sampling everything before me, savoring those flavors drawn from the Empire's far corners.

While Julia and I spoke, Mellius stayed largely silent, barely touching his food. His mother didn't show outward concern but she did glance at him from time to time, touching his hand as she spoke to me of other things. In particular she peppered me with questions about Volerus. It had been so long since I had known such a tender soul, indeed, I wondered if this was something that I had ever truly known. Once again in her presence I found myself thinking of my mother, so much so that I couldn't help but tell Julia.

"Dear Valentinian," she responded. "I understand your struggle because I see my heart in yours. We have both lost but you must learn that in this loss you can find your greatest strength. Don't you know that we can only lose those who we choose to forget? It's up to us to keep them alive, in countless ways, large and small, in the freedom of our laughter, the gentleness of our touch, the depth of our grief and the audacity of our passions we make certain that those we have loved continue to fill the world in which we live."

Leo approached. Placing a hand on the back of both chairs, leaning in between us, he whispered playfully.

"Help me, the Patriarch will have me baptized or crucified before the night is through. Help me."

Julia turned towards him ever so slightly. Mellius emerged from his trance then, focusing his luminous eyes on Leo.

"Leo, you are a grown man and I know for a fact that you have escaped unscathed from situations more dire than this."

Feeling the nip of a gentle arrow, Leo's tone changed as he continued.

"Yes Julia, yes, you're right as always. But let's not talk of the past now, let's talk of brighter things. For hours I've wanted to tell you that you have a fine boy that I'm glad to have met. And please forgive me for prying into personal matters, I didn't mean to intrude. I suppose that I relinquished that right when I left this place."

Returning her attention to the table, Julia responded in a voice that I strained to hear.

"Yes Leo, I suppose that you did."

Leo looked like he had more to add but he refrained. Nearby the Patriarch engaged Belisarius in a conversation that ran sharp. The General had to lean in front of his wife to make eye contact with him. Antonina stood and switched places so she could sit closer to her sister, letting the men talk. Even though he was practically on top of the General now, the Patriarch curled his robust frame over and around the table as he spoke heatedly.

I struggled to hear them over the roaring fire and the table chatter. Next to me, Mellius' eyes bore into Belisarius so loudly they sang. He seemed to have come alive even though he had barely moved a finger since he first sat down. Across from me Layla eavesdropped more blatantly than any with a hand cupped to her ear. She had all the subtlety of a well struck hammer and on a night of intense, the flavors, the scents, the people, nothing was more intense than Layla. I had this idea then as I watched her that if I strained I might be able to smell her. Some people take pride in personal pieces, a chin set so, a noble nose, eyes, but my favorite piece was my sense of smell. And though it might sound deranged, at that moment, in my completely stricken state, I decided that I might just be able to smell her across the table. So I tried. And there, amidst the spiced wine, salted boar and charcoal scent I found her, like the desert after a lightning strike, flinty, sweet. I lost myself in that desert for more time then I knew while our little microcosm moved on. I saw it then, Belisarius' lips moving, Antonina's jutting chin, an instant chill. All the emotion in the world swirled and I couldn't hear a word. But when the Patriarch flushed, beyond the wine's encouragement, I heard him perfectly.

"Of course I worry. There are agitators, General, and they harbor evil thoughts towards our Emperor. You can't convince me that this Saint Laurentius affair isn't connected to that evil. It has me concerned, truly and gravely concerned and this tranquility of yours baffles me. Clearly you haven't seen Laurentius with your own eyes so why don't you take a boat for Rome's sake, take my boat tomorrow morning and go there to get a sense of the ugliness. The citizens that claim to guard the place have bloodlust in their eyes. No good will come of it, absolutely nothing good mark my words. You know that I understand the city's pulse as well as any. Through my confessionals I hear many voices Belisarius and right now they are not comforting."

Belisarius' faint smile faded. He looked over the Patriarch's shoulder to catch Leo's eyes and the Patriarch noticed. The communication between the soldiers encouraged him to press on.

"Please General, you have been back in the city for weeks. And we've known each other for too long. You must know that I'm not inventing this."

With a voice that barely carried the table, Belisarius responded.

"Not everyone is cheered by our recent success in Persia. And yes, there are some that don't see this army, or this Emperor, as the true champions they are. But are these elements a cause for concern or are they part of the background noise? I just don't know and to be honest with you I don't care. Asking me to count my enemies is like asking me to count the stars in the sky, some things just aren't knowable."

At this moment John practically jumped in his seat, a peculiar motion that made his plump body snap as he harrumphed.

"NO, no, no, you are wrong. We can know and we do know. For the love of God, General, now is not the time for circumspect, we have a real problem on our hands. You are a man of action and I am telling you that Caesar must act."

By now all of us at the table had turned our attention to the Patriarch as he wagged his finger at the night sky.

"*They* are out there. Tonight, on this God-given night in the heart of the Empire there are those that conspire against Justinian and I believe that the conspirators are preparing themselves for action. I told the Emperor as much last week. The events of last Sunday were no accident and the story is simply too good to go away. Imagine, Caesar kills two men that refuse to die and then he insists on killing them again. If that can't inspire a rebellion I don't know what can. Please speak with the Emperor - he'll listen to you. As a man of God I can appreciate his forbearance but there's a point where this Christian charity can be carried to an extreme. The Emperor must reconsider his benevolent view of the opposition before something terrible happens."

The entire table vibrated. All eyes shifted from John to Belisarius but the General looked elsewhere, seeking the one man that deliberately avoided him. With a word the General pulled Leo out of his seclusion.

"Good Leo, I see those clenched hands of yours and can't help but think that you have something to add."

Leo shook his head as if he were throwing off a demon.

"General, I've been away and out of the game for so long that I'm wary, I don't know if I trust my own eyes."

Belisarius' showed his first frown of the evening.

"Leo, I ask you to speak."

Leo pulled a breath.

"General Belisarius, I think that you and the Emperor Justinian would do well to heed the Patriarch's words. I know the capital well and I know her conspiracies - I spent a good part of my youth trying to protect a different Emperor from his enemies. And I'm not certain that I believe in harmless *noise*, with all due respect. Noise is a concern and in this city every concern merits attention, investigation and swift responses."

Leo's sentence was cut sharply as a soldier bearing the insignia of Constantinople's Prefect rushed into the courtyard. After bowing low to the Patriarch, he hurried to Belisarius' side and whispered in the General's ear. Belisarius listened carefully and turned to the soldier.

"Sergeant, are you absolutely certain?"

The soldier stiffened.

"Sire, there is no doubt, I heard it straight from the Prefect who in turn heard it straight from the Emperor's lips. He sent me here with strict instructions for you."

PART III: HIPPODROME STRAINS

...those who suffer the most grievously from evildoers are relieved of the greater part of their anguish by the expectation they will sometime be avenged by law and authority.

- Procopius of Caesarea

NIKA BREAKS

For as long as Rome has been we have had the Games.
Greeks might have invented the Olympic concept but we
Romans gave it spice and blood. We inherited the discus, the mara-
thon and wrestling and they are all fine as far as they go. But it took
our warped minds to add gladiators, naval battles, chariot races and
even crucifixion to the mix. And then, once we had our savagery
perfected we built amphitheaters across the Empire to replicate it
so that no one would miss the fun.

Sarcasm aside, the fact is that those stadiums really are brilliant
things, bold experiments in social order. Only in the Hippodrome
can everyone that matters in Roman life and everyone that doesn't
cram into the same uncomfortable seats to see the show. In the
capital, that means that Senators rub shoulders with bakers and
masons who come close to rubbing shoulders with divine Caesar
himself.

For most creatures there's nothing more intoxicating than that
kind of proximity to power. And while Romans aren't easily intoxicated, they are an enterprising lot that sees proximity for what
it is, an opportunity to cut through our bureaucracy to get things
done. Things aren't quite the same now, but when I first arrived
in Constantinople it was still true that within the sacred ring of
the stadium the people had the right to petition the Emperor to

solve their little problems. And most remarkably, those men-that-would-be-gods frequently did.

On the Sunday before Belisarius' wedding that ancient custom brought our Empire to the brink in the Hippodrome.

Sunday, January 11th 532, was an especially frigid day, even in the Hippodrome that teemed with bodies. Everyone that could cajole their way in had done so and those that couldn't loiter outside, listening to the roaring crowd, trying to guess the outcome. These were the semi-finals of the racing season and partisan passions ran high.

When Justinian entered the Imperial box known as the *Kathisma*, high above the stadium floor, the crowd hushed. Horns preceded him, drowning the usual whispers of awe and envy that accompanied Emperors. Once Justinian sat and his standards were unfurled the games resumed.

And then the petitions began.

Tentatively at first and then with pluck the plain folk stood and called on their Emperor. Imperial pages relayed messages from the stands in a human chain until they reached Justinian who was in a fine mood that day and it showed.

"Good Emperor Justinian, please extend these marvelous races!"

And Justinian declared that it would be so.

"Mighty Emperor, more bread on feast days please!"

And the Emperor acknowledged that he would provide.

But then a new voice, smooth and strong as porphyry, floated above the tumult. It had been years since oratory, a dying art, had flourished in Christian Rome. And this petitioner, a home-ly lump of a man, was clearly a master. The proof was that no guard needed to transmit his message for anyone's benefit. That magnificent voice of his made the journey unaided, booming deep in the Hippodrome's distant spaces, echoing in the Kathisma. And once there, far away from its owner, it proceeded to pick a fight.

"THERE IS A RAT IN CONSTANTINOPLE!" The petitioner bellowed, claiming that the rat was so craven, so despicable, that he deserved to die like Judas. According to the heckler, the rat's name was *Calopodius*.

An implicit protocol controlled these interactions. Complaints were limited to banalities but this man spoke of matters close to the Emperor's heart. Calopodius was a member of the Imperial staff appointed by Justinian. Hence, an attack on Calopodius meant an attack on the Emperor himself. And the Emperor was inviolate. A deadly line had just been crossed.

After fifteen minutes Justinian had heard enough. Through his bodyguard he announced that he wouldn't sack Calopodius even though half of the Hippodrome had joined in the call. When Justinian ordered the petitioner's arrest the crowd erupted, showing its dissatisfaction as the Emperor left the Hippodrome. The remaining races were cancelled and the crowd was expelled from the stadium.

But not everyone returned home.

A dozen malcontents gathered outside and complained that Justinian's treatment of the now incarcerated Hippodrome petitioner was unjust. More protestors joined in, so many that their chants penetrated the Palace walls. The Emperor directed the city guard to quell the tumult, which they swiftly did, taking six key instigators into custody.

The machinery of justice moved quickly from there. A military tribunal was convened to judge the rioters. Evidence was presented and the accused spoke their piece but the crime could not be undone. They should have, and could have, spoken to the authorities about Calopodius. They could have spoken to their patrons who could have talked to a Senator who could have wielded influence. But they chose a different path and a different message, one that had never ended well under Imperial justice. And so, mere hours after their arrest, the original Hippodrome crier and his six supporters were judged guilty of sedition and sentenced to immediate execution, with three to be hung and four to be beheaded.

Before regret set in or news traveled a military barge slipped the seven across the Golden Horn to Pera. It was barely a town then, a clutch of stout houses, fishing boats and a church to bind them all, that was Pera. It was also an Imperial execution site, one of a few that lay about the City.

Now, executions were, are and shall forever be finicky things. Some are best conducted in the center of town where all can see and some are best conducted in dark corners. The magistrate decided that this particular execution was a dark corner job, but Pera wasn't far enough and twilight wasn't nearly dark enough.

When the guards trundled the condemned off the barge they had to push through a bristling crowd to reach the bluff. There was nothing docile about the shopkeepers, bakers and voyeurs who gathered to watch their neighbors die.

And yet the executioners did their job.

Four men were quickly dispatched with an axe to the throat. Blood flowed openly across the cobbles, coating the spectators' feet.

They say the small crowd moaned to see the loss of their own. We Romans don't often shrink from blood. If it's deserved then it's deserved. But we don't tolerate senseless bloodshed - it raises

our hackles. That's one of the things that make us Romans different from the Persians. They tolerate their tyrants better. We by
contrast are an impatient lot, particularly, especially when our traditions are abused. And unfortunately for the Emperor Justinian,
regrettably for us all, that night at Pera proved the perfect case in
point.

It rarely snows in Constantinople but a few flakes fell then, delicate
and dry, dropping onto the cobbles and into the blood. The final
three prisoners were led to the scaffold, very carefully so that no
one would slip and fall. And then they were hung.

I have a healthy respect for fate. Over the years I've learned
that it's almost never linear and almost always peculiar. That's the
normal course of things but what happened that day, on a rise above
the Bosporus, was anything but normal.

The hangman pulled his lever.

Three men plunged to earth.

But one rope held and two snapped leaving two wretches remarkably alive. One belonged to the partisan Blues and the other
to the Greens. If only they had died it might have ended right
there, on the bluff.

But they lived.

Every culture has its traditions. Some last for a generation then die
and others capture the imagination and last for centuries. Rome
has many of these, more than any other place on earth. People may
change, attitudes may change but Roman customs remain.

As the two condemned men wriggled in the dirt, the mob
invoked one of those ancient ways. We have always believed
that a man who cheats a death sentence merits his accidental
life. The large crowd that witnessed the execution let the guard

know that Roman tradition should be respected - the two survivors should be released in the mob's opinion. When it became clear that the soldiers intended to re-hang the blue and green a punch was thrown, the soldiers responded and partisans joined the fight.

In the ensuing melee, sympathetic monks from the nearby Monastery of Saint Conon managed to bundle the two condemned men into a small boat that lay nearby. Before the guard could react the monks had rowed the escapees up the harbor to sanctuary in the Church of Saint Laurentius, tucked in the northwestern corner of the city, just within the Theodosian Walls.

The Prefect Eudaimon controlled the city militia, a modest force, built to arrest pickpockets, to safeguard the commercial forums and to control the casual crowds. Eudaimon was also the chief judge of the capital and in this role he had presided over the earlier trial of the Laurentius two. He wasn't a malicious sort, but he took his responsibilities seriously. The Law of Rome said that two men must die. They were still alive and it was his job to correct the error. As soon as he heard about their escape he dispatched fresh troops to capture them. Mind you, the soldiers didn't dare enter Laurentius without an invitation from the clergy but they did make certain that no one could enter and no one could leave.

In the arc of a civilization there have always been moments like that, moments of raw energy, when a whisper of wind could raise the low and lower the mighty. And to think I was in Constantinople from start to finish. Of course, I was unaware at first but that would change soon enough.

News of the blockade raced throughout the city and citizens flocked to Laurentius. A few hundred at breakfast grew to a few thousand by dinner on the first day. They were ordinary folk for the most part. Some of them had been at the Hippodrome the day before and knew firsthand about the origin of Justinian's anger. But most had heard the story second-hand and to them it seemed that the Prefect's actions were plain wrong.

'So typical of the powerful to punish the little man, and not once but twice for the same crime," they said.

'You wouldn't see a Senator trapped like an animal in Laurentius,' they said.

The more they milled about the angrier they became. By midday the soldiers were completely surrounded by a heavy crowd demanding a reprieve.

At night the spectators and the soldiers lit fires to ward off the cold. From the surrounding hills the watch fires and makeshift shelters resembled the encampments of opposing armies. Shouts rang out through the night. The monks within Laurentius chanted and their baritones rolled into the deep dark.

This was Sunday.

The picket continued on Monday but the day passed without incident as partisans and soldiers eyed each other and the two condemned men cowered inside, not daring to show their faces.

Tuesday was the Ides of January.

It was also Belisarius and Antonina's wedding day.

The city convened at the Hippodrome before dawn for the final round of championship races, and by sunup the stands were filled to capacity. The Emperor and Empress were also there.

Evidence of the storm manifested itself from the start. Between each race both Blues and Greens petitioned the Emperor to spare the Laurentius unfortunates. Of course it would have been an easy thing to do. I've thought about it a thousand times and there's no question in my mind that if I had been the Emperor I would have conceded the point in hopes that the whole damn mess just faded away. But Justinian was a man of process, not of personal gestures. I knew that about him even before I got to Constantinople, thanks to Zeno and one salty afternoon, years before.

"Most Emperors, most kings and most dictators are indistinguishable from the rules they propagate. The problem with that model is that when the man dies the rules die with him, leaving the poor bastards he governed to learn a new dictator's preferences. Not a pleasant position for us simple folk and not good for the stability of the territory. Now, we Romans have made more laws then any culture on earth and a fair number of them are good. The problem is that good laws are irrelevant if no one remembers, understands or enforces them. Put in simpler terms, Justinian respects the law of our forefathers and he wants them respected, that's what makes him different."

So Zeno told me.

To rectify what he saw as the Empire's most pressing problem, Justinian commissioned his leading jurist, Tribunian, to codify the full thousand years of Roman civil law in a single work, the *Corpus Juris Civilus*. The colossal effort, one without parallel in human history was almost complete by the time I arrived in Constantinople. Once done Justinian would disseminate it through the Empire so that any literate Roman could know their rights as citizens.

What irreverence! Now that I'm older I understand better but at the time I had no idea how wild Justinian's concept truly was. As a young boy whose voice still cracked this whole legal revolution seemed very theoretical to me. But there was nothing theoretical about the Emperor's dilemma. Justinian could have pacified the mob by overturning the capital sentence with his little finger. And yet, he knew that a handful would benefit while the vast majority of his citizens would suffer. They might not see it that way but they would suffer, and their children would suffer and their children's children.

In every fiber of his body Justinian believed that Rome teetered on a precipice. He wasn't one more in a line of emperors, he was *the* Emperor that would decide if Rome careened off the cliff or if she would adapt and survive. He would decide if Rome slipped into the Darkness that enveloped our Lost Lands to the West, or if we maintained the ancient light that we inherited, from Rome and Greece.

The outcome in this battle between Darkness and Light was by no means certain.

And so Caesar decided that upholding the law was worth the risk. The verdict would stand.

By leaving the races early that day Justinian sent his message - Caesar would not succumb to the mob's demands.

Understanding very well what the Emperor's departure im-plied, the Mob sent its response between the twenty-second and twenty-third races of the day. Justinian and the Empress Theodora had just the Palace when the chanting in the Hippodrome assumed a new, menacing tone.

From the youngest to the oldest, man and woman, the Romans in the Hippodrome raised their voices in what sounded like a war cry. They no longer directed their appeals to the Kathisma or to the charioteers down below. Standing shoulder to shoulder, with voices raised to the open January sky, they howled the Greek word for victory, again and again.

"NIKA. NIKA. NIKA."

There were no more partisans, no more fans, just a stadium filled with irate citizens. Some were city residents, some were farmers, some were there by accident and others had more sinister intentions. But all that mattered at that moment was that a group of many thousand spoke out loud, telling the Emperor that they disagreed. They took issue with *Him*.

From that moment on everyone knew that it could only end in blood.

Seats emptied and the liquid mass streamed from the exits, howling their way into the Imperial Quarter expecting confrontation. But no policemen, no private guard and no militia attempted to stop them. Now, you might think that rabid bunch saw the lack of opposition as a good thing but when you are a mindless mob the absence of a fight can be anti-climactic. So they deflated a touch in the vacuum, pausing outside the Hippodrome's southern end, the *Sphendrion*, to take stock. Casual rioters began to tire of the effort but someone in that crowd understood the moment's potential. With a well-timed suggestion the mob changed course and made haste to the Praetorium because that's where Eudaimon lived. And Eudaimon, the Urban Prefect, had a special place in their hearts for his role in the Laurentius affair.

The Praetorium's guard consisted of two older men who looked sharp in uniform. The mob approached them and demanded to know the Prefect's intentions regarding their St. Laurentius compatriots. Those two poor souls couldn't have spoken intelligently about the Prefect's intentions for lunch, let alone something of importance but they promised to find out. One ran inside, pleased to have left his compatriot with the lunatics.

The Prefect received the news from the confines of his bath but he was an important man and he thought that he might answer them after dinner. To his defense, the answer wouldn't have made a difference to the mob. Within minutes they surged into the gate until it buckled and quickly occupied the inner courtyard, pulling Eudaimon out of the building for punishment. But before they could decide a proper fate for him, the Prefect took advantage of squabbling amongst the mob's leaders to tip toe out a side entrance to the street and safety.

That's when the crowds' anger turned, taking on substance. A clutch of the loudest and most irascible had assumed command over their compatriots. That naturally pleased them, and when Eudaimon's escape threatened their authority they sought something new to abuse. Someone produced a dozen torches and the ringleaders combined intellects.

Were they simple hooligans, were they professional mercenaries or were they decent folk caught up in the moment? I suspect that they were a bit of everything but as I've said before, it doesn't matter who they were - the outcome was the same.

A fire was started.

It would burn for five days.

It would destroy the heart of the city and bring the Empire to its knees.

Within an hour of the first spark, a lone soldier named Lucius was dispatched to fetch Belisarius from his wedding feast.

COMMAND RESUMED

B ELISARIUS RUBBED HIS hand roughly along his jaw, observing the room as if for the first time, that dining table, those frescoes, the mosaics underfoot.

"The city burns."

He called out to all of us and none of us.

"The city burns and the Emperor fears that there's worse to come."

I had been in Constantinople for the critical events I just described but I was oblivious to them all. Even after Belisarius broke the silence I still didn't understand. But I'm not certain that anyone, including the General, could have guessed what was to come.

Petronius returned with Belisarius' chainmail and sword; trembling, eager to be done. Time barely trickled as he extended his arms, holding the sword flat. I coveted that blade, imagining its heft, its history. Petronius coughed. Layla leaned in close to her father.

Belisarius was quiet as the rest of us but his face was alive, tightening, preparing. Crow's feet rippled beside his eyes. His hands flew, replacing his wedding tunic with chain mail. He ran his eye across the blade then plunged it into the scabbard. One pull cinched it fast by his side.

For the first time in my life, but not the last, I wasn't smart enough to be scared. Too transfixed, too enchanted with war

and warriors - that's what I was. But that would end soon
enough.

"I see your faces I see but I can't answer your questions, not yet.
All I know is that we aren't safe here, we need to move. And I owe
the Patriarch an apology. John, your damned suspicions were pro-
phetic and then some. Once again you proved that you are more
than a man of the cloth. Now listen please, all of you, there is much
to be done."

The General of the Eastern Armies barked and beside me
Mellius snapped to with a crisp military salute that I envied. This
boy, barely more than a child was a soldier and I was a country
clown. Again I looked at him and felt like he was a rival. Not to
be outdone I mustered my own sloppy salute but the General didn't
notice. He cleared his throat.

"It is time for safe havens, but I need help to get you there."

The General spoke in measured tones and assessed the material
at hand. A plump Patriarch, a sister in law of unknown qualities, a
whiskerless soldier, a wife that could hold her own, a surgeon with
delicate hands, a young girl that braced for wind and two back-
woods guests stared back at him, awaiting orders.

The General's eyes passed amongst us and my face ran hot. Next
to me, Leo hummed with a concentrated energy I recognized. The
General focused on him.

"You are no stranger to me, Leo Cantecuzen.

"I know of your time in the Excubitors and your father's time
before. The impact of good work lingers longer than you might
think, especially amongst us, the Emperors' men. You gave your
metal to Rome years ago and tonight I need it again. Can I count
on you?"

Leo inclined his head ever so slightly and rumbled.

"There is no question about that now, is there. My life for the Emperor, it has always been that way."

The two of them spoke words I understood but expressed sentiments beyond me. My ears arched forward as I tried to will myself comprehension.

The General smiled grimly.

"Very well then. You left the army as a captain, from this moment on you are a Military Tribune of the Eastern Army, a fair promotion for a worthy man. If anyone challenges you, tell them your authority comes from me. If they still question do what you need to convince them. Your job transcends niceties tonight. Before the sun rises you will bring every soul in this room safely to the Palace. Valentinian and the messenger Lucius will keep you company."

Belisarius proceeded with clipped instructions.

"Now, Private Mellius, you will come with me. Though I've been in and out of the capital for years I'm no native so tonight you'll be my guide through the back ways."

"Yes sir, General sir." Mellius spoke and though its pitch belonged to a boy it had a soldier's metal.

"We must be wary. Mobs congregate in open spaces and you should avoid them if you can. I have no idea how they will react if they see the Patriarch, but just in case..."

Belisarius beckoned Leo and me to an anteroom just off the courtyard. Ten swords hung from leather tongs on the wall. He selected five and handed two to us. I had never used such a thing in battle but having it in my hands gave me a comfort it shouldn't have.

Leo tested his sword, cutting the air. I held mine close, pressing it to my chest as Belisarius rejoined the rest of the group and offered the third sword to the Patriarch, the fourth to Leontius and the fifth to Mellius. Mellius bound his swiftly with a strap, John accepted the weapon with a bemused chuckle, the Surgeon returned his with disdain.

"General, we've known each other too long to mince words. So please keep your sword, I'm in the business of saving lives not taking them."

The Surgeon's beard flashed as if it was made of metal and he took Layla's arm in his. "My daughter and I will be leaving now and we don't need an escort, thank you General."

Layla removed her arm from her father's but she didn't move. She looked more comfortable standing alone. Leontius' rebuke didn't appear to surprise Belisarius.

"Leontius, you two travelling alone will attract less attention. But behave – don't make me regret obliging you. Now it's best you're on your way but Layla, please do make certain that your father practices some caution."

Layla conserved her motion.

I scrutinized her and wondered if her insides raced as much as mine. But only her white cotton gown floated - all else was still as her father prepared to leave. I thought of a thousand ways I could go with her so that I needn't contemplate *separate*. But there it was, the General smiled at her and her head inclined just so. Antonina received the same reserved curtsy. Then Belisarius clasped Leontius by the forearm and they were gone. Petronius saw them to the door as his last official act of the evening.

The Patriarch eyed his sword curiously before pressing the hilt into the General's outstretched hand. "General, if there were a stuffed fowl to be carved I would know what to do with that thing but in battle it's useless in my hands. And surely no one would dare to harm a man of the church. Remember the Persians! I handled them, in a manner, and I am sure that I'll handle these people who are *my* people, after all. So keep your sword, General, and keep your armed escort. Like my friend Leontius I have no need of their services. I'll be on my way now, with a little luck I might catch up to that incorrigible man. I do want to check on my church before sleep."

Belisarius stiffened and took a half step closer to John.

"Holy John, you wouldn't ask my advice on how to conduct a mass and I have not asked your advice on how to conduct my mission. I would go to the ends of the earth to ensure your safety but it must be on my terms. You know that I wouldn't lead you astray."

The Patriarch nodded to the General who lingered one more moment, searching John's eyes. Then, evidently finding what he sought he turned to his new bride who had stood, statuesque, immobile by his side. Belisarius took her hands in his, firmly.

"My Antonina, you have nothing to fear but you know that already. A braver woman doesn't exist. So be patient and safe."

Now, I didn't know much about matters of the heart then. But it was clear, or so I thought, that there was no poet in Belisarius, he was a man of action through and through. He spoke to his bride like she was just another soldier but that was the way between them I supposed.

As Belisarius moved to go Leo caught his eye. Noting the concern on Leo's face the General explained that he, Belisarius, had complete faith in him.

"Don't worry that I'm simply judging you based on your reputation, Leo. I know your truth, Leo Cantecuzen, and that's enough for me."

Leo's frown deepened in response.

"General Belisarius, with all due respect, I don't feel burdened. These are the easy things, the bloody things I know. Count on me to do all that I can and I hope that's enough. But before we separate maybe I can offer you something more. You spoke of traveling outside the city. If your journey takes you to the Theodosian Wall ask for Basil, Captain of the Guard. He is a friend of mine and a friend to the Emperor. On an uncertain night you might just need one more friend. Call on him and use my name. He'll stand with you as surely as I do."

The gratitude on Belisarius' face was palpable. He looked at Leo, narrowed his eyes then clasped my mentor's forearm with both hands.

"When this thing is through, you and Valentinian must join me, Leo."

With those parting words and a rustle of chain mail Belisarius motioned to Mellius. Mellius embraced his mother fiercely before disappearing in Belisarius' company.

Quiet fell in their wake.

◆ ◆ ◆

My tongue stuck to the back of my teeth and I left it there, worried about the noise un-sticking would make. The room was that silent. Only the fire spoke and when Leo stepped before it, his back to the flames, it went silent too.

"The Patriarch, the bride and her sister need clothes that won't attract attention. Antonina, go and fetch your simplest robes, take them from the domestics if you must."

The bride shot him a glance that might have killed a man who cared but Leo clearly didn't. Shooing her away with a finger he turned to face me

"From the sound of things the Palace is the last place for any of us tonight but the Emperor wants the Patriarch so we shall deliver him there. But first you, Valentinian, will deposit the girls in my house. That will give me time to move the Patriarch towards the Mêse. We have no choice but to cross it to reach the Palace. After leaving the sisters in my home you will meet me at Constantine's Column and from there we'll make our way together to the Palace."

A mission of my own.

There was no heavenly host, no shining star, no Oracle to read the entrails that said *your life begins now*' but it did. I tell you that I have relived those few minutes a hundred times or more in my dreams, painful dreams, especially in recent years. The dream is almost always the same. I stand in Belisarius' house, in a pool of light with black nibbling at the edges. But rather than Leo before me my father Claudius is there, looking younger than he ever did in my lifetime and he is staring at me, mouthing a warning but no sound transcends the roaring fire. Just before I wake my pool of light tightens until it's a physical thing, pressing in, squeezing the breath from me.

The only variant in my dream is the expression on my face. Abject fear appears most frequently and that's fair, I was afraid. There is nothing wrong with being human, screw the dolts that pretend to be something else. Those asses tend to be the first to die so if my fear keeps me alive then I'll embrace my inner coward. On other nights I've seen me as dullard, whip, thug, hero, child, even a young man in the throes of first passion and I wake up rested from them all. They are all genuine fragments of the man I've been and they deserve their moment.

As the ladies rejoined us I tried to compose my features into something manly but I didn't succeed. Julia looked frightfully pale when she passed a rough cloak to the Patriarch. Leo explained his plan in a few curt words. Antonina coughed, raising her chin high and beyond.

"So Leo, you're sending me back to the dogs are you? You know as well as I do that my rightful place is in the Palace. Have you forgotten that my husband commanded that you take me there? Obey him or regret it, Cantecuzen. This is not backward Isauria. This is Constantinople where my husband speaks for Caesar."

Leo spoke slowly, like water tempted to freeze.

"Antonina, you will leave here now. Valentinian is taking you to my house, its doors would stop a rushing bull and its location is discreet. This is the safest course. And lest you forget, Isauria runs in your blood too, nothing more or less noble."

Antonina turned away from Leo with a shake of her head but he would have none of it. Stepping in front of her to block her retreat, he bent low and placed his face squarely before hers.

"Antonina. Now means now.

"Julia. Please see to your sister.

"Valentinian. On with it."

Antonina shrank into herself and didn't say another word. Julia offered Leo a quick scowl and a swift curtsey to the Patriarch before grasping her sister's cold hand. With her other hand she hooked my arm in hers.

"So we'll make it a bit of an adventure then."

With that we were on our way, out the back door, into the alley, in the dark.

SISTERS SAY

"BY WHAT CURSE was I given dreams only to have them stolen? By what curse was I given this skin, this face, this beauty and these brains that should have brought me to the highest highs but left me here instead, wallowing in the gutter."

Antonina screeched in the dark alley behind her house while rats claimed their kingdom. Stealth would keep us safe, that's what Leo told me and Antonina's violent moans put us all in jeopardy, if anyone was looking for us we would be found. My chest was damp with sweat and I jittered with nerves and cold that shot through my thin cloak.

Not the man I should have been and not dressed properly for the occasion. Odd the things we worry about in our defining moments.

Asia spat bitter wind upon us, calling steam from my bones. With muscles pulled tight and spiteful when I needed them most, I coaxed my legs over and around the garbage, crunching cockroaches under my sandals. Ahead of me, in the shadows, someone retched from the overpowering stench and I prayed that the weak stomach belonged to my group, not to the enemy. The truth is that Antonina hadn't exaggerated; we really were making our escape in a gutter. The twisting path with high walls on either side was reserved for the servants' daily commute and because it was hidden from sight every kind of filth was stashed there. Trash, feces, pottery fragments and building supplies made it impossible to follow a straight line. What a damned disappointment. It wouldn't have killed the little royals that cavorted in this neighborhood to show respect for the littler people that kept their world dazzling.

I felt close to the poor bastards of the world that night, much more so than I did to the ladies I escorted. My fingers toyed with Africanus' gold medallion beneath my tunic as we skittered along, every time I touched it I felt unnecessarily comforted. Just maybe the story was true, just maybe, and yet as I came to realize with time that fantastical past didn't matter.

As Leo says, 'life is for the living', and if I was to live the legendary Africanus and all things esoteric had no place in my waking hours. Sticking to the things that can be touched and felt, my rudimentary facts, kept me alive during the Riots and the Wars that followed.

My father is a rope-maker. I am a soldier in the employ of Rome. The General cares but cannot save me. My sword has killed and that doesn't make me proud nor does it shame me. My heart aches and you are distant, distant, so distant.

That was my refrain for so many years, my litany of facts that kept me grounded.

Romans are obsessed with the concept of distance. Zeno says that we were the first people in history to measure length in a scientific way. Our desire to travel, build, measure and mark is a good part of what makes us unique in his mind and I agree. When we're all dead and gone those practical contributions — the maps and milestones, the network of highways, bridges and tunnels — will remain.

Engineers always raise an eyebrow when they hear me describe their infrastructure romantically but I can't help myself, I've always felt that way. Since I was a very young boy I used to traipse around our Volerus garden, drawing paths in the earth, imagining I was taking an Imperial road to adventure in Italy, Gaul, Germania, Africa. Someday, I thought, someday I would be *bold*, someday I would take my first step *there*, towards my destiny. And then I truly was there, faster than I ever could have imagined. In such a hurry to arrive I missed so many things in between and when I arrived, when I opened my eyes at my destination I was standing in a gutter, barely eighteen years old, on a mutinous night in Constantinople.

And I was not nearly the hero I had hoped to be upon arrival.

Despite everything I have seen and done since I am still not that hero but I'm effective I think, determined and effective. Thus far in my life those traits have been enough to traverse the distances, actual and imagined, that the gods have placed between me and destiny. Distance to the Palace, distance to trouble, distance from the world I knew and at that precise moment, distance between me and Antonina who insisted on walking ahead of me through that horrid muck, dragging Julia in her wake, not in the least bit intimidated by the rats. I used the back of my sleeve to filter the stench and called to her. She was too loud, walking too fast, acting far too brazen on a night that required discretion.

I told her as much and she slowed, allowing me to move ahead while Lucius, the messenger, brought up the rear. I had barely caught a glimpse of him before we left the house but I could feel those clear eyes of his scouring the night while I saw everything with a glaze.

He was only five years older than me, but he was rugged to my smooth. Not many young men in Constantinople wore a full beard but he did in what was considered the *Hunnic* fashion. I felt better knowing that he was with me, somewhere at the back of the line while I walked point with a sword sticking from my cloak.

Walking point on my first mission.

Walking point on my first mission.

I repeated it so many times, under my breath, that the sisters were well into their private conversation before Antonina's volume drew my attention.

"You will never, ever understand what I've endured to get here. We're too different after all, we dreamt different dreams and we chased different stars but then I catch myself thinking that maybe you never even bothered to watch the stars. You always seemed so content with the mundane that fills the world and the asses that populate it. I've always strived for special. I always knew I was *special*.

"While I lived, drank, ate and loved in every city between the Black Sea and the Nile you stayed in Constantinople. You accepted obscurity when I insisted on the stage. You ate your bread with a smile when I screamed for venison. When I suffered the loss of our parents you gave yourself to a mother that wasn't ours. And when I fought for love you contented yourself to life without a man. And yet, after everything, I go from fulfillment to emptiness in a single night. By what curse I ask you because I must be cursed."

If they knew I could hear them they didn't seem to care. For Antonina at least I must have been a regrettable necessity. Julia was different I think, I know Julia was different. But she focused exclusively on her sister as we snuck through the city. High on adrenalin, scared and proud, I walked on the tips of my toes, expecting enemies in the deep shadows. My nose told me when the first clouds of smoke rolled through the neighborhood and it was not hearth smoke, the heavy cinders were the first ominous sign of the City's trouble. I thought I had taken care to stay close to the group but when I reached our first milestone, an important local street where three could pass abreast, I arrived alone.

The Imperial Quarter lay to the left and Leo's house to the right. In the faint streetlight I looked as far as I could in either direction but just past midnight I couldn't see a soul. Better, we had been lucky so far but that didn't stop the tremor in my hands, I watched them a moment as I waited for the rest to catch up to me. Then I heard Antonina's voice lashing out at Julia for reasons I couldn't fathom. Now I know more about her envy, her insecurity. But then I just listened, puzzled, wincing as Julia accepted the assault.

"Yesterday I started a new life with my gallant husband by my side and today I'm running away from my home like a vagabond with my sister, the spinster. Just like the old days this is and I detested our old days Julia, I detested them."

They rounded the last bend, into sight. Julia was walking ahead of her sister with a jaw that looked set to shatter. She pressed her hands to her temple then threw them into the air with a groan. Antonina practically ran into her as Julia exploded.

"Enough Antonina. For God's sake that's enough you are unbearable. Could you try for just one second to focus on someone other than yourself? Because I promise you that you aren't the only one suffering. But how could you truly know because you never truly cared.

"As you said you were making your way from the Black Sea to Alexandria and now you're back. And now you dare to instruct me about pain, about disappointment, about how crushing it is to admit that life will never be what we planned? That withering frown of yours doesn't intimidate me anymore, Antonina. And don't you worry, I don't hold any of this against you, it's simply your way. It has always been your way."

I called to them. Though we had to keep moving my fear of the sisters, of women, prevented me from insisting. I grew up in a household filled with men, that's all I knew. Men acted, and reacted in simple, predictable ways. They are quiet, borderline incommunicative and they avoid confrontation. The confrontations that I did witness growing up between my father, Leo and Zeno were infrequent, civil and conformed to certain rules. No raised voices, no histrionics and when the confrontation was over it was over. That I understood. Yet this thing between the sisters was wilder than an elephant in the Alps. There was nothing soft between them, only fierce. And while Constantinople was supposedly on the brink of war I hadn't yet seen any signs. In reality we hadn't passed a single man, woman or child on the street. But here before me was something very tangible to be afraid of, the regal Antonina, the rare Julia and the ancient wounds that they had just ripped asunder. I would have used my sword to defend the sisters to the death but I wouldn't interrupt them, not yet. We could spare a minute for them to settle their differences.

Antonina realized that she had overstepped her bounds and tried to make amends.

"Julia. I beg your pardon I…"

Julia cut her sister's apology short with a raised hand.

"No, please, be silent for a moment and I'll explain why you aren't alone with your troubles. Can you imagine what it is for a mother to carry the knowledge in her heart that her son will never have a father? No matter what I do for him I will never be able to assure him that he is no bastard. Of course he knows that he had a father of sorts but as far as Mellius is concerned the whole concept is a fiction. And if it's indeed true it's too far in the past to be of any use to him now. And now he needs it most.

"Just look at him and you'll see that my little boy is no longer, he is a man, Antonina, and a strong one at that. Didn't you see him at your wedding? The way he watches over me, the serious cast to his brow and the sense of duty that pervades him. And tonight, my little man wanders this city, determined to protect the Empire but who will protect him? I would lay down my life for him but I'm afraid that I can no longer travel where my Mellius goes, he has moved beyond me."

So that the sisters wouldn't know I eavesdropped, I coughed before approaching. Though I hated to interrupt, Leo was waiting for me and I told them as much. To their credit they did look at me, briefly, before continuing their conversation as Lucius stepped out of the shadows. He had been trailing us like a ghost but it was time to part ways. Leo would pass through here on his way to the Palace and Lucius would join him. Lucius and I exchanged a quick salute that he complemented with a smile and that was it, we were moving again, three rather than four. The sisters walked ahead of me, quickly now, and within minutes Antonina's voice picked up the thread.

"Julia, I may seem the self-absorbed wench to you and to be honest, sometimes I am that. But I do know that you've struggled and I'm convinced that you've done everything that you could for your boy. With that huge heart of yours you didn't have a choice; you just did what you were born to do.

But as I listen to you I can't help thinking something else. Part of me wonders if the thought of your son is the only thing that weighs on you. You know I wasn't born a subtle girl so don't frown at me. Cantecuzen is back, that is fact. His departure wasn't easy on you. That is also fact and come now, don't look so surprised. We've had so few people in our lives that mattered and he was certainly one of them. He cared for us, protected us, and provided for us for so long. He was so many things, a guardian angel, friend and hero and just perhaps something more for you? I wasn't here during those last years before he left but I must admit that I always wondered."

Antonina paused to give Julia the chance to object but there was no objection. Observing her sister carefully, the flare to her nostrils, the heaviness in her eyes, Antonina continued.

"It doesn't matter what did or did not happen. All I know is that his return has been unsettling for me and I imagine it was for you. Seeing that relic from another age in my home made me shiver, to be honest with you. So I suggest that you follow my lead, ignore him. Our debt to him is paid. Leave Leo Cantecuzen in the past where he belongs."

Julia looked back over her shoulder at me while I made a great show of looking preoccupied with other things. Julia seemed satisfied by my act because she turned to her sister and spoke with a lilt.

"There are times my sister when I wished that I could see the world through your eyes where everything is brilliantly clear. To live a life where there is no doubt, no regret. But that was not my fate, where you were decisive I have wrestled and reasoned. But I do feel the truth in what you say and I know that you say it with affection for me and for my boy. Yes, of course I see the truth in it but I just can't tread the path you would have me take. As I chose it once I choose it again, a life of complexity. I can't change the past. And I don't know what Leo means for me anymore. He is a peculiar man, inconstant constancy, noble and coarse. If I were to make a decision based simply on my needs perhaps I would follow your advice. But the needs of my boy will always come first.

As I told you I feel that Mellius needs a man in his life. And when I watch Leo with his young protégé, Valentinian, who is lurking somewhere behind us, I see tenderness and stern love, the wisdom that only an old soldier can give. I think that my son would benefit from knowing him, Antonina, and for that reason I will not keep him from our lives."

Antonina took Julia's hand and brought it to her chest. She watched Julia carefully a moment and twisted her mouth at the corner before speaking.

"My sister, believe me when I tell you that this selfish wench stands beside you, in this, in everything. And now, I propose something slightly rebellious though you know to expect nothing less from me. Rather than waiting for the men to send for us I suggest that we thank young Valentinian here for his company and instead of going into Leo's house, we march to the Palace. I am, after all, the wife of General Belisarius, commander of all Roman armies and that is where we both belong, ensconced in luxury."

Antonina laughed. Julia joined her and both turned their defiant faces to me. With the sternest look I could conjure I told them that they must do what Leo and General Belisarius demanded. We were indeed standing before Leo's door and as I had watched him do barely a week before, I bent on one knee, took the long key from my cloak and carefully unlocked the door.

"Ladies. Please."

Antonina wrinkled her nose at me but promised to behave.

Julia placed a kiss on my cheek and promised to behave.

I didn't believe either of them but I had no way to compel them to stay. More important matters called me away and after I saw them close the door I sped away, back towards the Imperial Quarter.

NIGHT FLIGHT

A SHARP WHISTLE ECHOED in the back alley, ringing across the broad backs of moneyed homes. Just the tip of a nose protruded beyond the doorframe, testing the air. It was the third time Leo had sent the signal and there was still no response. Lucius was to have accompanied me half way to Leo's house before doubling back to join Leo for the Palace run. But it had been too damned long. Standing squarely on the threshold, fighting impatience, Leo judged the silence.

Though I couldn't have imagined it at the time my hero who looked as sure as granite was wracked with doubt. He explained to me later that the more time he had to think, the more bitterly he disagreed with this entire plan. It was wrong, plain wrong, flawed from the start. He could skulk and shimmy across the entire city but sooner or later the Patriarch would have to cross open ground near the Palace. We would all be exposed, we would likely be spotted and if we were stopped… Leo knew Constantinople's labyrinth as well as any, there were a thousand possible routes that ended at the Palace and all of them were wrong.

We were risking our lives to deliver the Patriarch into the Emperor's hands. Unlike me, the thought of death didn't put Leo off. It would come sooner or later and he had lived a singular life. What bothered him was that this rescue mission would put the Patriarch at even greater risk.

Just then Lucius' whistle rose above the city sounds. Leo heard, stepped back within the house and whispered roughly.

"Listen carefully, the time for flight is here and you, good Patriarch, will lead us into the dark."

A most audible grunt was followed by the Patriarch's shaken voice that had lost all hints of round-bellied joviality.

"Good Lord, my son, you cannot be serious. What experience has a man of the cloth in such matters?"

"Your Holiness," Leo hissed, "brave Lucius waits for you at the end of the alley and if someone tries to lay a hand on you we will kill them without hesitation. Move now. We have no time to waste."

The Patriarch wrapped the borrowed sackcloth around his ample frame and hustled down the alley. He ran for his life, unaware that Leo raced silently alongside, stopping periodically to confirm that no one followed.

As they drew to the end of the alley Lucius stepped out into the street to greet them. A winded Patriarch stood by himself, leaning against the wall of a nearby home, taking sharp breaths and muttering. With an eyebrow raised Leo asked Lucius for an update.

"Sir, all is well. I left them halfway to your home, as ordered, and we didn't encounter anyone or anything between here and there. If I hadn't seen the riot with my own eyes I'd think that the city slept peacefully. But of course it doesn't. It just means that the damage is still confined to the Imperial Quarter. They will have no problem reaching your home and Valentinian should have no problem reaching our meeting point."

Leo nodded his head as he eyed Lucius, noticing his face for the first time, the puckered lips, and the furrowed brow. There was something familiar in it and something foreign, but he couldn't tell which was which. Drawing himself up to his full height Leo called the Patriarch near.

"Until we reach the Palace I will call you by your name, John."
The Patriarch's eyes opened wide.

"No, I am not deliberately trying to insult you. Quite the contrary, Holy John, I am trying to save your life. If someone on the street hears your title and recognizes your face it might be ugly for us all. So listen now, this is our plan, sparse as it may sound. Valentinian is waiting for us by Constantine's Forum, from there we cross the Mêse and cut towards the Palace. The path looks clear but we'll take nothing for granted. Come John. Lucius, trail us by one hundred paces. We leave now."

Leo and his band sped through the neighborhood, moving as quickly as the Patriarch's bulk allowed. Leo led, plunging first around every corner and into every deep shadow with his sword drawn. When they arrived at the Column of Constantine they didn't find me. Had Leo known of the stupidity I was engaged in he would have killed me. But he didn't know and so he took care that his little group couldn't be seen from the Mêse and they waited. It was so calm on the Forum's edges, so apparently benign that Leo began to expect the worst. At midnight in a city of a million souls there should have been something, someone on the streets. Drunks, City Guard, animals, there was always action on Constantinople's boulevards and the absence of life screamed of trouble.

They didn't have long to wait for trouble to appear.
Looking east to the Imperial Quarter, Leo saw an orange glow stretch across the city's crest and called his companions' attention to the light. It stretched and receded and when he listened carefully he could hear the fire's dull nothingness, its death.

Constantine's Column was no more than fifty paces away and men appeared now, flowing past the Column towards the Augusteum. Leo knew that he should be moving soon but he couldn't bring himself to leave. He would complete his mission, his duty was to the General, to the Patriarch, to the Emperor. But he thought of my father, Claudius, and he stayed.

Just them a thousand terrible voices erupted from deep in the heart of the city and on the horizon a new plume of fire spiked into the sky. The Patriarch leapt but Leo grabbed him, holding him still. The awful noise returned in waves, sweeping westward and over them.

Leo expected an onslaught.

He and Lucius held their swords ready.

Though minutes passed with no sign of an enemy, Leo knew that the horrid noise didn't come from friendly forces. He had seen enough battles to know. Now they simply had to bide their time, to wait for me and pray for luck.

"Patience John. Patience Lucius. Patience."

◆ ◆ ◆

Long before Leo hustled the Patriarch out of Belisarius' home, I slowed to a walk on the Mêse. The sisters were safely locked away, leaving me time to explore before meeting Leo. The first neighborhoods I crossed were quiet but the city came to life as I moved east. Men emerged from dark corners, spilling onto the road, scurrying here and there.

First we were a few, then dozens, and then many hundred washing towards the Mêse's terminus in the Augusteum. I had expected to see a rabid mob but those people looked more like spectators than actors in the drama, on a late night stroll to see what they might see.

Then we came upon the first flames, crackling and spitting fury just inside Constantine's Wall. Passing through we came across the Praetorium, the original source of the mayhem. We skirted its smoldering remains and the mob moaned as it flowed by, awed by the destruction and I think I moaned with them. When I came to my senses I stood in the center of the Augusteum, the city's ancient Imperial Square. The ground swarmed with Romans and the encroaching flames cast their hellish glow upon us all. It was well past midnight now and this was clearly no ordinary gathering.

And yet, milling amongst their neighbors with no apparent malice, the so-called rioters spoke of small things as if they had just met in the market. The world came to an end but we discussed the price of bread. The unnerving calm of the mob convinced me that, just maybe, the Patriarch's journey wouldn't be so complicated after all.

I was rehearsing possible routes when I felt the mob shiver, stopping me cold. The men and women around me fell silent as the first torches began to circulate, passing towards the mob's boldest members at the front. Just then I saw a flicker of movement at the north end of the Augusteum. From the direction of the Senate a small troop of men marched towards us in single file. Faint torchlight revealed their jet-black tunics as they slipped deftly into the crowd close to the Imperial compound. Like a military stitch they wove themselves through the mob's breadth then stopped, standing still with arms locked. I didn't know their intent but I saw something remarkable in their precise movements. Held in place by my neighbors' shoulders, I watched that stitch tighten, slowly at first then faster as the troop pushed forward, forcing the torchbearers towards the Palace gate. The spell that had kept the mob docile

until that point broke. With raucous hoots the rioters in front began to swing their brands, showering ash and embers overhead.

On the other side of the Chälke, within the Palace compound, the
Imperial Guard eyed the situation nervously. The world felt as if
it was about to explode but I couldn't wait there to see what came
next. I had clearly made a grave mistake in coming here. A sen-
sible man would have gone directly to the rendezvous point instead
of improvising like a fool.

'Just let me get out of here,' I thought, 'and I'll behave, I
promise.'

But leaving wasn't so simple. I had to physically muscle my
way out of the crowd that compressed at the Palace gates. With
elbows jabbing I managed to reach the crowd's fringes when a shout
erupted behind me. I turned in time to see torches flying towards
the Chälke. The gate had already begun to burn, starting with the
guardhouses at its base. A handful of the guards were covered in
flames, running in panicky circles till they fell to the ground, condemned to death.

The true battle had been joined. And there would be no deliv-
ering the Patriarch to the Emperor through his front door. I could
only hope that Leo waited for me - if they came this way all would
be lost.

Sprinting up the Mêse with the Holy Wisdom on my right and the
Aqueduct of Valens on my left, I tried to keep to the shadows and
away from the raging fire that leapt from one building to the next.
The fire's voice kept changing, first a wind, then a howl, then a raging whistle that spit embers across my path. My only thought, my
selfish thought at that time was escape.

For an eternity I ran, staring at the ground ahead, completely oblivious to everything around me.

Then I stopped. My legs stopped of their own accord, abruptly. I was standing halfway between the Santa Sophia and the Forum of Constantine.

And that is why I did not die.

◆ ◆ ◆

Broad shoulders, black tunics and rattling scabbards thundered towards me.

They numbered many hundred, maybe many thousand, I couldn't tell. The atmosphere compressed and a set of drums beat time for an army on the move, in the middle of Constantinople, minutes to midnight.

With barely a second to spare I leapt out of the roadway to let them rush past. For just a moment I was tempted to curse the front line for not taking more care. Didn't they see me standing alone in the road? In my righteous anger I wanted to plant my fist in the face of the closest man but I refrained. After all, these were the City's saviors and so I let the army flow by, speeding on its way to subdue the rioters.

The soldiers entered the Augusteum and turned towards the Church of the Holy Wisdom. Within minutes the fighting men had pooled before the most important house of the Christian god. They assembled before marching on the rioters and when they did march there would be no contest. The rioters would quietly submit - they would have no choice.

Yet something was amiss.

The soldiers didn't rush to attack. Of course they must have seen that the Palace was threatened but they stayed in place. And they didn't wear the Imperial insignia. Leo had told me that General Belisarius had cultivated an elite troop that formed the core of the rejuvenated Roman Army. I began to think that I must have stumbled upon them, which would mean that the General himself would be near.

I had to know.

Though I had promised not to be a fool my curiosity got the better of me, again. Carefully I crept back towards the Augusteum just in time to see the troop part with a hush. A solitary man passed through the aisle they formed. *Belisarius.*

It had to be.

He lingered, rolling from side to side, slapping the backs of those closest to him. When he finally reached the Basilica he mounted its steps. I could only see him from a distance but I could see that his form was broad and blacker than black. If it really was Belisarius maybe I could consult with him before returning to Leo.

The commander raised both hands. Holding them above his head he called to the crowd in a voice that boomed off the facade, rolling down its steps into the street.

"My good friends! Welcome in the name of Rome."

The soldiers drew their swords in response and stabbed them into the sky with a roar. The man I still believed to be Belisarius clapped his arms together to quiet them before continuing.

"We have waited too long for this day and let me state what we all know - WE SHALL WAIT NO MORE!"

The soldiers bellowed again. I was close enough now to see them organized into ten distinct units. There must have been five thousand men there, maybe more.

I was so awed by the sight that I didn't see wickedness approach, as I stood alone and exposed in the street.

At that early hour, long before sunrise, the city was deserted as far as the eye could see except for the mob that menaced the Palace across the Augusteum.

So it's no surprise that they found me as quickly as they did.

"You there, come here."

The voice that called to me was not kind.

"You are quite the snoop, aren't you, so you must have heard the General. Great things are afoot tonight – the Emperor is in for quite a surprise, isn't he boys. And we could use you oh yes, we saw you sprinting down the street like a little cat. Come here little kitty, the army needs you."

They were clearly not my friends. I couldn't imagine that Belisarius' troops would speak that way to an innocent Roman that they caught on the streets. I didn't know who they were, I couldn't begin to guess. But I did know that they meant me harm and they were barely two steps away from grabbing me. Before I could will myself to move I was moving, leaping backwards and away. A set of brawny arms stopped me in mid-flight.

"There you are my elusive cat. What do you think Silas, is he a cat or is he a mouse? I suppose it doesn't matter, you are with us now boy, you can be certain of that."

With both arms held firmly from behind I stared into my captors' faces. They grinned heavily, letting their yellow teeth shine broadly in the torchlight. I could smell the sour wine on their breath. From a childhood spent with Zeno I had expertise in cheap wine.

"There is no need to run young one, you are in for some fun tonight. We'll make you jump some more before this night is over, for sure and for certain."

◆ ◆ ◆

"You stand before an instrument of the false Emperor."

The restless host outside the Church of the Holy Wisdom howled in response.

"Here he was crowned. Here he receives undeserved blessings. I ask you my brothers, what should we do? Shall we let it stand?"

The crowd bellowed a resounding "NO."

"Shall we spare the comfortable Patriarch from the wrath of the Just?"

Again, they shouted "NO."

"Very well then, fellow Romans, I beseech you to tell me. What shall we do with the Usurper's church?"

"BURN. BURN. BURN." The horde responded in a guttural that shook the street. Dispersing as they pronounced their death sentence the torchbearers marched slowly around the church's periphery until they surrounded it completely, holding their flames aloft, waiting for the signal.

A hundred paces away, my sole remaining captor hissed in my ear. "Have you ever seen such a stirring sight?"

My body flooded with that insidious hopelessness that saps muscles, churning my stomach. I had no idea how much time had passed but it must have been hours. For certain Leo had given up on me.

"Brat. I'm missing the action because of you, brat. Maybe I should just let you go? I don't imagine you are really going to be any great help to us and you're certainly no threat. Isn't that so? You're just skin and bones but I'd be a poor soldier if I didn't make absolutely certain."

As he spoke he shifted. With one arm wrapped brusquely around my neck the other made its way down my torso, searching for weapons. That is precisely when I remembered Belisarius' short sword strapped to my waist. If he realized that I was armed he would simply run me through and be done with it.

I fought to breathe as his arm tightened on my neck.

His other arm patted my cloak, looking for trouble and then, as he reached my stomach he paused to watch his compatriots, leaving his hand a hair's breadth from the sword. Now was the moment, now. The brute continued his search and immediately touched the sword's hilt but before reaching for his own weapon he sputtered.

"Whelp. What is this?"

Gathering all my force, I twisted with a grunt and thrust my elbow into his stomach, wrestling myself free. I had only traversed a dozen steps in the direction of the Column when a terrifying *whoop* stopped me, a blunt, primordial thing that struck my back and ground past me.

Not yet halfway to my destination, I couldn't help but turn and gaze in morbid fascination as the Church of the Holy Wisdom exploded in flames. The crowd that set the fire drew back to admire their handiwork that spread the night's savagery.

Transfixed, I caught sight of the black shape backlit by the wall of fire nearly too late, growing larger as he moved with surprising speed towards me. My attacker didn't ponder technique his second time round. This time he rushed at me with his sword drawn, held high as he bore down upon me.

My entire life I had handled a sword, and with Leo's help I could do so with skill. But I had never drawn a weapon in battle.

'Watch over me father.'

He was inches away with a blade that had already started its downward arc. At the last conceivable moment, I stepped to the right. Pivoting as the brute's own momentum carried him forward,

I slapped the flat of my sword across his back, sending him sprawling headfirst onto the roadway.

Before I could run for my life, two more men materialized from the gloom and began to edge towards me with swords drawn, one on either side.

"Alexius you gluttonous slob, do you think perhaps that you can cut him if I hold him still or might that be too taxing for you?" A thick guttural rumbled beside me. "Drop that pretty blade whelp; you won't need it where you're going."

Alexius, my nemesis, drew himself to his full height with a puff. Taking a moment to wipe the blood off his jaw where he had struck the pavement, he recovered his sword and prepared a great thrust.

◆ ◆ ◆

"Valentinian. I worried that you would die if I left. And I almost left you."
Leo is very few things with great, defining intensity. Amongst those traits that overwhelm his details is his honesty. Honesty sharp enough to alienate friends, honesty noble enough to convert enemies. So I wasn't surprised when he told me how close he was to leaving me to sure death.

And so he would have if the nearby crash of metal on metal hadn't arrested him on the spot. Without hesitation, he crouched low and crept around the Column, into the Forum, to see what he could see.

Barely ten steps beyond he saw four figures traced in fire-glow. Leo edged towards them, angling for a glimpse of their faces. When the three made a concerted rush at the fourth he didn't have a chance to make certain, he acted to save a stranger.

And that is why I live.

I had just parried Alexius' attack when I heard a grunt and Leo's voice above the fracas.

"COURAGE!"

In an argument I have never had the smart retort at the ready. But in war, for reasons I'll never know, I have always had the response, even before I had the experience. That natural response has saved me more times than I can count and it saved me that day with Alexius. His attention lapsed for a blink and my sword moved, sweeping across the length of his body. The man who would have cheerfully murdered me fell forward, instantly dead.

I turned to see Leo with two men lying crumpled at his feet. I called to him but he was moving, past me, sword held straight. The point slipped into Alexius' neck just as his massive hand closed around my ankle. A long, wicked dagger fell from Alexius' other hand, clattering on the Forum's cobble.

"Boy, I've told you before but you damned well better hear me now. Never look for battle but once the battle is joined, never turn your back on an enemy. I'm overjoyed to see you safe but we have no time to talk. Come now. Reinforcements for those three can't be far behind and we have a Patriarch to rescue."

Mighty Constantine peered down upon as we flew from the Forum, drawing to an abrupt stop before Lucius and the Patriarch who sat cross-legged in the dark nearby.

"Leo." I called to him, my mind churned with everything that I had just seen. He needed to know what I had witnessed but Leo raised his finger to silence me. The Patriarch stepped around Lucius to greet us with a broad grin.

"Valentinian. The Church welcomes your return young man, and we rejoice in your safety."

I mumbled something inadequate. I had almost died and I had almost killed.

The Patriarch continued. "Now, Leo, do you not think it is time for us to be on our way? My stomach rumbles when I think of the breakfast waiting in the Palace and it seems to me that it would be ill mannered to let the Emperor wait. Plus, the good Lucius here seems to think that we are not in an ideal location and that we should be on our way. Jittery young man he is but I do think he has a point."

Though little could be seen in the low light I could hear Leo's frown.

"I can't say much, I'm certain Valentinian will tell us more. But your Holiness, you must know that your church is burning and can't be saved."

The Patriarch looked like a man condemned to death but he held his tongue. Leo watched him a moment and when he was satisfied he continued.

"You are right, we can't stay here. The city is alive with trouble for anyone connected with the Emperor. We will bring you to the Palace before the sun is up, John, but we have a new problem. I had originally planned to cross the Mêse here but Valentinian's experience tells us that we can't. We need to find another way across and right now I'm out of ideas."

I was standing close enough to the Patriarch to see the smile return to his face. He was a remarkable man, resilient or crazy, I couldn't tell which.

"Leo, if they are blocking the obvious routes above ground, why don't we try the non-obvious? I do believe that I know a way…"

BASILICA CISTERN

"How? Well, I was a man before I was a priest and I was a boy before I was a man. And that boy was born in Constantinople, raised in the streets, drinking out of its fountains, eating its bread and scavenging in its dark corners. As you might imagine, or perhaps you can't entirely imagine given the look on your face, I know the city's ins and outs better than most. And it's well that I do."

The Patriarch spoke in a whisper as we huddled behind the low wall that ran along the Mêse just west of the Holy Wisdom. Before going any further the Patriarch had insisted on seeing his church and there it was, engulfed in flames, close enough for us to smell its enormous store of incense consumed in the fire. My nose filled with frankincense and myrrh, lending the whole scene a perverse holiness.

The ground rose between us and the Basilica, and the Basilica stood between us and the heart of the Imperial Quarter. So when we looked eastward all we could see was the burning Santa Sophia at the hill's crest. The Augusteum, the Palace, Senate House and Hippodrome were all hidden from sight. Though we couldn't see the citizens that massed before the Chälke Gate we could hear them. Gone were the tranquil neighbors. The sound that rolled down the heights belonged to a mob, hoarse and shrill, interspersed with the slap of military sandals.

Behind us the Patriarch released the breath he had been holding. There was nothing he could do about it now. As a disciple of
Christ there was no room for revenge. Though much of the Old
Testament spoke of such things that path was not his. But people
would avenge him, the Emperor would avenge him. Willing himself to focus, he picked up the thread of our salvation.

"As I was saying, Constantinople doesn't have fresh water wells,
we import our fresh water. Those magnificent aqueducts bring
water to us from deep in the Bulgarian forests. We bathe in it, we
cook in it, we drink it and it sweeps our detritus away. Without
that water the city wouldn't survive for more than a week."

Leo placed his hand gently on the Patriarch's shoulder as a
team of a dozen rebel scouts marched up the road, passing within
a stone's throw of us. We waited for a break in the flow of rioters and what could only be rebel soldiers so that we might cross
the Mêse to the Patriarch's promised safe passage to the palace.
We still didn't understand what that hidden way might be and the
Patriarch seemed to be enjoying the moment.

"Now, those aqueducts work well in normal times but it is
the abnormal times that bring down empires. The cisterns were
designed precisely for those occasions and as with so much else,
we have Constantine to thank for the concept. He built the city's
first cistern anticipating that an attacking army of any intelligence would cut the aqueducts in a siege. Subsequent Emperors
have continued Constantine's, including Anastasius, who drew
up plans for the Basilica Cistern in the last years of his reign. The
Emperor Justinian continued the work and as fate would have
it, he and I visited the site together not more than three months
ago. I might not have contributed to its construction but in his
goodness Justinian did let me contribute its name. Not terribly
creative of me I suppose but I called it the Basilica Cistern for its

close proximity to God's house, the Church of the Holy Wisdom, our *Santa Sophia*.

"Since that first visit I have returned from time to time. It was supposed to have been finished and filled with water weeks ago but according to the Emperor his fine engineers have found opportunity for endless delays, bless their avarice. Tonight their greed might just provide us with an escape route. Deep in the Cistern there is a passage that opens on the catacombs built by the ancient Byzants. As I said, I grew up in this city and I have traveled its length above and below ground a million times. Very few men in this city know the catacombs and I daresay that no one knows that through those ancient burial chambers there is a passage that leads to the Palace. All of this is accessible through the Cistern and the Cistern's entrance lies there, just across from us."

My eyes followed the Patriarch's outstretched arm across the Mêse to a small shack on the side of a road. That was the entrance and that entrance would lead to safety but between us and safety was an endless stream of enemy.

Leo saw the same. "My boy, we need to get the Patriarch into the Cistern. But we'll need a diversion to make it safely across."

Leo drew my attention to the enemy troops spreading around the western edge of the Augusteum. They were stopping pedestrians, brutalizing some and arming others with torches before encouraging them in the direction of the Palace. A group of these mercenaries carrying their own torches were systematically setting fire to each and every flammable structure along the Mêse between the Basilica and the Forum, moving them closer to our position. They would be upon us in a matter of minutes. All about us the mayhem spread as the first signs of light appeared in the Asian hills east of the city, across the Bosporus.

And still there was no Imperial response, no Palace guards, no City Guard, no Roman Army. The devil himself controlled the center of the Empire and if anything moved on the Mêse his black shirted thugs would see it and they would surely respond.

Leo was right. We would need a damned fine diversion.

And as usual, he had a plan.

Moments later the four of us huddled together, digesting Leo's instructions.

"Does everyone understand their part?" Leo spoke, knowing that none of us could really grasp the moment but that was war after all. Clarity comes in hindsight.

"This is as it must be and as commander I won't discuss alternatives. Now, I repeat the question, does everyone understand?"

He turned to me and pressed his hand above my heart. I knew nothing of the turmoil that raged within him. It still shocks me when I think about the complexity and melancholy that he hid from me for so long. But I'd learn of that later, when all was said, and all was done.

"May the gods protect us," Leo whispered.

And then, without another word, he was over the wall, skirting along the boulevard's edges. He moved with that loping gait of his and it wasn't long before he drew close to the rebel troop, sauntering all the while.

◆ ◆ ◆

The Patriarch broke the heavy silence left in Leo's wake, speaking to all and none. "When that fine man returns he and I must have a talk about matters of the faith, these oaths to many gods are of some concern to me."

Very well I told him, certainly Leo would relish that talk in particular. But my attempts to make light of the moment fell short, I was worried about Leo and worried about what came next. All I could do was to focus on my mission. I reminded the Patriarch, and Lucius, that we would be on the move once we heard the signal and we wouldn't stop until we were safely underground. I would go first, followed by the Patriarch and Lucius would bring up the rear, protecting our flank. Not another word was said. Lucius hadn't spoken since we had met at Constantine's Column. He must have been nervous - we were all nervous.

The Patriarch put a damp hand on my forearm. All I could hear were our labored breaths as we waited anxiously for the sign.

We didn't have long to wait.

Within seconds the street erupted in tumult. We recognized the sign and set off, over the wall. Soldiers scattered left and right but there was no sign of Leo. 'In a blink we had crossed and passed through the nondescript door into darkness.

Fortunately the Patriarch had the presence of mind to pluck two torches from a nook in the wall before the street door snapped shut, robbing us of light. As we descended the steps to the cistern's floor, I produced a flint and coaxed sparks from the torches spit. Somehow we managed to reach the cistern floor without killing ourselves on the pitch-black steps. But our relief was short-lived because it was immediately apparent that somehow we had lost Lucius. Three had started across the street and only two stood together in the cistern.

Leaving the Patriarch to scout the web of walkways that threaded through the cistern, I dashed back up the steps to see if Lucius had remained at the street entrance. But he was not there. Bearded Lucius had either deserted or been captured and neither event boded well!

With no time to waste I raced back down the stairs so quickly I took a tumble at the base and was thrown flat on my face. The torch that I had held in my right hand went sliding across the stone floor and into the water where it extinguished upon contact.

And then there was blackness everywhere and no sound but for the pounding of my own heart. What's more, the Patriarch was nowhere to be seen.

Then a distant drip broke the silence followed by the faintest of lights. It was so far away that I doubted my eyes but gradually the flicker steadied and the Patriarch's cherubic face materialized behind it.

"Valentinian. On some days God chooses some days to be subtle and on others to be clear as the nose on your face. We should thank him for choosing this hellish night to be bold. It appears that Justinian's workers neglected to seal off the entrance to the catacombs."

He peered past me and frowned.

"I take it our jittery Lucius has left us? Just as well, the boy made me nervous. Come now, our way is wide open. But not another word, follow me and watch your step, I'll have you in the Palace before sunrise."

To be honest I didn't have such profound faith in the Patriarch but I was exhausted and ready for the night's adventure to end. So I did as I was told.

With the Patriarch in the lead we exited the lobby of the Cistern and entered the main hall. Looking far out and then far up I began to understand the peculiar majesty of the place. It was built to hold water but I swear that it is the most marvelous of temples. It's flooded with water and inaccessible now, yet I wish you could see it. Three hundred and thirty six columns rise from the floor and disappear in the dark where they meet the ceiling some hundred feet above. By torchlight we saw that there was already some water luminescing in the basin.

The Patriarch ruminated. "It appears that they have indeed begun to fill it slowly, testing its integrity I imagine."

As we turned a corner he slowed and moved to the edge of the walkway. "Valentinian, come here, there's something you must see."

I told him that it was best we hurried on our way but he would have none of that.

"Just a moment, we can surely spare a moment."

The Patriarch bent to one knee. Teetering precariously, he thrust our last torch out over the water.

"Do you see it?"

Following his instructions, I looked into the water and gasped out loud. At the base of the nearest column, anchoring it to the floor was a massive block of green marble, a perfect square at least five feet a side that glowed as if light from within. As I stared at it I realized the true marvel of the thing. Carved onto the four sides was the head of Medusa, placed upside down with writhing snakes wrapped around the base.

"Legend says that it was carved for King Byzas and that Medusa's magic has protected this spit of land ever since."

It was the most singular experience of my life. Rambling underground, in the dark, with the Patriarch of Constantinople, examining Medusa while the world burned above. He was an enigma that man, upholder of the Christian faith. And the most open-minded priest that I have known. I must have been staring at him, thinking similar thoughts when he caught sight of me.

"Of course it fascinates me as well! I am a citizen of Constantinople. I take pride in her history, her architecture and her culture - only a cretin would not! You know, the Emperor Justinian himself pointed out the Medusa to me. Ah, and if you look just over here there is another identical head. It is a touch of the profane that fits oddly well here. I'd like to think that this holy space is the sister of my Santa Sophia. Or at least it was until the villains destroyed her. But Justinian will rebuild her. She will be beautiful again. Yes, I see your face and you're right, Valentinian, we dawdle when we are still in danger. So let us proceed, onwards to the Palace."

I'm not too proud to say that the Patriarch took my hand and together we flew along those treacherous walkways to the farthest corner where we stopped before a narrow sliver of an opening. The tools and materials that would be used to close this last gap in the chamber walls lay strewn about the ground.

"I smell my youth through that opening."

The Patriarch crowed, placing his first foot on the threshold.

"I hope that you're not weak stomached young man, because the smells in there are ungodly, the rats are dogs and the bones of the ancient Byzants litter the ground. But we will be safe there and the way to the Palace is short for someone familiar with the labyrinth. But for someone who is not familiar, these dark passages mean certain death."

A shadow passed across his face as he looked up at the ceiling.

"I trust that I have not forgotten the way..."

PALACE INTRIGUE

WE TRUDGED DOWN yet another corridor, dark and dank, quickly and hopelessly lost in the Byzants' subterranean tombs. They were all dead now as we would certainly be; it was just a matter of time. That realization washed over me as the Patriarch flashed me his crazy man's grin for the hundredth time

"My good Valentinian, this is one of the true marvels of our city, built and rebuilt over a thousand years. There are at least that many ways to travel from one point to another in fair Constantinople. Now I may be wrong, but this time I truly believe that we have arrived."

With that he slapped his meaty hand across my back, winked comically, and began to scan the floor like a dog, moving his head quickly, back and forth. Eying a stone block the size of man's head, he asked me 'if I would mind' moving it to a spot that he marked with an 'X' in the dirt. I humored him, what else could I do? When he asked me for my sword I humored him again, the sword was of no more use to me. In exchange for the sword he handed me the torch that began to sputter as a prelude to death.

Then he looked up and I did as well. I supposed that he was looking for his God but there was no Almighty in the catacombs with us. The only thing above John was a smooth patch of ceiling, a bit lighter than the rest. Concerned with my own fate, I had started to turn away when he took hold of the scabbard's tip and thrust the butt into the ceiling, once, twice and three times. Then he handed the sword back to me and began to whistle a tune.

That tune was shortly accompanied by a thunderous crack.

The crack melded into a creak and that creak rose to a sharp whine just as a circle opened in the solid rock ceiling. A rush of light, mercifully fresh air and a river of voices poured down upon us.

"WHO GOES THERE?" A booming voice menaced from above

"It is the Patriarch John for God's sake, raise me up. I'm here for breakfast with the Emperor."

After a muffled debate, four thick arms reached through the ceiling. In the blink of an eye they had plucked John by the wrists and lifted him through the roof. I was alone for an interminable moment before those helping hands returned for me, whisking me upwards towards the light.

As I ascended through the roof I didn't know if we were being drawn into heaven or hell. But as my equilibrium returned I understood.

A burst of pungent steam hit me in the face accompanied by the most exquisite smell of fresh bread, rosemary, olive brine and charcoal. The two Palace Guards that had pulled me through the floor now held me suspended. Though I stretched, my feet didn't touch the pristine white tiles below me, in the middle of the Palace's kitchen. An army of chefs, servers, assistants and cleaners pressed in towards me.

Grapes in the hand of one.

A fish valiantly flapping in the hand of another.

A cleaver that could kill an ox.

They looked at me quizzically. I wiggled my feet, waiting just a moment to see if I might wake up from the dream. But no such luck. Running through my options, panic, flight, negotiation, I heard a familiar voice boom from deep in the kitchen.

"Divine. This is truly divine. And with some of this bread, and rosemary of course, there is no need to skimp on the rosemary or the salt. Master Chef you are a master indeed, don't let me interrupt you one moment more, breakfast cannot be delayed, an army cannot fight, an Emperor cannot rule and a priest cannot preach on an empty stomach."

The cooks, assistants and cleaners parted to let the Patriarch enter the circle of my confinement. His obviously full mouth worked its way through something that was to his great liking. After licking a thick finger clean he waved his hand at the two mountains of men that still held me suspended.

"Soldiers - put him down. Thank you. He is with me of course. Valentinian, we have been delivered into the arms of angels and to think you doubted me! I know that you did, I could see it on your face but no matter, I doubted myself. Quite convinced we were going to die down there, I was and I don't mind telling you now. Yet here we are and the Emperor knows we have arrived. We are to join him straight away. Gentlemen, we are ready, please lead us."

I was not ready. My feet reacquainted themselves with the floor and did a barely tolerable job supporting me. News that we were to meet the Emperor didn't help. Reality stabbed me, sharply, in the heart. Leo was still missing, there was still rebellion on the streets of Constantinople, and I was still the son of Claudius, rope maker, humble man. And we were now being rushed out of the kitchen with two soldiers ahead, four alongside and two behind, plunging deeper into the Palace compound in search of Caesar.

We passed out of the kitchens into an open garden filled with intense aromas of spice and herbs planted densely about, fed with glistening streams that flowed freely. Four of the most beautiful girls I have ever seen, before or since, tended the herbs in pure white togas. They looked like the Vestal Virgins, creatures from another time and place. One of them must have smiled at me, I was convinced and then, maybe, I was hallucinating. The paths were inlaid with mosaics of every animal on earth, it might have been a trick of the sun but they danced beneath my feet, happy creatures. I was hallucinating. Paradise, that garden was paradise and if I could have I would have died there but death could wait, the Emperor would not. Our troop swept into the next building, a dining hall with a wood table, carved from a single tree, black as obsidian that could have comfortably sat one hundred. I remember feeling my jaw slack, country rube, and then I was dragged out again into the next open space, filled with fruit trees and bird song.

And inside again.

And outside again.

And so we proceeded until I had lost all sense of time and space. Leo had explained to me that the Palace wasn't a single structure but many scattered across the tallest of Constantinople's hills but I didn't appreciate the concept before. In life it was an astounding thing, a fitting center for the center of the world. Each building served a unique function, kitchen for the Emperor, kitchen for the nobility, kitchen for the guests, reception hall for petitioners, reception area of dignitaries, dining for the Emperor and family, banquet hall for the Royal courtiers, residential quarters for Palace servants and the eunuchs that controlled them, barracks for the various branches of Palace Guard, Imperial sleeping chambers and residence. The Palace was a city within the city with more than one thousand full time residents and another five thousand who filled its many hundred rooms from dawn to dusk.

And then there was the Throne Room.

And then there was the Emperor.

It took me some time to realize that we had stopped moving and longer to understand that I was now on my knees, encouraged there by a not so gentle prod.

The Patriarch was beside me, also on his knees, so close that I could see the perspiration bead on his flushed jowls. In front of us I saw the curled forms of other men, a dozen or so, similarly prostrate.

The room was small but infinitely grand, unlike any man-made space I had ever seen. The ceiling soared above, pulled together with a cupola of glistening indigo, wrung with windows that splashed the young sun onto our faces. Gold plates covered the walls, each as wide as a man, each square stamped with the Emperor's seal. Phoenician purple carpets graced marble floors of soft, luminescent green.

This had to be the Palace's Throne Room and that man who filled the end of the room, surrounded by golden light, floating above the dais like Zeus himself had to be Justinian, Emperor of the Romans.

I knew well enough not to look at him directly but around the corners I could see him in pieces. His features were striking, large and strong and they dominated that face as it dominated us all.

A bell sounded from somewhere behind me, resonating deeply in my chest.

"RISE."

Someone spoke accompanied by the rustle of silk. A friendlier touch guided me to my feet. It was the Patriarch. He stood by my side and together we stood before the Emperor *Justinianus I*.

I had seen Justinian's face before on sculptures and coins but there was something both ferocious and familiar about him up close that those renderings didn't capture. His skin was dark like olives, wind worn like the faces of mariners I had known as a boy. His brow was short and broad, and underneath the laurel crown of the Caesars sprang mahogany curls. He had the wayward nose of a pugilist, underscored with a poet's full lips but at that moment they were drawn tight and pale. As I watched them they parted and the Emperor of Rome broke the room's silence.

"Holy Patriarch John, I am pleased to see you safe. When I requested your presence I did not know how bad the situation was on the streets. I've subsequently sent scouts to check on your progress and when they didn't find you I despaired. Your arrival is indeed welcome. Now please tell me, who do we thank for your successful journey?"

I heard the Patriarch speak my name from very far away.

"Sire, this is Valentinian Constans, pupil of Captain Leo Cantecuzen, formerly of the Excubitors. Valentinian and Leo are responsible for my safe passage though sadly, we were separated from Captain Leo who risked his own life to save mine."

I was tired and bewildered as the Emperor's eyes bore into me.

"Patriarch John, take your seat here by my side. Valentinian Constans, accept our thanks. Narses, Master of the Domestics, will see to your needs. Your presence is no longer required."

Orthodox Imperial protocol is elaborate beyond belief. Courtiers spend a lifetime learning how to behave in the presence of the Emperor. At that moment I should have bowed, scraped, stepped back once, stepped back again, all the time with my eyes glued to the floor. Needless to say, that was not my approach.

The eunuch Narses, head of the Imperial household, moved towards me with serpentine grace. I have never liked serpents. He was one of the tallest men that I have ever laid eyes on. His head was egg shaped and his sallow skin was the color of a wilted leaf. Thick lids could not hide the underlying menace of his eyes.

This man was a predator. I knew it at as soon as his bony fingers closed on my shoulder, indicating that my presence was no longer required. But I had just spent the night fighting against the mob in the Emperor's name in order to deliver the Patriarch to Caesar. Now my master was missing and a debt had to be paid, it was only right, I could not be dismissed so lightly.

When I think back upon what I did next I still shudder.

I pushed away from the wall where Narses had maneuvered me. My sharp move caught Narses by surprise and he was pulled with me, leaving us both in the center of the room facing the Emperor. Perpetuating the insult I looked the Emperor full in the face and my eyes found his eyes. My actions were so unprecedented that not a single soul moved as passion spilled from me.

"All powerful and benign Emperor, please forgive me Sire but I have no need to be tended by the Domestics and I don't need rest. Mighty Justinian, I have seen things tonight that the Emperor would certainly like to know. I've seen your enemies my Lord, I've drawn their blood and they've drawn mine. I've been out in the streets, I've seen the city burn, my master is missing and if it weren't for him the Patriarch might be captured or worse. Forgive my insolence Sire, but I beg you not to send me away and not to forget Leo Cantecuzen."

It would have been well within the Emperor's right to have my head lopped off for sport. The crowd around me murmured loudly, while swords belonging to the Palace Guard rattled in their scabbards. The Emperor's brow furrowed deep and dark and for a long moment, an eternal moment he didn't say a word.

Then he lifted a finger and all of the whispers and the rattles ended. The Patriarch looked like he was about to speak in my defense but one look from Justinian stopped him cold.

Caesar returned his attention to me.

"Valentinian Constans. Your service to the Patriarch earned you thanks, now it has saved your life."

The tittering voices of the crowd flared but Justinian's voice cut through them.

"But on a night when so many of our friends cower under their covers I would be a fool to ignore a man who risked his life in my service. You may stay and I will instruct the Palace Guard to keep watch for your Captain Leo. You have both been of use to your Emperor. Perhaps you shall be again. I will now hear what you have to say of your experiences last night. Please describe what you saw on your flight from Belisarius' home."

"My Lord."

A shrill voice broke behind me.

"My Lord, surely this boy has no place in the Council. He could not possibly know anything that is relevant to us. He has no place here."

Justinian didn't bother to answer. A different rhythm returned to the room as he sat back into the golden expanse of his throne. The Emperor used silence like my father and the thought of Claudius brought some warmth back to my cheeks. Just perhaps the worst had passed for me.

The Patriarch evidently thought the same as he approached the Emperor. Justinian watched him, coolly appraising the holy man. When John was close enough the Emperor gestured to a low divan, below him and to the right, which the Patriarch gladly occupied. When he was seated the Emperor bid me to speak.

"Valentinian. Continue."

And so I did, quickly, running through our experiences on the street. I described the mob, the troops, the burning of the

Santa Sophia, our flight. When I had finished the Emperor nodded gravely. Turning to the Patriarch, he addressed him, loud enough so that everyone could hear.

"Your Holiness, your home is destroyed and your altar desecrated. But with God's grace we'll right these wrongs. The perpetrators will pay dearly for their crimes. And in the meantime I extend the protection of my arm and the comfort of my home to you. As I do to you, Valentinian Constans, your brave service and that of Leo Cantecuzen is noted and appreciated. Many could learn from your bravery."

This cue I understood. With a deep bow I thanked the Emperor then stepped to the perimeter of the room as the business of the court continued. There couldn't have been more than two-dozen souls who made up the center of the Emperor's circle and a dozen or so were there. Of course every Roman worth his salt knew the names of those that moved the world, but I didn't know their faces until that moment. Red-faced John 'the Cappadocian', keeper of the Empire's purse strings, was there. So too was Tribunian the Jurist and *Quaestor* of the Sacred Palace, Julius, Captain of the Excubitors, Leontius the Imperial Surgeon.

Leontius refused to meet my gaze even though I sought his. All I wanted was news of Layla, I didn't have a second to think about her until I saw his face and at once I was obsessed again. I think I even admitted the obsession to myself for the first time as I stood in Caesar's presence. But there was no sight of her and there was nothing to be learned from Leontius' stony face. *So be it.* In addition to those few I recognized there was Narses who I detested on sight, and a handful of other men, richly dressed. I knew nothing of court protocol but even I could appreciate their act, the way they spoke through cotton and moved through honey as they jockeyed for position before the Emperor.

Justinian broke the silence. "Very well John, let us begin where we ended, before this young man brought us the only reliable news we have heard since the fires started. I want my Prefect to tell me more than what I already know. A blind man could see the fires. So listen to me closely, because I have three questions and no time for speculation. What is the damage thus far? Who is our enemy? What is our plan of action?"

While the Emperor's last question lingered, a narrow door opened behind him and an ethereal bell tolled. At once, everyone in the room except for the Emperor got down on both knees.

Before we saw her we felt the hushed, delicate chill that accompanied the Empress Theodora. Honey lemon and pepper scent filled the Throne Room.

As much as the country folk talked about their Emperor they talked about his mate and as was usual with rumors, they painted a jumbled picture of her. But there was nothing confusing about the pale beauty that approached Justinian. Though she was stunning she was also more severe in expression than her husband. Her face was almond-shaped and dominated by luminous green eyes that blinked slowly and definitively. Nothing and no one escaped her notice and even I felt measured as her eyes passed over me. This was no trifling queen. From her gaze, her gait, the liquid motion of her limbs that much was clear to me. It must have been clear to them all because not a single man moved while Theodora took her place at her husband's side.

"Rise."

And so we did again, each man taking his place. We were positioned in a semi-circle facing the Imperial couple. John the Cappadocian stood in the center, before us, below the Emperor.

Justinian took Theodora's hand as the Cappadocian knelt and continued his report.

"My Lord, the damage to the city is great and it continues to grow. This is more real then we initially thought, My Lord. As of our last count the Prefecture, the market in the Forum of Constantine, the Santa Sophia, the Chälke, and a host of minor structures have either burnt to the ground or are on their way. I'll have a proper accounting done shortly with cost estimates, my Lord, though events are running ahead of our ability to catalog. The fact is that the mob is still out in the streets and actively trying to spread the flames. I have said it before and I will say it again, only drastic action can save the Imperial Quarter.

"As far as who is behind the mayhem I'm ashamed to say that we simply don't know who the true culprits are - reports are conflicting. Some say that this is the work of the Laurentius mob we have seen off and on over the past week. But there are other reports as well, Lord, reports of a more sinister group on the streets. Overnight I lost a handful of my personal guard. I sent them into the Augusteum to gather information and they have failed to report which means that they may have deserted, or worse."

"They have been found. They are dead. Confirmed." Narses spoke with an audible hiss and the Cappadocian turned on him like a bull, his face in flames.

"How can you possibly know?"

"My spies have confirmed it."

"And why in hell didn't you tell me?"

"Because you didn't ask me, John, *Cappadocian*."

John laced his fingers and cracked every knuckle. Then he sucked in a deep breath and held it while his eyes bulged from his head, blazing anger. The Emperor intervened.

"Narses, we all know your network of spies is effective. Share or be removed. John, contain yourself, your men are lost but we have learned something here. Now continue."

Narses' face contorted into something approximating a smile, while John's color moderated from bright fire to smoldering coal. I thought that I would not want to be enemies with the Cappadocian. He continued.

"Very well. People, like Valentinian, whisper of soldiers on the streets and I know they cannot be Imperial troops because those haven't been called into the city. We all know that our army hasn't entered the capital in centuries. If it is true that my men have been killed I can't imagine that they died at the hands of a mob. My stomach tells me that the true enemy hasn't revealed himself, my Lord. And I cannot believe that this tumult is spontaneous."

While the Cappadocian paused, the commander of the Palace regiments, Julius, strode to John's side and bowed before the Emperor. Justinian showed his impatience.

"Julius, this better be worth our while, speak."

Julius stood and he was quite a sight with his pristine armor shining in the full sunlight that now streamed into the Throne Room. He spoke with the exquisitely tuned emotion of a professional actor.

"My Lord, six transports seek permission to dock below the Palace in the Harbor of Bucoleon. My watch commander reports that it is General Belisarius, my Lord, accompanied by General Mundus and an armed host of some magnitude. Before granting them passage I wanted your permission given the unusual nature of the request. Shall we open the harbor gate or shall we send them back to sea? The request is, after all, *most* unusual."

Justinian drew himself to the front of the throne with obvious relief.

"Open them, Julius. Open them or lose your command. Open them immediately and bring Belisarius to me, now, with haste."

◆ ◆ ◆

Those that attended the Emperor rumbled like rocks as they stepped back to let Belisarius pass. And he passed, sweeping through them with barely controlled fury. Sinking to one knee, he placed his sword squarely before him on the floor.

"Great Caesar, your humble servant, General Belisarius of the Eastern Armies lays his sword at your feet. One thousand soldiers, the finest under my command, muster under your walls with General Mundus at their head. And we are ready to show your enemies the sting of Imperial might, my Lords. Command us."

Theodora bent towards Justinian and whispered in his ear. The world froze in anticipation, all accept for sallow Narses who flickered to the left of the dais, observing the faces that observed the Emperor.

That is how I knew that Layla had arrived. His yellow eyes narrowed like a lion's before a feast, piquing my curiosity. I looked over my shoulder in time to see her approach Leontius.

And she was stunning!

Forget the vestal virgins forget everything and everyone. I would have plucked her from the Palace and taken her far away, to a simple place, for a simple life with no war, no heroes and no chances for glory. Euphoria, delusion, call it what you will, it lasted for the briefest of seconds and ended when she wove her arm around her father's. They conferred intensely. She looked anxious. Together they left the Throne Room and I fought a burst of antipathy for Leontius then felt absurd for considering her father competition.

"She is lovely and she is decent."

A voice whispered at my elbow and I nearly leapt through the roof, wound as tightly as I was. But Mellius' firm hand stilled me.

"Hello Valentinian, I hear that you have had your own adventures last night as I had mine. They told me that Leo is missing but don't worry, we don't leave our men behind. We will find him you know and I will help you."

Mellius and I stood at the edge of the Throne Room, pressed so deep into the heavy drapes that we were virtually invisible. But somehow Narses noticed us. I felt those scorching eyes on me and I stared back at him, knowing in my stomach that he was my enemy. Mellius saw Narses and knew it too.

"A vile creature but we can learn from him. He rose to his position in part because he trusted no one. The Palace can be a dangerous place Valentinian. This is no Volerus."

I winced at the mention of home. He felt it and responded.

"Constantinople is no better than your Volerus, only different. I can tell that you are brave. You and I both want to be warriors. But I have lived here all my life and I hear the city gossip, I know what they say about these characters and I think it would serve you to know as well."

I felt like I had just met Mellius for the first time and he was not the sullen child I had imagined him. He didn't shame me intentionally but he shamed me. I was a perpetual skeptic, a suspicious ass, while he was purity incarnate. Here was an example I could learn from and I told him as much.

'Please, Mellius, I know nothing, I know no one, help me understand.'

My question made him happy.

"Nothing in this room happens by accident, Valentinian. Proximity to the Emperor is rank and rank is power. First in the Emperor's heart is his queen, Theodora. The Empress is as intelligent and influential as she is beautiful. You know that he fought for her, Valentinian? So many disapproved of Theodora, the Senate was scandalized, his own family disapproved. There were terrible rumors, she wasn't chaste, she was manipulative, she was a striver and climber but who really knows her truth? The Emperor Justinian knew and the fact is that when you truly know, when you truly love you don't care what anyone else says or thinks. At least that's the way I imagine it. Theodora is first and she helps the Emperor in everything - they rule together.

"Then we have Justinian's Cabinet of Ministers. On any given day any one of them might dominate but I believe that Narses is the one to fear. He is Master of the Domestics, master of Palace minutiae, master of the spies and keeper of the secrets. Theodora might dominate Justinian's ear but Narses has frequent access and he speaks first for himself.

"Next in power is the Cappadocian, red-faced, barrel-bellied and cantankerous. People say that he controls the Empire's purse and he does that, but I believe that he makes enemies because he doesn't bow to the nobility. He is the Emperor's man and honest.

"Of course you know Belisarius. The General is technically a member of the cabinet but because he spends his time in the field he isn't an insider. That is why I admire him most of all - he isn't a player in the game, he is one of the few with power to define the game. Just look at the way the others eye him, separate, suspicious. That is the kind of man I would like to be Valentinian, someone not afraid to stand alone in the room.

"Your hungry friend the Patriarch is another important person though he isn't in the Cabinet. The Emperor clearly respects him, though I don't know how respect translates into influence. Justinian has a legal mind and even though he's a committed Christian he believes in the primacy of Imperial power over the Church.

"Speaking of legal minds, that weed of a man is Tribunian, the Emperor's jurist. Three years ago Justinian commissioned him to gather together all of the laws of ancient and modern Rome, to make sense of them and to put them in a single book. Captain Basil claims the book was just finished and that Tribunian is a genius. I have never met a genius but he does have a thoughtful face.

"The nervous man with the fluttering fingers is Anthemius of Tralles, chief architect to the Emperor. His family has produced generations of builders and artists but even amongst them he is special. Leo must have taken you to the Church of St. Sergius and St. Bacchus. Anthemius designed that, you know, in honor of Justinian's marriage to Theodora. Just imagine how much confidence the Emperor must have in him. I don't know about you, Valentinian, but I have always admired architects and artists. They leave our world richer when they pass. We soldiers protect the gains of the creative spirits, Valentinian, but we don't create. Maybe someday I can have a second career, a second life. Maybe."

Mellius left me speechless. He kept whispering, making me wonder what happened on his night ride with the General to release this torrent.

"Behind the first tier is Julius, commander of the Palace guards. He looks splendid in his armor. In my regiment, I have never seen a soldier wear such armor. No dirt, no dents, strange man.

"Next is Eudaimon, the city Prefect who must be miserable, he was the mob's first victim though to look at him you wouldn't know. He looks as pompous as ever.

"On either side of him are the literary men. To his left is the Historian, Procopius. All I know about him is that he served General Belisarius as personal secretary in Persia - that says much. To the right is Paul the royal Poet, confidant to the Empress. Poetry and the Poet Paul are both mysteries to me.

"And that leaves us with the nobles not noble enough to wear the crown, the Senators and the men of ability. There is Origenes, the senior Senator and voice of the blue bloods. And there are the Imperial brothers, Hypatius and Pompeius, nephews to the old Emperor Anastasius. They have another brother, Probus, but I don't see him here. They are the last surviving male heirs to the Anastasian line."

The Imperial brothers didn't impress me on sight. They bent towards each other, like two trees seeking refuge from the wind. One was tall, broad shouldered and stately. The other was whip thin with translucent skin that revealed his veins.

Origenes, the first Roman Senator I ever saw in the flesh, was another matter. He so perfectly embodied everything I thought an elder Senator should be, richly dressed with a noble face and a wise cast to his brow. His movements were deliberate, even majestic, exuding experience and devotion.

The Senator conferred quietly with an elegant, elderly woman with hair pulled back severely in the ancient style and held in place with an unadorned gold tiara. Mellius described her as the Princess Juliana of the *Anicii*, daughter of the Western Emperor Olybrius and granddaughter of the Western Emperor Valentinian III. No living Roman had more noble blood coursing through her veins and her palace was the center of the capital's cultural life.

"I know it seems like a big group, Valentinian, but this is just a taste. I've seen Justinian in audience before and there are at least two hundred, sometimes five hundred regulars in the hall. They are landowners, knights, lords, princes, bankers, barbarians, ambassadors, merchants, socialites, all looking for proximity, a way to rise through the ranks, and glory. To each their own but that's not for me. Sometimes I worry that we've forgotten the meaning of Rome. It's a concept Valentinian, not a place. It's a concept worth dying for."

A concept not a place.

The world unfroze then, just in time, when Theodora touched Justinian's hand. The Emperor looked at her and lingered a moment before beckoning to the General.

"Belisarius, Rome places much trust in you and that is why we accept your army here. As everyone in this room knows the army has been prohibited from the capital for centuries to protect the Empire from military tyrants. But in extraordinary times we need the army to preserve order and it saddens me to admit that today is such a day. Fortunately, our army is led by an honorable servant of the Empire. Your Emperor thanks you, General Belisarius, for your courage and honesty. You give us the added comfort and strength to pursue the diplomacy this crisis requires.

"But before pursuing anything I must have hard facts about the nature of this mob, their motivation, their objectives, their leaders. Where are my spies, where are my wise men? I see too many blank faces staring at me when I need intelligence. Facts, gentlemen, give me facts so that I can make educated decisions."

Eudaimon cleared his throat.

"With all due respect my Lord I had some experience with the rabble last night and I do believe that I know *a fact or two* about them." The Prefect wagged his heavy head around the room to emphasize that he was being droll and that his experience was quite substantial. There were no knowing smiles in response and so he continued, visibly disappointed. But he would not let it detract from his dramatic delivery.

"Sire, they are animals. And it is my belief that the Emperor should not stoop low and attempt to dialog with them. I believe that we should act decisively and I believe that we should act now. With the troops under my command I can place an armed force in the streets and…"

With a wave of his hand Justinian cut Eudaimon short.

"With all respect due the Urban Prefect, it's not your place to determine with whom the Emperor would entertain dialog and how. Moreover, your 'armed force' has shown itself to be inadequate to the task. We *shall* speak to the people of Rome. Let us hope that there remain some sane voices amongst them."

Turning to Belisarius, Justinian continued.

"General, it's too early to call upon your arms. But I would send Mundus to the Hippodrome to speak with the rioters. I don't know how some here can speak confidently about what '*they*' want when we haven't spoken with '*them*'. So we will send Mundus and give them a chance to redeem themselves."

Belisarius pulled himself up to his full height, thrusting his chest forward in anticipation of action.

"My Lord, I would gladly undertake this mission myself."

Justinian shook his head.

"No, Belisarius, you are my secret weapon and I don't want your presence revealed just yet. Mundus will go, leaving you and I to discuss matters further. It's nearly midday now, we can't afford to delay any further."

Belisarius bowed.

"As my Lords wish. I will give Mundus his orders and I'll return shortly."

I heard my own heart thumping and I was convinced that the whole room rang with the same beat. Not a molecule moved, not an eyelid twitched, until a gravelly voice filled the vacuum.

"Mighty Justinian, illustrious Emperor, if I may have a word, Sire."

Origenes stepped into the spot that Belisarius had just relinquished. The Emperor's eyes acknowledged the Senator. Origenes used a cane to support his considerable weight, and with pain he began lower himself to his knees, according to protocol.

The Emperor offered a tight smile.

"Origenes, we do not wish you pain on our account. Remain on your feet, Senator, and speak your mind."

The relief on Origenes' face was so genuine that I felt immediate empathy for the man. His voice was deep, still robust, full of a life lived.

"Mighty Justinian, the Senate meets at noon and though I am an old man and a simple Roman, my presence is requested there. But before I left I wanted you to know that we, the Senate, speak with one voice in support of the Emperor. We applaud his handling of this dreadful Laurentius matter and in condemnation of this mob and the damage they have inflicted. We, the Senate, stand with the Emperor and we ask you to command us, Sire, in anything, as always. With your permission my Lord, I shall now leave the Imperial presence."

Justinian nodded. "Honorable Origenes. We regret your departure but leave is granted. You will of course communicate our thanks to the illustrious Senate for their stout support against the rabble."

Looking about the throne room as if he counted heads, Caesar continued. "I do believe that all that found themselves here in the Palace on a social occasion would do best to leave now, including the noble Princess of the Anicii. Juliana, while your presence always gives us great cheer I would *never* forgive myself if you came to harm. I would feel more comfort if you were safely ensconced in your own considerable palace, Princess, and not at risk here in the house of the Caesars. Perhaps the good Senator Origenes might see you home on his way to the Senate?"

How curious of Caesar to single out the frail Princess for that special treatment, their relationship must have been great indeed! How little I knew then, how much I would learn in the years to come. But at the moment I was too fascinated by the palace drama to have asked more pointed questions. Most fascinating of all was the Emperor himself who sounded like no living creature I had ever heard. I wondered if the Emperor spoke with the same careful choreography in his sleep. It seemed exhausting.

Even then I knew that I would not want to be him.

The Princess joined Origenes in the center of the throne room, moving with the aid of her own cane but with no affectation or visible pain. The cane seemed to provide her only connection to the earth below. When she reached the Senator, below the dais, she offered Caesar and the Augusta an exquisite curtsey and crisp thanks. "As mighty Caesar wishes, so shall this humble servant of Empire do."

That was it. Not a word more as the Senator and Princess, both older-than-stone, linked arms and with canes clacking, exited the room. A dozen or so other nobles and dignitaries that had hovered on the periphery joined the exodus.

"Can we trust him? Can we trust any of them?" The Cappadocian spoke first.

"We will trust everyone until they prove themselves untrustworthy." The Emperor responded, giving his words a chance to take effect. "And we should have those answers soon. Narses?"

The eunuch stepped close to the throne and the Emperor spoke to him, deliberately low. When Justinian finished Narses bowed to him and then to the Empress before darting from the room.

◆ ◆ ◆

A short time later, Mundus, Belisarius' close friend and next in command, climbed the steps to the Kathisma, the Emperor's Hippodrome box. The Kathisma sat on the eastern edge of the Hippodrome, connected directly to the Palace with a vaulted walkway that spanned the city streets below. In that way there was no need for the Emperor to set foot in the street when he attended the races.

Mundus found himself thanking Constantine for the wisdom of his design as he led two trusted officers up the winding staircase. With swords drawn, they rushed around each corner to surprise the enemy that they didn't find, arriving at the door to the box undetected. A rap at the door was answered by two knocks in return, whereupon the door swung open to reveal three members of the Excubitors, the Emperor's elite bodyguard. The Excubitors were known to be the bravest and boldest of all branches of the Palace Guard but these three looked positively sheepish when Mundus entered.

He announced his intentions to them and they expressed their concern. Leaving them in the deep shadows, Mundus walked to the balustrade high above the arena floor that was covered by a throng of partisans, easily ten thousand strong, who mixed with the rising dust. This was not what he expected.

Mundus did not hide from them and word of his presence quickly spread, drawing the crowd in a tight cluster to the foot of the Kathisma. When sufficient numbers had gathered, Mundus raised his arms and bellowed.

"Romans. Good men and women of Constantinople. What would you have with your Emperor? There are no games planned here today, go to your homes in peace."

They responded with a roar that gathered strength as it ripped through the arena. When they finally quieted, one single man pushed his way to the front to address Mundus.

"General Mundus, we have no issue with you and we don't need games. But we, the Blues and the Greens, the united brothers and sisters of Rome, have demands. The Emperor would do well to heed them."

Mundus leaned out over the railing, calling in response.

"You speak dangerous words, Roman. But continue, what then, are your demands?"

It was not one voice responding for many but many voices responding as one that erupted below him.

"DOWN WITH THE CAPPADOCIAN. DOWN WITH EAUDAIMON. DOWN WITH TRIBUNIAN."

Mundus had heard enough, the People had spoken and the Emperor must know. He signaled to his men and plunged down the back steps but the chanting didn't end. As the demands were repeated the voice of the mob grew, rending the very air, melding with the heavy smoke that filled the sky.

◆ ◆ ◆

"You look about as natural here as two Huns in Cairo. And lest your vaunted Roman education doesn't reach that far, Huns are not indigenous to Egypt."

Layla's laugh softened the insult.

She caught us by surprise, deliberately creeping up for maximum effect. In reality she didn't need to try so hard, we were so oblivious that she could have announced her arrival with military horns and we wouldn't have noticed.

Mellius and I had been frozen in place along with the other Throne Room supplicants since the Emperor left hours before. The room stewed in gossip and the fact that we didn't participate in any of it made our position even more awkward. We were ignorant of Palace protocol but for the scraps that Mellius had gathered, disconnected from the power structure and we had no natural allies. If there's one thing I have learned about politics since that day, it's that you always need a sponsor who has the power and will to shelter you from the occasional assault. Men without allies have short lifespans in the Palace.

All of which is a convoluted way of acknowledging that Mellius and I looked as odd as Layla described. When she joined us, unexpectedly, it felt like we had stumbled out of the Great Desert into an oasis.

'*You see Layla*', I told her after flashing the desert metaphor, I was not so completely ignorant of Egypt. Deserts. Camels. Oases. Pyramids. True, I had never been there but I knew a thing or two.

She was on the verge of an even sharper retort when Mundus, Belisarius and Narses strode back into the Throne Room together.

Then the heavy bell sounded and we all dropped to our knees.

The Emperor was expected.

An invisible panel behind the dais slid open and Justinian emerged quickly, brushing aside the valets that sprang to his aid. He walked with purpose, visibly angry.

Mundus and Narses had been in conference with the Emperor and General Belisarius about their recent errands. I searched the faces of all four for some clue of what was to come. The coarse murmurs that filled the Throne Room stilled with the Emperor's raised hand.

"General Belisarius, please clear the room of anyone not in the Cabinet. Narses, you will make certain that our esteemed guests have an adequate escort to their homes. And I want the entire Palace emptied of all but essential staff. John, Anthemius, Tribunian, Procopius, Eudaimon and Paul, you will remain here. Valentinian and Mellius may stay according to the General's wishes."

The Emperor had asked Belisarius to perform a task normally handled by ushers. Had I been paying attention I would have known that we were on the verge of momentous. But I was so relieved that Justinian had remembered me that I completely missed the signal.

"Julius, your presence is required outside. Pay close attention to the Palace perimeter, we are at war. Layla, I have a message for your father. Leontius should prepare his tools and medicines, we may need them soon."

Layla bowed then dashed out the door, leaving Mellius and I as awkward as she found us.

General Belisarius promptly ushered all out the door but for Anastasius' nephews. In their elaborate way the brothers begged for the Emperor's attention. Hypatius, the elder heir, spoke in mahogany baritone that rang off the marble floor.

"My Lord, my brother and I beg your permission to remain here in the Palace. Just maybe we can be of service to you. We do retain some standing with those that served our Uncle and we would gladly use our influence in your favor."

Justinian pressed his hands together in an almost prayer, and peered out from above his fingertips.

"Dear Hypatius, dear Pompeius, though your offer is kind, I think that the Romans would be better served with you both in their midst. You shall therefore obey my command. Fare thee well."

The brothers bowed in unison as Hypatius spoke again.

"As you wish, Emperor Justinian, leader of the Romans. But should you require our services I assure you that *we* are for *you*, steadfast and true."

"How comforting, royal Hypatius, but I need no such assurance."

The Emperor was inscrutable.

Hypatius offered a modest flourish, and Belisarius saluted before whisking the brothers from the room into the hands of the Excubitors who would see them home.

With the throne room now empty of all but the essential members of Caesar's cabinet, Mellius and me, the Emperor waved Mundus forward.

With unadorned words General Mundus swiftly described his Hippodrome adventure, whereupon Caesar called on Narses.

"While Mundus visited the Hippodrome, Narses slipped into the Senate to observe the vipers in session. He will now recount what he has just told me in private. Narses, proceed."

The eunuch smiled beatifically as he bowed his gaunt frame to the Emperor.

"The guards at the back entrance to the Senate had to be eliminated. In reality, I might have slipped past them with a bribe but I thought this approach best. With such carnage on the streets their loss won't arouse suspicion." He swung his yellow head about the room as if expecting someone to challenge his methods - none did. "After entering I found a spot where I could hear well and when necessary I could see without being seen. And this is what the Senators said, word for word."

"Senator Severus swept into the rotunda while other senators swirled about. Their mood was volatile, almost violent. When a clutch of them began to shout and push he remained tranquil, biding his time until the first punch was thrown. He spoke then and they fell quiet.

'My friends, peace to you, peace! This is our time. This is our triumph. Our kind has sought liberation for an eternity but this time we shall succeed. By God the Almighty I swear that we'll succeed. May my family be banished from this fair earth if I'm wrong.'

"He blathered endlessly about sacred vows and his leadership. Then he described the activities of the army, *the Senate's army,* under a 'Titus', who all will recognize as the disgraced commander of the *Limes Arabicus*. Finally the Senator Origenes stood, lumbering right up to Severus with that cane of his clicking. From a distance I could smell the old man's fear when he exploded like old Cato himself.

'Dear Severus, you have carried us far, far we must go. And tell me, if we are not successful, how far shall we go then? Do you think that the victors will be kind enough to banish us instead of murdering us in our sleep? If I were them I don't think I would incur the expense of banishment.'

"The chamber erupted again, neighbors bickered with neighbors and fingers wagged. Severus looked like he would slaughter Origenes on the spot but the old man gathered momentum. His voice boomed, quieting the crowd. Their families had served together for generations, he reminded them, and it was time to speak hard truths. He wanted to know if they were truly convinced, if they truly understood the risks that Severus took in their name. The old man was eloquent.

'I say, let us take decisive action. Yes. But let us move decisively to forget this thing. Let us admit that we erred and save ourselves, and our heirs, a worse fate. We were wrong, we were hasty and there is no shame in admitting that now. If we do so our families live to fight for justice another day, and another, and another for as long as this glorious thing that we call Rome lasts.'

"The chamber was so still and his words so powerful that I thought Origenes would carry the day. He finished, gave a slight bow and upon rising he caught Severus' arm. He spoke quietly but given my fortunate position and the room's acoustics I could hear what the crowd could not. Origenes hissed.

'Into the lion's den you take us Severus, I won't forget that this was your idea from the start.'

"Then Severus grabbed Origenes by the shoulder. The old man winced.

'Indeed Origenes, how very good of you and I shall return the favor. When we succeed, for we shall succeed, I will not forget that you have been against us from the start. You shall be rewarded in kind. As sure as the sun sets in the West I will ensure that you have your just reward.'

Narses didn't stay to hear the rest. He concluded that the Senate was part of the rebellious mix that tore Constantinople asunder. But the Senate had its factions and Severus was in control of the traitors.

Leaving them thick in debate he slithered back to report to the Emperor.

NATURE OF THE BEAST

"NEVER IN A million years would I have thought that Romans could contemplate such a thing. Barbarians murder their own but not the Romans. Doesn't anyone else here agree that this idea is detestable?"

Tribunian's hands chopped the air, casting his anguish across the room. The entire assemblage, the Emperor included, hung on his words. We were far past the time for niceties when Justinian asked his closest counselors to opine on the two, terrible options we faced. Tribunian spoke last, holding nothing back.

"My Lord, I am no natural politician but some things I know - in my stomach I know that this is what our enemies want! They hope that the Emperor will debase himself with a rash response. If blood runs in these streets then they will have won. Forgive me for saying it but has everyone here lost their minds? Where is the wise counsel that our Emperor requires? Can't you see that there are two issues here? Leave the Senators aside for a moment and focus on the common Romans that fill our streets. These men and women are the salt of the earth, the foundation upon which our forefathers built their first wall to separate the civilized from the animals. Who are we to throw this so recklessly away?

"Mark my words, the last thing the mob expects is for us to accept their terms and that is precisely what we should do. Separate the little people from the rest and if what Narses says is true then we'll have an easier time addressing the Senate's treachery. My Lord, I say that we should grant the demands of the Hippodrome mob. Let me resign, let Eudaimon resign and let the Cappadocian resign. As honorably as we all might serve the Empire, if our early retirement can preserve the peace then isn't it a small price to pay?"

According to Mellius, Tribunian wasn't prone to histrionics so when he stamped his foot in disjointed punctuation, everyone took note.

The Emperor's head rested heavy in his right hand.

Those thick fingers of his cradled his forehead, splaying wide to better support its weight. He listened as Tribunian's voice faded into the rising murmur. I couldn't swallow past the lump in my throat. Mellius stood bolt straight by my side. We had no right to be in that room but we were there, forgotten. And that is how we witnessed history.

With visible effort, Justinian pulled his head straight and paused, letting the moment gather its gravity.

"Tribunian, you do indeed serve honorably and your Emperor thanks you for your service. Now listen to me, all of you. We who seek to do more than *preserve* Rome, we who seek to take those metaphorical walls that Tribunian described and to use them to protect something grander than a village on the Tiber must look beyond. Beyond the bricks and mortar, beyond the apparent and tangible, that is where we must strive so that we are judged more kindly by history. Abhorrent, dear Tribunian, it is. And it is right that you question this thing that we ponder. You have revealed yourself once again as a true friend."

Justinian stood now on the edge of the dais and the room stood with him. The nature of the thing was finally, definitively clear to

Justinian and now he would make it clear to the crowd. Let the friends, and enemies, fall where they may. But before he spoke he wanted everyone in that room to openly commit themselves to an opinion, a course of action. No one would be spared. And so he called on them one by one.

"Tribunian, what would you have us do." Caesar questioned.

"Fire us, spare the people, arrest the Senate leadership, and put them on trial." Tribunian answered.

"Narses."

"Put the army in the streets, kill as many as we can."

"Paul."

"I am reminded of Thermopylae and I am inclined to a noble fight, a noble death."

"Cappadocian."

"I am in uncomfortable agreement with Narses and Paul."

"Patriarch John."

"This is not a matter for the Church."

"Very well Holy John. Procopius?"

"I think of history, my Lord, and wonder what we can do to avoid bloodshed."

"General Belisarius."

"I agree with Tribunian, make this a matter of law but use the army to bring the mob to heel."

The Emperor of Rome looked to the dome that hung above, letting his gaze fall on the gold eagle emblazoned at its apex. "Very well. Thank you for your opinions. I have decided.

"All of you that stand before your Emperor, listen. The challenge might be clear but there is no simple solution, we are in for a fierce storm. Very well. We will start by accommodating the mob's demands even though it will not satisfy their hunger. As

Procopius says, we will make a gesture for history, knowing full well that blood will soon flow.

"John, Tribunian, Eudaimon, you are relieved from your official duties, though you shall remain in the Palace. I won't deprive myself of wise counsel when I need it most.

"I see an organized enemy behind this mob. Their motives might seem capricious, but I know that this poisonous rabble aims to bring back the House of Anastasius.

"We are no fools. We knew that many took issue with my Uncle Justin's accession to the throne and those same men reject my own authority. That opposition has grown every time We exercised the Imperial power to benefit the common man.

"For the commoners then, John has sought to improve the collection of taxes. It was our moral obligation to do so, to make certain that the wealthy amongst us pay their due, something they haven't done for far too long. In Asia we seized large country estates, broke them into small plots and gave them to army veterans so that they may retire comfortably after risking their lives to defend us. This was important but I'm especially proud of Tribunian's work. By clarifying the laws of Rome they are now accessible to all, not just the law's dark clerics who twist it to their own ends.

"Of course I knew that We would make enemies when we pushed for these changes. But I thought, naively, that the nobility would be persuaded to accept less in their ample pocketbooks for the greater good. Clearly they have not.

"Now, I do believe that the original Hippodrome demonstration was spontaneous and true. We should do what we can, when this passes, to address our citizens' concerns. Mark my words. If graft exists then we shall find the perpetrators and they will be punished to the full extent of the law.

"Our well funded enemies have seized upon this organic tumult to reshape the Empire as they see fit. Now we have only to discover which puppet they would place on the throne. They have three nephews of Anastasius to choose from, Hypatius, Pompeius or Probus who was absent here this day.

"Before proceeding, perhaps it is worth recalling the circumstances surrounding my uncle's accession to the throne. Let us not forget that he was the Emperor Anastasius's chosen successor. For those of you too young to remember, humor me as I retell the story.

"Anastasius had been ailing for some time. Childless as he was, the Emperor was a student of history and knew that if he died without an heir, chaos would follow. The Emperor invited his three nephews to the Palace for a feast. Anastasius was a pious man and he trusted in God's will - he would let *Him* decide. The Emperor prepared three couches for his nephews so that they might sleep overnight in the Palace. Beneath one of the pillows he placed a scrap of paper upon which he wrote '*The Chosen One.*' The boy who selected that bed would be his successor.

"The night of the feast came, the dinner ended and all retired for sleep. Yet when the old Emperor went in search of the Chosen One he found that bed empty, for two of his nephews had chosen the comfort of each others' arms, and bodies, for the night. Distraught but encouraged by his faith, the Emperor resolved that the first man who entered his bedchamber the next day would succeed him. When his doors swung open the following morning, it was Justin, commander of the Excubitors, who strode into the room. Understanding the wisdom of God's choice, the Emperor embraced my uncle and before God and man, Anastasius proclaimed Justin heir to the throne moments before his death.

"There were no sinister machinations here and there was no Palace revolt. The Imperial diadem passed bloodlessly from Anastasius to Justin and from Justin to me, according to the will of the Romans. Would any here deny that? Speak now. I won't punish anyone for their views, but if anyone here doesn't believe in my right to the throne they should leave now. I only want the faithful in my war counsel."

Bristling silence fell upon the room. Neither the sound of shuffling feet nor the rumble of clearing throats broke the calm. In the Emperor's house Justinian alone interrupted silences and so he did.

"Very well. We are at war and it is time that the battle is joined. General Belisarius, I give you the power that you require and I ask simply that you proceed with caution. Go forth with our blessing. Tame them."

Belisarius bowed to his sovereign.

"It is late afternoon now, I shall return to report before the next day dawns."

Without pausing he snapped straight, turned, and strode to the threshold. Before reaching the door he passed directly in front of Mellius and me. I couldn't do anything in the Palace for Leo and I said as much to Belisarius. He looked at me a long moment then nodded curtly before proceeding through the door.

Mellius and I bounded after him.

◆ ◆ ◆

In a breath, I was one of one thousand troops that slipped out a narrow door behind the Palace then westwards into the smoke-filled quiet.

There was no common face in the unit I had joined. We were a blend of colors, from the swarthy Huns of the Asian hinterland, Heruls from the east, the ivory white Alani from the north and the olive-skinned Italians, Africans, Dacians, Thracians and Greeks. In addition to the common swords and armor, all soldiers strode about the campsite with sturdy bows strapped across their backs.

The more I observed them the more I noted the missing elements. There were no battle standards, no infinite infantry and none of the ritual signs that had marked the Roman Army for centuries in all the epic battles that I had studied. The Army still possessed those things but they were left on the frontiers to fight the increasingly rare set-piece battles. These men, this troop, represented something very different, something that few people in the world had seen before.

No verbal command was issued but the troops split soundlessly in two. Though there were so many nations represented I saw that the Huns and the Heruls seemed to concentrate in separate groups. After exchanging a few low words with Belisarius, Mundus led the Heruls away, around the Palace towards the east side of the Chälke ruins.

I thought of something that Leo had explained to me only days before. Roman armies had always been distinguished by the specialization of their troops, heavy infantry, light infantry, cavalry, archers, spearmen, grapplers. Yet our armies had suffered since the loss of the West and especially the loss of Africa had pressured the Imperial treasury.

Belisarius was the first general to seek truly novel solutions to the problem. On the frontier with Persia he began to develop a new, highly mobile, elite corps that fought alongside the traditional military structure. These troops were expert with sword, bow, shield and spear and capable of wielding them with equal force on foot and on horse. I remember the hair spiking on my arms as I watched them muster and move. When Mundus had completely faded from view Belisarius called Mellius and me to his side.

"One thing is certain, victory won't be ours today and it won't come in a set battle. We have to wait for our moment and when it comes we'll strike a decisive blow. Until then we'll do our best to assess the enemy and to secure the Palace."

Though it was late afternoon, heavy smoke covered the city in premature dusk. Belisarius dispersed patrols in the neighborhoods bordering the Palace. In the alleys and lesser streets they met mild resistance as they established their perimeter. If they could control the minor ways, then any attack on the Emperor would be forced to approach on the open ground of the Augusteum, where Imperial troops would be more effective.

From our perch we could see clear ground to the Miliôn, deep in the heart of the Augusteum. The Miliôn was a stand of six columns, two bronze, two silver and two gold, arranged in a semicircle, capped by a marble dome. Distances throughout the Empire were measured from its base. It was the very center of the Empire and from Belisarius' vantage point the center had not yet been taken. He could build on that.

As Belisarius monitored the execution of his evolving plan, a runner arrived from Mundus. Mundus' troops had fanned out on the Bosporus slopes below the Palace. Inching their way to the Propontis on the south shore, they would attempt to secure the Emperor's access to the sea. Though they had encountered some armed resistance it had quickly disappeared. Mundus wasn't certain if the skirmishers they met might were armed citizens, irregular troops, professional mercenaries or a combination of the three. Mundus had also noted the spread of the fire along the city's western edge. A stiff wind off the Bosporus fanned the blaze that had just consumed the Senate House and showed no sign of slowing.

"Very well," Belisarius growled, "tell Mundus to proceed with caution. This damned smoke is going to bring an early night and his troops should be secured for the evening well before. Go."

The General had a peculiar face. At times it gleamed like desert stone, a mature man at the peak of his powers. At times it softened with the youth he in fact possessed, as it did when I met him on his wedding day. And at times, as it was that moment, Belisarius' face pulled and strained, laced with the dust and angst of too many campaigns.

Observing the three short, clean lines of his advance guard as they broke, melting into the smoke, he pounded his stiff steps with purpose, trying to shake the heaviness from his limbs.

PART IV: BURNING FAITH

If we should go out against the enemy, our cause will hang in the balance, and we shall be taking a risk which will decide everything in a brief space of time; and as regards the consequences of such action, we shall either fall down and worship Fortune or reproach her altogether. For those things whose issue is most quickly decided, fall, as a rule, under the sway of fortune.

Senator Origenes in the Nika Riots (according to Procopius of Caesarea)

Byzantine Faces

THE FIRES THAT had raged for three days continued to burn and those that could afford to had already fled the city.

By land they left in a steady stream of carts and chariots. By sea they escaped in small skiffs to safety in Asia. Yet for the vast majority of Constantinople's citizens, there was no recourse but to retreat indoors.

Entire families, generations upon generations, clustered in the stoutest homes they could find. Across the city the innocent took to their hiding places and praying for the best, they left the streets to the wicked.

All work in Constantinople had stopped. Fisherman no longer hawked their catch because the fleet had dispersed for safer harbors. Merchants no longer sold their wares because all city gates were sealed shut. Farmers that had once brought their produce to the capital stayed home on their farms, hoping that chaos from the capital wouldn't reach the countryside. And so the news spread, from capital to country, from small town forum to farm - throughout the Empire the citizens knew and they waited, they speculated, they feared the inevitable.

◆ ◆ ◆

In the forum of Volerus the news was loudly proclaimed as in so many other city centers yet one thing, one man, by the power of his presence, made the recitation different and distinct.

After my father heard all that he could hear he retreated to his workroom and sat on the bench he had built for me when I could barely walk. I think that I could be one hundred years old and I would still be my father's boy, with dimples, chunky thighs and all. He told me that was the picture that he couldn't erase from his mind on the day he heard about the Riots.

It stayed with him, it vexed him and he searched his mind for some relief. Finally, he pulled the chest of Scipio Africanus from beneath a stack of parchments and opened the top, looking for inspiration

◆ ◆ ◆

Two hundred miles to the east, on the outskirts of the capital, Basil, captain of the Theodosian guard, swung his arm across the desk, pushing his maps to the floor. Basil's lieutenant, Pyrrhus, was also an old friend of Leo's. Years later, in the same tavern where I had met Basil, Pyrrhus described the moment Basil decided he couldn't wait any longer.

"I was as ready as Basil was to get out of our little fort and to see if we could do something to settle the city down. But Basil told me that I was going to stay put. '*You're promoted, old Pyrrhus.*' That's what he told me.

"Promoted! I had been his number two since time began and I didn't want promotion. I wanted action. He just shook his head and I knew better than to challenge that stubborn ox.

"He told me that he was going to leave me in charge of the Wall while he went with twenty men to join Belisarius. The General had passed through the Wall the night before and he told us he might need our help. From everything we heard the time for help had come. Before leaving Basil told me that the gates were to remain closed for everyone but the Emperor's men. He said, *'if anyone tries to force their way they should be taken and held. If they resist, kill them, we'll sort out the mess after.'*

"So that's what we did, Valentinian. That's what we did."

◆ ◆ ◆

Across the city, in a cavern deep beneath the burning remnants of the Senate, Severus coughed.

"Titus, that's quite enough for now. I want them breathing when they're found."

When Titus refused to stop his gruesome work, Severus stamped his foot in the dust.

"I SAID ENOUGH. You have more important things to attend to. Hear me and obey General, its time."

Titus stood up and pushed his stomach out. His hands were covered in blood and when he rubbed his jaw he left blood there, flashing the Senator a knowing smile.

"My Lord, no time has been lost here I assure you, utterly, most entirely, yes. This has been time well spent and time delightfully spent. The troops have mustered, they await, and I was just preparing my Lord, simply preparing. And now, I do believe, that I am prepared."

A bloody dagger appeared in the General's hand. He pressed it against the wall and swept the blade back and forth, leaving crimson in its wake.

"Very well, away we go then. Most honorable Senator Severus, the city will be ours soon. The throne shall be yours in one day or two at the most. Truly, it's almost tiresome in its own way, isn't it Senator? Those who would wear the mantle of Rome have always been so predictable, so disappointingly predictable. They rise and they fall, sometimes of their own accord and sometimes with a gentle push. We shall now give Justinian that gentle, final push."

Kicking dust from his feet, the rebel general looked back to see if his words took effect. With no reaction from Severus, Titus ordered Leo bound though it was no longer necessary.

"Are you certain he's still alive, Titus? I would be terribly disappointed if he died. Lucius declared him to be a friend of Belisarius and we know his history with the Excubitors. We can use him. I want him to die when it matters most. And we can use our friend Lucius again as well. No one but this Cantecuzen knows Lucius spies for us, and I don't think any risk of Leo talking remains."

◆ ◆ ◆

Steps from the Gate of Perama, in the midst of homes that screamed nobility, a mob of many thousand paused before Probus' door. No one in the vicinity dared to stop them when they tore the door from its hinges. Chanting Emperor Anastasias' name they shredded furniture, desecrated walls and scavenged rooms from attic to basement but it was clear that Probus was not there. He might have become their champion had he stayed in Constantinople, but Probus had decided weeks before that was not the fate he desired.

His house was the small price he paid for his life. Within minutes flames hissed through the grand corridors, leaping from story to story, bursting through its roof to the sky above.

"TO HYPATIUS!"

They roared as the fire went hungrily about its business. There were two other Anastasian nephews after all, why not try the eldest of the three? As the pack jostled its way free of the narrow alley, sparks from the fire they set chased them into the city.

◆ ◆ ◆

In the Sacred Palace of the Caesars, the Emperor received a thin wafer of bread on his tongue that was, as the Patriarch intoned, '*the body and the blood.*'
Justinian knelt in the middle of his private chapel as the Patriarch officiated unaided for the first time since he was ordained. I could just imagine John's soft fingers raising the cup to the Emperor's lips, brushing crumbs from the gold plate that held the offering, adjusting the miter on his head.

Long after these events the Patriarch and I met at a minor ceremony where the world fawned on him. John saw me and broke through his circle of sycophants so that we might share a drink. While I refreshed his wine we relived those dark days, with a smile that only time can allow. For me the highlight was this, the Patriarch's description of the Emperor on the eve of the Riots.

"Justinian occupied the marble floor alone, devoid of pews, enjoying the absence of those hundred helping hands that followed him from dawn to dusk. A heavy light, palpable as quarry dust, flowed through the string of windows that punctured the nave, settling about us, complementing the ritual.

"The Emperor made the sign of the cross, pressing two fingers to his forehead, to his breastbone, to either side of his heart and stood in one fluid movement, energized. Raising his hand, pointing to the jewel-encrusted crucifix that dangled from the ceiling, Justinian addressed me.

'Do you know what set him apart John, do you know what distinguished the Christ, Jesus of Nazareth?'

"I remember my head twisting and I told him that I neither knew the answer nor was I completely comfortable with the conversation. But of course, the Emperor could guide me down any philosophical path he chose. Always better with wine, those conversations and of course, at that moment there was none to be had. I was quite nervous when the Emperor pressed."

'Come now John, leave the orthodoxy aside a moment, half the city is ready to hoist our heads on a pike, so please, humor me and answer my question honestly.'

"The idea of my head on a pike did not comfort me. Again I thought of wine. The Emperor pressed me for a response and so I guessed, knowing I would be wrong. I suggested that Christ was distinguished by his unwavering, absolute, unshakeable faith. Justinian looked disappointed as he paced to the back of the chapel, plucked his sword from its niche and cinched it to his waist.

'Yes, of course that was useful, but I assure you that it was of secondary importance. There were many men of faith in his era, perhaps even more so than in our own. Since the dawn of time the land has crawled with the unkempt penitent. But what set the Christ apart was so utterly simple, so terribly, disturbingly simple that the truth of the matter has caused many men greater than us two, a profound crisis of the spirit.'

"The Emperor was standing so close to me that I do believe I took a small step backwards. What he said next I would never, ever forget. And I'm not entirely certain that he is wrong.

'Here, then, is the answer.' Caesar said. 'Luck. Pure, blind, dumb, brilliant luck. The carpenter had the good fortune to be struck down in his prime, in fulfillment of the prophecies, to the delight of his fellow Jews, to the chagrin of our Roman forbearers and to the utter mortification of his apostles who would spread his word to the four corners of the world. Everything according to its own time, its own particular geography, its prevailing wind. Jesus' luck was martyrdom and his death served him well, John, as it would ultimately serve the Empire well. I've been thinking about this a great deal the last few days and I tell you that we don't have that luxury. Our death would, I am certain, I am confident, spell the eventual end of Empire. We must, somehow, with God's blessing, with the citizens' charity, with the efforts of our loyal servants, find the dumb, blind, blessed luck to live.

'To live for Rome.

'We will survive for Rome, so that the light is not extinguished.'

STREET TO STREET

THE DRIFTING SMOKE was the metronome by which the scouts, traveling in pairs, timed their departure.

The fighting thus far had been grinding, not dramatic. In the few, spontaneous battles that they had fought, the Emperor's enemies were quickly dispatched. But as Belisarius consolidated his minor gains, and began to probe more aggressively, he found himself reconsidering his tactics. Sporadic duels weren't going to end the rebellion in time to save the city. Some said that over a quarter of the Imperial Quarter lay in ashes and the fire continued to spread.

There had to be another way.

It took me time to realize that I was standing almost exactly where I had been the night before but I barely recognized the spot. The Augusteum's manicured gardens were a wasteland now. Screams rang out in the distance, I couldn't see the men that drew their blades for the Emperor but I could feel them. It hit me then, that life had irrevocably changed, that it continued to change, that I would never be the same. And yet I had one connection to the past, one immutable part of me that was lost somewhere in Constantinople. I owed Leo more than I had given him and it was time, I explained to Belisarius, it was time. The General's concern was palpable.

"Valentinian, Leo disappeared in the midst of the mission that I sent him on, you aren't the only man here that owes him. I should send you with an entourage but I can't, so in the absence of numbers you'll have a fine young swordsman, Mellius. I can vouch for his discretion and valor. Now go and return before nightfall no matter what you find."

I saluted the General with a nonchalance that I didn't feel. Mellius was by my side, he hadn't left my side since we met in the Throne Room. And on the verge of my leap into the breach, I felt his presence by my side as an irksome physical thing. Imagine, the country bumpkin felt burdened by the professional soldier because he was younger, more earnest, and because I was envious of course. It was shameful but what's done is done.

'Just stay near me Mellius,' I spat. 'I have no time to worry about you.'

He barely blinked in response. His cherubic face was so close that our heads touched. With one eyebrow raised and his lips pursed he put me in my place.

"Valentinian, here is one difference between us. I have, apparently, much time to worry about you."

Leo had told me a million times that anyone could be a teacher and that a true warrior was forever a student. I remembered it then, not too late to change.

'Very well Mellius, very well.' I tried to speak calmly, confidently. I can only guess what he heard. 'We'll go together then, as partners, on my signal.'

Constantinople was alive with voices that day, the calls of the advancing scouts, the mob's dispersed rumble, the gulls' plaintive wails. And through it all the menacing baritone of the fire spoke the loudest, whistling and cajoling, battering and seducing. Awash in that dull roar I turned to Mellius, gathered my courage and nodded my head.

'Now Mellius, now.'

We dashed in tandem through the broken Chälke, past the smoldering remains of the Baths of Zeuxippus and across the Mêse in search of Belisarius' scouts. Mellius saw our rendezvous point and tugged on my sleeve, maneuvering us through the Senate's crumbled outer wall.

The grizzled scout that waved us to safety whispered as we approached.

"If I were to guess a number I would say there are at least a few thousand devils mulling about in the smoke. Bastards that would see Constantinople burned to the ground. But as the General says, all that matters is the quality of our brains and tactics. So here I employ an old fox's tactic, I hide and observe when all I want to do is run out there with my sword swinging, screaming like a banshee. My blade could teach them let me tell you, death would teach them a thing."

The scout reeked of the intensity common to Belisarius' men. I tried to muster what I thought was great energy and conviction as I explained my plan to Mellius and the scout as we cowered behind the crude shelter of shattered columns. We would slip into the Forum of Constantine and we rummage around until we found some sign of Leo. The Forum lay five minutes up the Mêse, through the heart of the opposition whose bellows reached us quite plainly.

Of course the idea was suicidal but Mellius didn't say a word, those luminous eyes of his just absorbed the plan as fact and prepared to come along for the ride. It was the scout, Octavian, who set me straight.

"Friend of the General or not, even if the gods made you invisible that plan of yours would mean certain death. And that, my wet-behind-the-ears pups, will not happen on my watch. I've already lost one of my men this day to stupidity far less obvious than yours. Stay if you want but you won't move past me, I promise you that."

My bravado evaporated. And it was just as well, because events would soon demonstrate how precarious our position truly was.

I noticed the first sign of trouble as I conferred with Mellius. It was something in the distance, almost imperceptible, a hint of movement amongst the late-day shadows. At first I thought it was just the wind-blown smoke and I began to turn away when I noticed it again. Something moved in the ruins of the Senate.

Not wanting to alarm my companions I crawled a few cautious paces to my left and pressed up against a column's torso. The Senate's rotunda laid steps beyond me but there was virtually nothing left to distinguish it, no more than a small clearing in the rubble. 'Just my imagination' I thought as a gust blew off the Bosporus and clarified all.

In the middle of the rotunda where a staircase wound downwards to the Senate's foundations a group of soldiers rose from the very ground itself. There were at least two hundred of them and they moved slowly in our direction. I was too far away to hear their voices but I was close enough to see drawn swords that had to belong to the enemy.

Mellius and Octavian had joined me by then and they saw what I saw.

"If we run they'll see us for certain," Octavian exhaled. "We have to warn the General but know this. When I send the signal our position will be compromised and we'll be done for sure, no doubt about it."

Octavian placed one hand on my shoulder and another on Mellius' before continuing. "If the two of you leave me now there's a chance that you can escape. There is nothing shameful in it but you have to decide."

Mellius thin voice cut the silence with a clarity that I will never forget. "Octavian, we are Romans, we do not run."

Octavian's eyes darted quickly between us. "Very well. May the Gods take pity upon us."

He mumbled softly before cupping his hands together, pressing his thumbs to his lips and blowing with all his might. From the weave of fingers it came, rhythmically, once, twice and three times again, the call of a wood owl.

The sound had a surprising effect on the front line of brutes. They wagged their swords and menaced the phantoms they could not yet see. Behind them the enemy column came to a halt. Charged with violence, they huffed a stone's throw away.

Craning my neck between two blocks of marble, I looked about, capturing shards of light.

To my left Octavian crouched, taking deep breaths, each one slower than its predecessor.

To my right Mellius' knuckles bled pale, while his eyes fixed on me, his responsibility.

Then the sky above us filled with sandaled feet. Our enemies had leapt the barricade and soared above, spilling into our hiding place.

◆ ◆ ◆

Two men bore down upon me in the chaos.

More swarmed over decapitated columns, rushing into the open roadway beyond. Two came at me. Pressing back madly against them, one plump, one lean, perspiration and blood filled the air as I ducked a strike and struck back.

The heavy blanket of smoke reflected the war cries and screams. Nothing was clear. The men I fought looked like demons from the spirit world. Only the pain was real, I had been cut but I didn't know where and couldn't stop to look. Then Mellius appeared, rushing up a pile of rubble to meet one of the rebels. With a spark and a clash of metal the boy bent under the onslaught. Octavian pulled Mellius away then hurled himself into the troops that continued to pour over the ledge. Three fell with him in a tangle.

So this then, so this…

It was my only thought, detached words, calmly arranged. Soon we would die.

The timeline faded, little remained to us.

My enemies lay on the ground before me, dead and dying. Mellius and Octavian stood back to back beside me, returning the blows of five. Then, through the rubble, through the smoke I caught sight of the man I had seen addressing the rebels at the Santa Sophia. There couldn't have been more than fifteen soldiers between me and the man I later learned was Titus, the rebel general.

Fair odds damn it all. I remember thinking as I began to run.

Titus saw me sprinting towards him and didn't bother to suppress a giggle. Orders lolled from his tongue through tears of joy.

"Take him oh this is too good, what fun. Take him alive if you may, we can add him to our collection."

As his troops advanced to meet me, Titus asked his valet to bring the prisoner forward. The squat troll of a man, rumbled.

"General, I'm afraid he's not long for the world that one, you worked him over too well."

Titus waved him away as he waited for me to die, and I did everything I could to delay that moment. Ducking to a squat I swept my right leg under the feet of those closest to me. Two fell on their backs as a third charged forward. Too slowly, I moved to parry a blow that landed on my shoulder, cutting clean to the bone. Everything went dark and I almost lost consciousness. The pain was blinding, excruciating, and I just barely managed to keep my sword up and swinging back and forth before me.

My attackers waited for my sword to fall.

As my strength failed, a mighty roar and a piping counterpoint hurtled over the barricade. Octavian and Mellius fell on my attackers with blunt fury, striking two dead on the spot.

"KILL THEM! KILL THEM!" Titus shrieked as his reserves rushed past him into the fray.

It was the scout, Octavian that took the brunt of the onslaught. He tried to spare us, jumping into the empty space with his sword flashing. Trading blows with a dozen dogs – all that remained of Titus' guard – he managed to fend off the first rush. But they rallied. He attempted orderly retreat, stepping backwards, warding them off with bold strokes.

That is when he slipped and they fell on him, cutting him to shreds before we could offer help. And we were next. There was no question of rescue. The most that Mellius and I could hope for was to sell our lives dearly. All around us the mercenaries closed their ranks. Mellius' back pressed into mine.

That is when Mellius spotted him.

I would see him seconds later but those seconds would make the difference. A litter lay on the ground beside Titus. On top of it was a broken man whose bloodstained face I had known in a way since birth.

But before I could react, Mellius had raced ahead of me, darting past our pursuers. He broke into the clear and accelerated towards Titus, who hovered over Leo's motionless body.

Looking up in time to see the boy, Titus drew his dagger with a portly tranquility.

◆ ◆ ◆

While Mellius, Octavian and I fought for our lives, Belisarius roared in the middle of the Augusteum. Darkness had fallen and he too was deep in battle with a detachment of Titus' troops.

"Parthias, bring the left flank around, prepare the archers, we crush them here."

With his head bent low, Belisarius pressed into the thick rump before him with a handful of bristling Huns by his side. Most fearsome amongst the ferocious, Belisarius laid two to the ground for each of his comrades' victims. And just as the center began to weaken the General's orders were transmitted, and executed.

While the core forced the battle deeper into the rebel heart, Belisarius' left flank moved into action. Looping wide around the General they wheeled and plunged into the side of the enemy cohort. Their charge dissolved the block before them into a chaotic sea of swords and spears.

With their attack stalled, buckling under the combined sting of Belisarius' central thrust and the pincer move of his wing, the rebels turned to the open plaza on their left, searching for an escape. At that precise moment Belisarius' archers released their bowstrings in a twanging chorus, sending three flights of arrows into the rebels' unprotected left flank.

Their shafts didn't have far to travel. When they cut into the rebels' side a good fifty or more crumpled immediately to the ground. The screams of the wounded competed with the battle cries of those who knew that there would be no surrender.

◆ ◆ ◆

Far across the Augusteum, in the remains of the Senate House, Mellius must have heard my warning but he didn't slow until he was paces from Titus whereupon he called to the rebel commander in a voice I barely recognized.

"Sir, in the name of Justinian, the one true Emperor of Rome, I command you to drop your sword. Drop it and release your prisoner."

Titus' mocking voice yelped in response.

"Oh dear! Mighty warrior surely you mistake me for someone else. I am a simple citizen that has stumbled across this frightful battle. The beast roams tonight. Do help me."

One pace closer now, Mellius didn't flinch.

"Sir, you are no such thing. I might be young but my mother didn't raise a fool. Drop your sword or prepare to defend yourself."

Titus' eyes narrowed as he appraised his opponent. "Yes, of course, as you command." Bending slowly, he stretched his sword arm out and from his knees, he laid the blade in the rubble. Seeing his adversary's fingers lingering by the hilt Mellius called sharply.

"Step away now. I command you…"

Before Mellius could complete his sentence, fresh sounds of battle exploded behind him, making him pause for a single beat of his heart.

Titus did not make the same mistake.

Pulling the dagger from his robe in one rapid motion, he lunged from his knees and launched his full weight upon Mellius with the knifepoint before him.

Life compressed to this.

Blades singing all around with Basil's roar above the fray as re-inforcements arrived.

Me screaming wildly, so far from Mellius, screaming wildly as I watched.

And the body of the boy, accepting the point it could not resist, pierced again and again as Titus called the blood forth.

Down Mellius went, dropping under Titus' crushing weight.

Turning his back then with a glance at the approaching mayhem, Titus moved to Leo's side.

Leo was gravely wounded and he faded in and out of consciousness. Unable to bring his eyes to focus he heard Titus' voice and in its dripping sarcasm he knew his enemy.

"Dear old Cantecuzen, the time for ceremony has passed. My moment is delayed but yours, yours has come. It is time for you to die."

Ever fastidious, Titus eyed the blood-soaked dagger in his hand. Uttering a low oath, "by the heavens this will not do", he wiped it clean, preparing it for worth.

Admiring his handiwork, he placed the tip against Leo's chest, shifted his weight behind the blade to force it more readily, and whispered.

"Fare thee well, Isaurian."

There, on the threshold of life and death fate intervened to claim its man.

Prepared to administer the fatal blow, Titus convulsed and dropped his dagger on Leo's chest as a sword tip emerged from his stomach. With a ragged gasp, he fell heavily to Leo's side.

And Mellius stood above them both, swaying from side to side, his life's blood streaming from his chest, his final act complete. Unable to resist he collapsed there, falling on top of Leo, arms stretched across his shoulders in an almost embrace.

"To hell with you boy. To hell with you."

Titus coughed as his head fell back.

My scream echoed in my ears.

Leo's eyes fluttered then shut.

All went black.

FINAL APPEAL

PURPLE CLAD, PENITENT but proud, Justinian took the bound scriptures and approached the Kathisma balustrade.

The Hippodrome held eighty thousand souls at capacity and it was far beyond that now. The citizens filled the stands and then, when there was nowhere left they flowed onto the track to catch a glimpse of the Emperor.

Since his coronation, Justinian had never stood before such a throng, nor had he ever faced such a moment.

"Good people of Rome. Your Emperor stands humbly before you."

Vibrations from the crowd traveled through his feet before striking his ears. It came again and again and when it seemed that it would never end Justinian thrust the bible aloft, high above his head.

The ensuing silence came gradually, reluctantly and when it was complete Justinian continued.

"I have heard your concerns. And as a gesture of the love your Emperor holds for you, I dismissed those that wronged you and I am prepared to do more. But first, you, my fellow Romans, must choose peace. The power is in your hands to end the chaos. Let the good people of Rome go back to their homes. Let us resume our lives, let us resume the countless things, grand and small, that make this Empire the master of the civilized world."

A cry rose from below the Imperial Box, breaking the Emperor's conciliatory rhythm.

"PERJURER! USURPER!"

At first Justinian shrugged off the lances, continuing unperturbed.

"CITIZENS OF ROME! HEED ME."

His voice strove to cover the dissent as he extended his ultimate concession.

"Should you disband now, your Emperor will grant a full amnesty to all. No man will be persecuted for what happened this week. I seek peace. Hear me Romans because this is our last chance."

This was truly the mob's last chance - Justinian had nothing left to offer. Neighbors turned to neighbors. He observed the nodding heads, the changes in posture. For a moment it seemed that the Emperor might carry the day.

Then their answer rose in the back, gathering converts and force as it approached the Kathisma. The chant was simple. It was clear. And it was for Anastasius' eldest nephew.

"HYPATIUS. HYPATIUS. HYPATIUS."

The mob's cries for a new champion ended all speculation. Caesar had much work to do and decisions to take. But before disappearing, he gave the hordes one final flourish of the purple.

'Bid farewell to Rome' he is said to have whispered, before disappearing down the back steps.

◆ ◆ ◆

Belisarius saw the Emperor late. I saw him early.

The wounded, dying and dead had been moved into the Imperial Stables after overwhelming the smaller Palace infirmary. I happened to be watching when the heavy doors swung open and Justinian stepped across the threshold. The Emperor had just left the Hippodrome and from his manner I knew that it hadn't gone well. Narses followed close on his heels and for a moment the two observed the room. The Emperor composed his face quickly but I saw the original emotion.
No one could help but shrink from the horror of the place.

The air boiled with the screams of those who clung to life. Their appeals to an unjust god filled the space and lingered.
Leontius ambled from palette to palette, tending to the wounded. John the Patriarch comforted the dying and placed sacred ointments on the brows of the dead.

And I sat on a bale of hay, one in a long line attended to by Layla and the volunteers she culled from the Palace to patch and stitch the lightly wounded.

I could only think of Mellius, nothing else. Not even Layla's touch could change the fact that the boy was gone. Mellius. It seemed such an injustice to call that old soul a boy, he was so much more. I'm not ashamed to admit that I cried there in the Stables when I recounted his final moments to Layla. Hell, I still cry when I think about him. Layla's eyes welled with tears but somehow she kept them from falling.

"We Egyptians believe in fate and it was his to live a comet's life. But just look at what he accomplished, look at his impact. Rather than mourning him, learn from him Valentinian, you can help make his life matter."

I was unconscious when they found me on the field. After they roused me I insisted on helping to carry his body, ripping my shoulder open further, half hoping I'd die. Then Layla saw me, skulking in the shadows of the Stables and she accosted me with her hemp satchel of bandages. Her dress must have been a similar color when she put it on that morning but now it was streaked with blood and dirt. Strands of hair fell in her face from a braid that refused to hold. She was covered in the filth of war, exhausted, pushed to her absolute limits and furious.

"Some *civilization* indeed. You butcher each other like you butcher sheep, like you have butchered the weak around the world for centuries. Just maybe you deserve this madness that you've unleashed on each other. Oh, I see the look on your face, am I offending your delicate sensibilities? You think I should perhaps be a little more demure, grateful that I am here in the *Sacred Palace*? You think a woman's place is in the background? What is it – speak."

But I couldn't speak and if I could, I would have had nothing to say. So she kept yelling at me.

'You could have lost the arm completely thanks to your stupidity. Only because I am skilled in the healing arts, only because I am Egyptian and not Roman, am I able to fix your arm. But you are lucky, Valentinian, you have no idea how lucky.'

Of course she was right. I wanted her to keep talking to me and I wanted the physical pain to continue, in order to distract me from the greater pain in my heart. I wasn't ready for war's aftermath.

The Emperor progressed slowly through the palettes of wounded, placing a hand on each bandaged head, each twisted limb. He spoke steady words of encouragement and the men responded. Justinian's innate power could not be conferred. As he drew closer I saw the blood on his hands, on his sleeves, the blood of *his Romans*. For the briefest of moments his ashen face hung low. Then he straightened, calling to Belisarius in a soft voice.

The General managed a swift bow but he didn't bother to hide his anguish, there was no need. Contrary to many of the old commanders, Belisarius never denied his humanity. According to him empathy didn't make a man weak. But understanding came with a price. When he lost a man there was no denying the pain. There had been too much of that today, and he told the Emperor that there would be more to come.

"More than three thousand irregular troops attacked along the west and north end of our perimeter. If they had attacked our main body we would have easily thrown them back. But I miscalculated, casting my troops out like a net thinking that we would gather information and catch stragglers. I underestimated the number and quality of the opposition and it cost us. The first wave pierced our scouting line by the Senate. There was no honor in what they did. Our boys didn't have a chance."

Belisarius wagged his head.

"They fell directly on Octavian. He has been with me since my first command. Mellius and Valentinian had gone there, under my instructions, in search of Leo Cantecuzen.

"My rearguard was bogged down in fighting beyond the Baths of Zeuxippus. We met the rebels that had run straight through Octavian on their way to the Palace, and I thank the gods of war that we were joined by a small detachment from the Theodosian Wall. Captain Basil led them and it was he who reached Octavian first and it is he who saved them. By the time I reached them Basil had carried the day but the damage was done."

"And the Senators, what of them, was there any sign?" Justinian glowered.

Belisarius shook his head. He had traversed every inch of the Senate grounds but there was no sign of any Senator, alive or dead. Their home was dust but they had known enough to avoid the blaze.

"We have won ourselves a breath Sire, no more. The reprieve won't last long, I'm sure of that. There must be between five and ten thousand rebel troops in the city in addition to a mob of thirty thousand or more. There is just too much city between us, too many buildings and monuments that give them too many places to hide. If I could only lure them out into a proper battlefield I would have options, we would have a chance."

Justinian listened to Belisarius but looked at the blood-streaked body at the General's feet, watching his chest slowly rise and fall.

"Is that Leo Cantecuzen?"

The General nodded.

"Will he live?"

Belisarius nodded again.

"He has been stabbed more times than you can imagine but the skin is too thick, his will is too strong. Men like that aren't made anymore."

The Emperor brushed past Belisarius, past Leo, towards the palette at Leo's side. He pulled the blanket back, revealing the boy's face. Whatever pretense of manhood that Mellius had carried in life had long ago deserted him, showing him as he truly was, with an inner sweetness that death couldn't steal.

"Poor boy," Justinian muttered as he brushed his fingers across Mellius' brow, his own shoulders hunched, frozen in place. A feeble groan broke his reverie. Leo's barely audible whisper raised the hairs on my neck.

"My life, he saved my life..."

The Emperor, who was still on his knees, placed a hand on Leo's chest.

"I know what he did, Leo Cantecuzen, and I know what you did. You saved the Patriarch and nearly lost your own life in the process. Your Emperor wants you to know that neither your service nor his sacrifice will be forgotten."

Just then a servant entered the stable and exchanged words with Narses. The eunuch listened a moment before beckoning to Belisarius.

"General, your wife has entered the Palace with her sister, looking for you. They know of the battle and they won't be comforted. She demands to see you."

Belisarius furrowed his brow.

"Tell them anything but keep them away. Julia's son lies here, dead and she has no idea. Do what you must, tell them what you have to but keep them away."

Justinian intervened.

"Belisarius, you can't keep a mother from mourning her son, and in my mind it is best commenced quickly. The decision is yours but don't take long, I need you in the Throne Room. Events have overtaken us. We have grave decisions to take and I must take them with you."

As the Emperor prepared to depart, he turned once more to Belisarius. "What about Valentinian?"

Belisarius' face lightened a touch. "He is right here my Lord, behind a post being tended to by Layla. Valentinian, boy, the Emperor asks for you."

My legs moved, carrying me out of the shadows and towards the Emperor. I fell to my knees, too overwhelmed to feel awe in the Emperor's presence.

"Valentinian, I have been told that you fought bravely. Because you earned the respect of your General you have earned mine as well. Accompany General Belisarius to the Throne Room when he is done here. And General, hurry, we don't have time to waste."

No sooner had Justinian exited then the stable doors burst open. In raced the sisters, Julia and Antonina, with Narses in pursuit.

"I couldn't stop them."

Narses called across the infirmary as Antonina dashed towards Belisarius. The General moved away from Leo and Mellius, into the center of the Stables to greet them. Antonina threw herself into his arms, sobbing.

"Thank God you are well my husband. I was so afraid. The city burns, the streets are alive with demons and I had a terrible premonition that I wouldn't see you again."

Belisarius stroked her head as he extended his spare arm to Julia, beckoning her to approach. Julia stopped paces away and gazed at the horror about her. Looking at her brother-in-law, she spoke in flat tones.

"General, my son, my only care. Do you have news of the Wall regiment? And what about Leo and Valentinian, are they here?"

"Yes Julia, yes, both of them are here and they will be just fine. Valentinian is there, you can see him if you'd like. He was wounded in battle but the wounds were benign. Leo was also wounded, he is here and resting. He'll be up and about in no time at all I promise you though it's probably best that he rests right now. Now, I don't want to rush our reunion but the Emperor has called for me and I must be on my way. Please allow Narses to take you out of this place and to see to your needs."

I overheard the General. The evasion was below him. He should have handled the horror directly but I'm not certain I could have done any better.

Julia realized that Belisarius' answer was incomplete. With a flush of blood in her face Julia locked Belisarius in her gaze and asked again.

"Please, General, you must tell me, what do you know of my son?"

Belisarius looked away, over his wife's head to the door beyond. Drawing a deep breath he returned his attention to Julia. Antonina gripped his sleeve and watched him with held breath.

"Julia. Your son and I travelled to the Wall. My men were camped just beyond it. He led me bravely and I invited him to continue with me instead of returning to his regiment. After we arrived at the Palace, he and Valentinian were sent to investigate Leo's disappearance. In the ruins of the Senate they were ambushed. Mellius fought like five of my best. He killed the rebel Titus and he saved Leo's life. But he sustained many wounds, Julia. By the time that we had carried him back here…"

As Belisarius fought for words, Julia broke past him and fled deep into the stable, led by her heart. Recognizing Leo where he lay, Julia threw herself to the ground.

She wrapped her arms around him and pressed her face to his with tender ferocity. In a profound sleep when she arrived, Leo awoke to Julia's caresses and tears. Too feeble to move his body, too weak to return her touch, he did succeed in turning his head ever so slightly, compressing the space between their cheeks.

"Never again, never again will I leave you."

Leo whispered as Julia whispered in response, burrowing her face deeper in his side.

"Promise me. I won't survive it a second time, promise."

It was Belisarius' gentle touch on her shoulder that pulled her away.

"Julia, we must let Leo rest, he needs sleep to heal."

With a lingering kiss on Leo's brow, Julia stood, her chest heaving as an impossible mix of emotion rushed across her face.

"Yes Belisarius, I..."

That is when she saw him where he had been left, in the shadows beyond Leo, face uncovered, her son.

The scream rumbled in her chest before her mouth opened. It leapt from her pores before her tongue moved and when her lips did finally part it was her soul that exploded into the room. All around her illuminated and froze at once for one eternal moment of the most pure despair, black as night, forlorn as Hell.

When the sound would come no more Julia collapsed where she stood, falling into the waiting arms of Belisarius who had rushed to her side with Antonina behind him. Leo watched from his bed, unable to move a finger in response, a look of terror spreading across his face as Antonina whispered to him through her own tears.

"Your son Leo, he was your son..."

As it Would Be

BELISARIUS STRODE INTO the Throne Room, brushing shoulders with those that didn't move swiftly enough to avoid him. I followed with my shoulder bandaged tight and my head buzzing. Together we bowed to Theodora and Justinian.

The Emperor's strained face broke into a tired smile as he looked down upon us. "Please take your place. Let this war counsel begin."

Gripping the arms of his throne, Justinian continued.

"We have made little progress in the last five days. The flames draw closer and the Hounds of Hell march behind them. The center of Constantinople lies in ruins, the Holy Wisdom, the Baths, the Chälke, and it gets worse. The Excubitors just reported that the Hospice of Samson was burnt to the ground overnight. Seven hundred patients that were too ill to escape died in their beds. The depravity deepens, the destruction accumulates. The City can't survive another week of this. Rome can't survive another week."

Narses slid up to the dais then and approached at Justinian's invitation. He whispered into the Emperor's ear. Justinian's face darkened and Narses withdrew as deftly as he approached. The Emperor looked up and took us all in before continuing.

"Hypatius has apparently delivered the final insult. He has entered the Kathisma with a wreath of gold upon his head, in the company of his brother and the Senator Severus. As we speak

Hypatius is addressing tens of thousands that are acclaiming him as their new Emperor."

Justinian stood and approached the front of the dais as all of us dropped to our knees.

"Dispense with the formalities now, I speak to you as my trusted advisors and friends. Stand. Stand and speak, your Emperor seeks your guidance. This war must end. For the sake of Rome, we must do now what is right."

Silence fell heavily in the Throne Room, blanketing the faithful with an impossible weight. We glanced at each other, wishing for inspiration. John the Cappadocian spoke first.

"My Lord, I don't fear any damned mob and those flames out there could be the flames of Hell and they wouldn't scare me. You all know me and you know that I'm a bullheaded son of a bitch. No hooligans intimidate me. But I must admit that I fear for the safety of my Emperor and Empress and I think that the only way to protect them is to retreat. Let Hypatius the Usurper have his day, let him try to control what he has started, and let Justinian and Theodora take refuge far from the city so that they may live to reclaim the throne. I have swift ships waiting in the harbor. You can be safely away as soon as night falls."

Justinian nodded to John then turned to the General.

"Belisarius, what do you say?"

Belisarius raised his head high and spoke.

"My Lords, as deeply as it pains me I believe that John is right. Though I despise the thought, the only way that I can ensure your safety is to get you out of the city. With the troops at my disposal I can't guarantee the integrity of the Palace compound for long. If they come at us in a concerted assault we'll be overrun. To retreat now my Lords would be to assure that you live to return when the moment is right. In my opinion you should follow John's advice."

Justinian's chest rose and fell, fighting air that was still with the pregnant expectation that this then, was the end. A deadly silence prevailed. The Emperor moved his head from side to side, catching each in turn with his gaze as he readied his decision.

The thunderclap that shattered the silence was the sound of Theodora's foot as she stomped it on the dais. "Enough." She roared, turned to face her husband and spoke with cool fury.

"In a crisis like the present we have no time to argue whether or not a woman has a place in a council of war. I am here, I am Empress, and I shall not be modest and meek in your presence, my Emperor. So I shall say what I must and ask that you heed me. My opinion is that this is no time for flight, not even if it is the safest course. He who is borne into the light of day must die sooner or later, none of us is eternal and that is an eternal truth. But it is definitively not true that an Emperor who is rightfully given a throne must relinquish it while his heart still beats. May the day never come when I do! My Emperor, my husband, if you want to make yourself safe, nothing stops you. There is the sea, there are your boats and there is ample money to pay your way. But mark my words, if you go you are going to bitterly regret it. As for me, I stand by the ancient saying that *purple is the noblest winding sheet.* I will stay here and if I must, I will die here, as Empress of Rome."[1]

Justinian crossed the small space between them and wrapped his arms about her in an open display of affection, causing us all to avert our eyes as the man, not the Emperor, pressed her close.

---

1 *This is nearly a direct quote from Procopius who in turn quotes the Empress herself. Her extraordinary speech changed the course of history. This is the only footnote in the Legend of Africanus and Theodora certainly merits it.*

Holding her inches away, Justinian pressed his lips to her forehead, and spoke softly.

"My queen, without you I am lost."

Turning now to the few loyal that remained, the Emperor spoke.

"Very well then, the decision is made. We will not run. Men of war, men of finance, men of art, what say you? If you choose not to make this stand that is your decision but know this, stand we shall."

Belisarius conferred heatedly with Mundus and Narses when Justinian called his name.

"Belisarius. Let us hear it."

Belisarius looked Narses and Mundus carefully in the eye and they nodded.

"My Lord. It is not a plan as I would like but I believe we have an option. As you said, the mob is currently crowded into the Hippodrome and the Usurper is addressing them from your throne in the Kathisma. Mundus' scout just returned, confirming as much.

"Just perhaps…"

◆ ◆ ◆

Dashing out of the Throne Room, the General called to me.

"Valentinian, I want every able-bodied man in the infirmary to meet me behind the Chälke in thirty minutes. It's time to take the offensive."

I had been floating around the back of the room, trying to shake off my anxiety. This wasn't some small battle after all, the fate of Rome hung in the balance. But when the General gave me a purpose those jitters fell away. And as if he could see into my heart, Belisarius had given me a mission that led me to Layla one last time before we would live or die.

Once Justinian dismissed me I didn't lose time. With an Imperial page as my guide I dashed down the Palace corridors towards the Stables. I assumed that the page was one of Narses' men that blanketed the palace, taking note of everything and all. One would think that I was too small to merit Narses' attention but I felt it nonetheless, his yellow eyes were always upon me and I could see their reflection in that page's eyes. Narses. When I think of that sallow skinned monster my skin crawls, may he burn in Hell.

We reached the Stables and I burst through the doors at full bore, making every head in the room turn. I must have looked like an ass but I didn't care what any of them thought, I only cared what one of them thought. And that one, Layla, approached me with fire in her eyes, drawing up short before me and stomping her foot in the dark earth.

"Valentinian Constans, this is an infirmary. What are you do-ing banging the door and rattling your sword. Have you lost your mind?"

She looked more exhausted, more beautiful than before.

'Layla. General Belisarius sent me to collect what troops I could. The Emperor's men are on the move and there is no time to lose. Are there any able bodied soldiers here?'

She looked at me like I had two noses.

"First of all, no, as you can see every man in the room except for my father is lying on his back because they are wounded, as you are wounded you fool. Mundus was here seconds ago to collect the troops you were looking for. And second, you had better not be thinking about joining whatever bloody crusade the General is leading. You struck me as modestly smarter than the rest."

Layla's hand touched my arm then. It was a fleeting brush but it was intentional. My heart soared. Her lecture continued.

"Valentinian, in case you forgot you are lucky to be walking and talking. And yes, before you ask, your friend Leo will live. But you, Valentinian Constans, will not if you persist with this lunacy. God gave you a brain, use it."

She hadn't shown me the smallest flicker of kindness. And yet, there she was in my face after all and maybe, after all, that was something.

"Valentinian. Son of Claudius."

The voice that called to me was fainter than it should have been but it was unmistakable. I looked past Layla and saw Leo standing against a granite column. Crossing the width of the place in three bounds I threw my arms about him as he chastised me.

"Valentinian, don't even begin to think that you can rush off to war without me." Leo's bloody garments had been replaced but at separate spots on his chest, blood had seeped through the bandages. With his typical brusque touch he pushed me back a step and held me there by the arms. There was that old crooked smile. "No my boy you will not go to war alone. Come, tell me now, what's the plan?"

As I quickly relayed what little I knew, I felt Layla's fierce energy by my side.

"Captain Cantecuzen, you are even more of a fool then your protégé. You can't possibly be serious, by all rights you should have died last night. You could still die if those wounds reopen. I am going to have my father order you confined. If it requires leg irons then you should be put in leg irons. Both of you actually should be put in chains until you come to your senses."

Leo attempted a gallant smile.

"My Lady, from the bottom of my heart I thank you for your gentle ministrations. But when the Emperor asks for help a Roman soldier answers the call, it is time for the troops to report."

Leo spoke kindly but curtly to Layla as he stepped away from the column.

Then he collapsed.

"LEO."

The first voice that rang out wasn't mine but Layla's and she was on the floor by his side before I could react. Her call brought Leontius, running across the stable.

From his back Leo waved the three of us out of his face with a perturbed huff.

"Enough, I'm fine I'm fine. Please, I know you all mean well but I am fine and I am leaving."

Leo was obviously in no condition to move anywhere as much as I would have dearly loved to have him by my side. I told him as much. I explained that even if he could move under his own power, Belisarius would never let him serve in this condition. Of course I didn't need to say any of it, Leo knew far better than I did that this was one campaign that he couldn't join. So he wished me the blessings of the many gods that he cherished and he let me go as Leontius carefully examined him.

Walking briskly towards the exit, I remembered something essential and beckoned to Layla who looked at me crossly in response.

"Am I a washerwoman that you can wave me to your side? Speak to me civilly, Valentinian Cantecuzen. Didn't your mother teach you manners?"

I had started out amused but the mention of my mother, no matter how accidental, brought quick melancholy to me. Wise woman, she sensed it at once.

"I offended you, somehow." Then a light returned to her face. "Forgive me, you must have lost your mother, I lost my own. I should have known better."

I wanted to soothe her but my time was short. Belisarius waited for me, the battle for Rome's soul waited for me. *'Layla,'* I spoke that name and it made me flush. *'You had no way of knowing. Someday I hope to have time, someday I would like to speak with you about other things. But right now I must ask a truly great favor of you.'*

Reaching beneath my tunic, I removed Scipio's medallion and handed it to Layla, asking her to deliver it to Leo if I didn't survive. My uncle would understand what to do.

"Valentinian Constans, I will not accept goodbye. Simply be safe and return quickly."

Then she took the medallion from my hands and leaned forward, freezing me in place. Her lips, the sweetest sweet, touched my lips. It lasted for half a heartbeat and it lasted an eternity. Then it was over, no one had seen. She was slipping the medallion around her neck. I could not muster a word, a war called me.

She touched the medallion through her blouse as I crossed the threshold and left the Stables, Leo and Layla behind.

Minutes later I arrived at Belisarius' staging area just inside the Palace walls. The General and his troops mustered within that typically Roman colonnade where petitioners sought the Caesars's ear in times of peace. Belisarius grimaced before pulling me aside into the corner of the courtyard.

"Valentinian, listen to me carefully - you are not joining this war party. I am leaving you here in the Palace to keep watch over my wife, Julia and Leo. You must know that the outcome of this war is by no means decided. There is a chance that we win but there is a greater chance that we will not. If we lose that will be the end for me and in that event you must take all three of them across the Bosporus to Chalcedon. I rely upon you Valentinian, do not fail me."

Not knowing the protocol in such times I nonetheless believed that the General would appreciate blunt.

'General Belisarius, I'm honored by what you ask of me but I'm a soldier and I belong in the battle. The Emperor needs every sword he can find in this fight. Let me accompany you. Let me serve you. This is why I'm here, for this alone, I beg of you.'

Belisarius grabbed my collar. "You are a pig headed ass. But you have guts boy, may they keep you alive. So you shall come but you'll stay by me, do you hear me? If you stray, if you take initiative I'll kill you with my own hands. Now stand aside and listen carefully, we go to war."

The General turned to the waiting troops whose ranks had swollen while we spoke. His Huns had now been joined by Basil and his small guard, Mundus with his Heruls and Narses who stood slightly apart from the rest. Basil smiled warmly at me and I saluted in return.

Belisarius called the commanders to his side to discuss the plan that even now took form in his mind. As they conferred a commotion rose from the yard and a ripple parted the mass of men. A lone soldier passed through them, wagging a blood-speckled face. The man was none other than Lucius of the Imperial Guard.

Despite his appearance Lucius walked proudly. Stopping short and saluting crisply, he called out so that there would be no doubt.

"General Belisarius, Sir. Corporal Lucius, present and ready for action."

Belisarius looked at Lucius with some amazement, examining him from head to foot. The man looked battered but he still stood straight and strong.

"Lucius, we are pleased to have you back. I must say that we feared the worst when you disappeared. Where have you been, soldier, and what fortune brings you to us now?"

"General, I was taken prisoner during our dash across the Mêse. The rebels have held me ever since and I've bided my time, waiting for a chance to escape. Finally it came - I bolted and left the dirty beasts behind; killing more than one in the process let me tell you. I've been days without news General so please tell me, were we successful? I trust that the Patriarch, Leo and Valentinian found their way to safety?"

Belisarius grasped Lucius' arm.

"We have sustained losses." Belisarius' face drew tight. "Though the Patriarch is safe, and Valentinian is here with us."

Lucius gazed my way - his eyes looked nervous to me but I couldn't possibly have known then.

Belisarius continued. "As you can see a battle is at hand. Can you fight?"

Lucius straightened with a snap.

"General, I would like nothing better than to fight those dogs. I am ready for war."

Belisarius nodded.

"Very well then, we could use the help. Now, fall in and prepare yourself, we leave momentarily.

Addressing Mundus, Basil and Narses, Belisarius gave a cryptic explanation of his plan. Even though I heard everything I can safely say I heard nothing. There was no plan. All I heard from Belisarius was instinct. There were no stirring words that made a warrior's heart thrum and there were no battle plans that I could understand. Yet as I looked at the faces of Belisarius' commanders I saw acceptance and conviction. They nodded their heads in unison, they sheathed their weapons and synchronized their movements to their commander's tongue.

I looked across the knights one last time, surveying the horde that would subdue a mob. They numbered no more than one thousand, stoic to a man, eyes focused far away.

Commanders began to peel away with their units, leaving only Belisarius and his troop. Then the General moved and we followed, exiting the Palace, past yesterday's command post, through the Chälke, past the Baths of Zeuxippus and straight into the northern Hippodrome gate.

◆ ◆ ◆

Belisarius led us into an arcade that opened into two separate passages. To our left lay a narrow corridor that ended in a small, wooden door. On the other side of the door was a stairway that rose to the Kathisma. The passage to the right led to the floor of the Hippodrome.

The roar of thousands cheering Hypatius issued from the stadium, rolling past us before erupting into the city.

The General didn't have the luxury of time to ponder right and wrong. He didn't have the Emperor standing over his shoulder, ready to give his blessing. Only a moment remained before the story was decided for him, for Justinian, for all of us.

Belisarius was no fool.

He knew that the threat to Caesar went deeper than the Anastasian line. He knew that the rebellion was organized, broad and well under way long before Hypatius emerged as its champion. And he knew that he couldn't win a war in the capital with the small force at his disposal. Once the mob scattered again across the city he couldn't possibly protect the Palace, control the fires and crush the insurgency all at once.

Since the first stone was thrown he understood that only a twist of fate could give him a chance at decisive victory and as he stood there, imagining the throng paces beyond him, he knew what he had to do.

This was no police action.

This was war, one that he intended to win.

Decision made, he whispered to himself, "may we be forgiven", before silently beckoning us to follow.

With catlike strides he sped down the corridor to the right, and without hesitation, he stepped onto the Hippodrome floor.

The time for negotiation had ended.

HIPPODROME REDUX

THOUGH IT FELT like an eternity, it only took a few breaths for the rebels to notice us once we stepped foot on the Hippodrome floor.

There were one hundred rebels to each one of us and I could *feel* their murderous eyes burning into me, appraising me. Noble Mellius should have lived to fight in my place and I should have died the day before. I retched bile into the dirt, my legs trembled. If I had the strength I would have deserted but I froze there instead, inches behind General Belisarius at the very front of the front line.

'*Better to die first*', I thought, on the verge of hysteria.

And then, with an audible snap, Belisarius' phalanx of Huns came to order behind us and all went silent and still.

In those last moments before battle I found the courage to look up from my feet to see where we stood. We had entered at the Hippodrome's north end. The horseshoe-shaped *Sphendrion* stood at the opposite end of the field. Empty rows of seats wrapped about - the vast rebel swarm was down on the arena's gravel floor. A marble spine marked the middle of the track, supporting the monuments that Zeno had described to me so many times.

There was the bronze Serpent Column, taken by Constantine from Delphi, cast by the triumphant Greeks after they defeated

Xerxes' army a thousand years before. Legend said that the column's metal came from the swords of the vanquished Persians.

There was the two thousand year old Obelisk of Thutmosis III, taken by Theodosius from the Temple of Karnak, whose pink granite emitted its own soft light.

In between them was a procession of bronze and marble statuary, Romulus and Remus suckled by the she-wolf, an enormous eagle with a serpent in its talons, and so forth.

Our enemies began to recover from their initial shock caused by our appearance. The very timid and the very wise were the first to move, evidently deciding that despite the numerical advantage they would rather be quite far away from Belisarius, Lion of Persia. Their movement allowed Titus' professional troops - now answering to an equally brutish rebel lieutenant - to filter up to the front, nearest to us. Within seconds we faced a disciplined block of black shirts with armor and swords glaring in the sun, stretching across the entire breadth of the Hippodrome. There was no way past them and slowly, they began to press towards us.

Before we stepped onto the floor, General Belisarius had told us that on this day, the forces of the Emperor would strike first. And so he did, howling "TO ROME" before plunging into battle by the ancient obelisk. No refined strategy, no noble ideals, no quest for personal glory remained under the still afternoon sun. There was only this, a fight to the death, and Belisarius' whistling blade.

That blade met its mark and continued, cleaving the nearest, burliest brute from the rebel line in two. Twitching still, his halves fell to either side with an animal whimper and I leapt back to avoid his body. With a quick jerk Belisarius freed his sword and threw himself, shoulder first into the mercenaries who had stopped to watch their colleague fall.

Only the gulls and the false sovereign in the Kathisma above were privy to the full scope of terror unleashed in those first dark moments, when the Empire teetered on the edge. Up and down the line of Titus' troops, Belisarius' Huns launched themselves like needles, darting between the Blackshirts that overran their position.

But there were dozens of Blackshirts to each red-cloaked Imperial man.

I followed the General into that maelstrom.

At first I could see nothing but dust and whirling weapons, dull here, flashing there, and bloodied, blood. Belisarius' back was my landmark, I clawed and hacked and pushed towards him deep in the enemy sea. Choking dust rose, men coughed and I could barely tell friend from foe. But I never lost sight of the General. And then, just when I thought we two were alone in the world, a god-sent breeze parted the dust to reveal the Kathisma floating above.

Three figures craned their necks over the balustrade – I can only imagine what they saw. Below them, in the precise center of the arena floor, in the precise center of a circle cleared of combatants but for the dead, Belisarius appeared. I'm almost embarrassed to write myself into history but the fact is that I was there too, by his side, fighting for my life. The rebel's numbers hadn't notably diminished. If anything they seemed to multiply as we moved deeper into the fray, packing the Hippodrome with their sinew and steel. And then, with another whimsical gust, the dust cloud closed and everything, everyone disappeared from sight.

◆ ◆ ◆

Poised at the southernmost Hippodrome entrance, Mundus heard the battle's first screams and understood.

Though he was a general in his own right, Mundus had fought long enough with Belisarius to know him as his superior. In the baking sun of the Persian borderlands their metal had been tested together time and again. Through it all, Belisarius' wit provided the margin of victory more oft than the weight of their arms. Some might have their doubts but Mundus would have nothing with them. The signal had just been given and it was time to play his part.

With neither time for strategy nor space for elaborate tactics, Belisarius had settled upon a brutally elegant solution, virtually the only one available. They would win here or die and every man that took the field that day knew as much. And so, after Justinian had ordered them again into battle, Belisarius explained to his commanders that they had only two conceivable options, neither favorable.

If Belisarius couldn't take the Kathisma directly, the Emperor's last chance would be to open a battle on the Hippodrome floor. Should it come to that, Belisarius and his detachment would act as the hounds, flushing the rebels from north to south towards the minor Hippodrome gates. There, in the west, the east and the south, he placed Mundus, Narses and Basil in command of each exit. As Belisarius swept forward the rebels would be pushed against their blades. And although the Emperor's elite was vastly outnumbered, if they could incite a panic, hold their ground and then prevent escape, Belisarius felt confident that they could prevail. His commanders had only to let the rebels come to them and to hold their ground. They had no other choice.

And so Mundus watched the unfolding panic and prepared. With a nod of his head, the Heruls advanced before him, through the deep arch and onto the arena floor, no more than fifty paces from a stampede of men that fled the erupting carnage.

"Men, we stand here. No one passes."

The Heruls didn't need further instruction as they unleashed their own terrifying yawp. These ferocious men, two hundred strong, were warriors for the Emperor but they were men first and they roared for good reason. For as they braced themselves, their feet moved to the thunder of the rebel wave dashing headlong towards them, driven mad with fear, all sound and fury and sharp swords drawn.

◆ ◆ ◆

Ensconced in his own world, in service of the greater good that paid best, Narses was at peace. A bitter smile crossed his face as he gazed upon the Eastern Gate. It was one of the mob's few avenues of escape and Narses coolly positioned himself to prevent just that.

Narses didn't laugh aloud. Indeed, no one in the Imperial court was old enough to remember the sound of his mirthless chuckle. Only those that knew the eunuch well would have detected the faintest twist at the corners of his mouth.

In command of three hundred of Belisarius' troops he covered the exit in two semi-circles of Huns behind their razor edged pikes. Brushing his nose with the back of his hand Narses wouldn't listen to his counsel nor would he hurry. Free from the Palace walls, acrid air in his nostrils, he was determined to savor this moment that history would certainly remember. So he watched, not stirring a finger as the sound of mayhem drew close.

The first rebels to approach were neither the strongest nor those of blackest heart. Before the true brutes knew the battle was lost it was the weak-limbed, the witless and terrified that made for the door, desperate for life.

Narses watched their faces and relished the shades of emotion as they passed. Initial panic yielded to faint hope as common men of the Blues and Greens, merchants and sailors, fishermen and carpenters approached the great arch that led to salvation.

"No need my dears, no need..."

Narses hissed at the first few dashing towards the light. And then came the moment, the one he would remember before all else, as the gate he deliberately left unlocked burst open beneath their weight and forlorn relief filled their eyes.

The first dozen spilled into the dust of the street before they understood that there would be no escape. No time was left to react as the Huns pressed forward behind their pikes.

His yellow teeth bared, Narses did not flinch but observed, tallying the dead. A handful fell, then one hundred, then one thousand and more until all those that sought their freedom through the Eastern Gate were cut down at his feet. With no way to be certain if Belisarius' ploy would ultimately succeed, Narses could yet say that no one broke through his line.

Of this he was certain and glad.

◆ ◆ ◆

With the waning of the noonday sun, Belisarius pushed past the middle of the Hippodrome field.

The effect on the half-hearted anarchists and traitors, for there were many of these common men that came that day to crown the Usurper, was profound. Though many had already charged for the exits, a massive group remained, milling in no man's land, eying the accelerating battle. They found themselves hemmed into a

small space, packed ever tighter by the broad backs of the retreat-
ing mercenary troops.

From this crowd of some twenty thousand, a gaggle of young, armor-clad Greens clacked their swords together, hurling insults at
Belisarius' troops from a safe distance. Despite their bravado and
the armor they wore, they had been held back from battle by their
leader, a certain Actius.

Actius was a veritable titan. But just because he had the body of a
beast did not make Actius any man's fool. From the battle's start he
took note of the Huns devastating effect on the Senate's mercenary
army and knew that his 'boys' did not dare face them. At first he
thought he would let the rebel army take the initial spit out of the
Imperial troops before he let his boys take their crack. But the
picture seemed to be changing quickly. Now, as he looked about
the battlefield, Actius began to think that Justinian's troops might
prevail.

So he began to plot an escape. Surveying the exits, his eyes fell
upon Basil's meager force at the Western Gate and decided that
here then was his opportunity.

Actius and his self proclaimed 'Defenders' were neither citizens
nor were they soldiers, they were hooligans of the highest order.
Most had chosen not to follow their fathers into the guilds for a career of honest trade but lived comfortably from their fathers' pocketbooks. They spent their days in the streets where they harassed
the common folk, beat the slaves they found alone after dark and
savaged the whores they frequented. They called themselves the
protectors of all good Romans yet they were the city's most feared
ruffians, the first to throw a fist in Hippodrome melees and Forum
brawls. And when the Riots had started the previous week Actius
and his cohorts were the first to light their torches.

Conferring with his lieutenants, Actius told them that the time had come for their glorious battle. Prudence might dictate that they flee but he would make certain that they drew blood before they escaped. With a sign to the rabble-rousers they were on the move, five hundred strong at a full, uncoordinated sprint towards the Western Gate, screaming vilely as they ran.

◆ ◆ ◆

From his position under the Western Gate, Basil monitored Actius' approach and called his men to attention.

The door he protected was the deepest, narrowest and most readily defended of the four Hippodrome exits. The heavy arch behind him opened onto a corridor that ran for one hundred paces, cutting straight through the heavy masonry to the perimeter road that rung the Hippodrome. No more than three could pass through the tunnel abreast and the resolute Captain knew that this would spell salvation or death for his defenders.

Basil's troop consisted of the same stout two-dozen that had fought by his side the night before. They had barely rested, they had barely eaten and even on a good day most were long past their prime. Despite his many entreaties none would leave him, none could be cajoled to retire to the safety of their homes.

Clearing his throat with a harrumph, he thrust his sword in the dirt before him.

"The hounds of hell draw close so I'll make this short. My men. Too many days, too many nights, too many draughts of the finer spirits and too many tears have we shared together for me to speak to you as anything other than equals. You are good men all, I dare say that you are great men to the last. And yet, the world may think us small. No riches here, no blue-bloods, no great artists, no silver tongues amongst you. You are only this - sons and fathers, husbands and friends. And above it all, when the men of letters write our stories you may be sure that they shall call us warriors and ROMANS, the Emperor's tried and true. I don't know if any of us will leave the field this day but by the gods I swear that not one of us shall be forgotten. By standing here when Rome has no other you have earned this, of this you should be eternally proud! Now to battle. Let them feel our blades. Ready yourselves."

To make their numbers count the most, Basil placed half his men in the corridor. Standing in squads of four with three up front and one behind for reinforcement, they formed stout clusters in the passageway's near dark, clapping each other on the shoulders for strength as they took their positions. Before the arch, on the edge of the arena floor, the twelve that remained formed two staggered lines. With back feet planted and their small shields and swords thrust forward, they readied themselves for the first clash.

Just moments away, Actius' thugs saw the token retinue that stood between them and the City and picked up their pace.

The wave crashed with a force so terrible that it threw Basil's outer lines back like flotsam, pounding the wings against the inner arena wall while those in the center, including the Captain himself, were thrown backwards into the dark corridor beyond. A throng of Greens burst over Basil into the passageway before he could move to respond. Then, just as the last infiltrator leapt over his torso, Basil's meaty arm shot up, grabbing the man's ankle mid-flight. He snatched his captive down with all his might and as the ruffian reached for a knife, Basil's elbow slammed into his larynx, stopping him dead.

The Captain bounced up and surveyed the battle. Nearly twenty had slipped past him into the tunnel and now traded blows with Basil's troops. Swords chopped frantically, whistling murder in the dark. Sensing that the greater concern lay outside, Basil snapped his blade from the dust and dashed back to the corridor's mouth where his broken lines struggled to regroup.

Emerging from the arch, Basil saw five of his men dead, trampled under the remaining seven who steadied their swords at eye-level, facing the Greens who prepared for another push.

They couldn't win, but they could give the General more time.

◆ ◆ ◆

Amidst the roar of battle, Belisarius didn't hear the gravel scrape behind him.

But in the corner of his eye he saw a shadow loom.

Instinct set his body in motion as Lucius' blade plunged swiftly towards his back. Too fast for the General to escape, the assassin's blade struck his arm first then continued into his torso as he spun. A long gash opened along his right side, exposing his ribs as he collapsed in the dust.

Lucius was indeed a traitor, born into a traitorous family, pledged to the House of Anastasius. In exchange for the General's murder, Lucius would receive a high position in the new army and estates in Thrace - he imagined those riches as he watched General Belisarius writhe on the ground.

Success was a sword's stroke away.

Then, with an impossible effort Belisarius managed to raise himself to one knee. He would die standing as Lucius' blade swung.

Belisarius and Lucius were oddly alone.

Only Parthias and I were anywhere near and Parthias was closer, faster and more alert than I. With a deft slip he pulled a small dagger from his belt and with a flick of his wrist he sent it hurtling end over end into Lucius' neck. Blood spilled immediately forth, across the General's face as the traitor spun into the dirt.

With a swipe of his sword Belisarius finished Lucius before he could rise.

"Damned ingrate."

Belisarius groaned, struggling to stand, using his sword as a crutch.

Parthias grasped the General by the shoulders, helping him to his feet. "We must get you to the surgeon, immediately. Valentinian, take his arm, help me."

"I'm fine, I'm fine damn it all."

Belisarius coughed, drawing himself up to his full height as his tunic filled with crimson, his face wrenched with pain.

"Quick, take this traitor's shirt, Parthias, double it and bind it about the cut. All I need is to stop the bleeding for now, later we'll deal with the details."

Parthias did as instructed while I helped Belisarius to clean his wound that was so deep that I don't know how he remained conscious. When I suggested that he shouldn't continue, Belisarius clutched my arm and snarled.

"If I die here I die nobly, Valentinian, now tie that thing around me and listen. We need to change our plans. I can't command the full line now but I'm no invalid. And yet, a friend needs our help and so I need yours. If we fail in this then the battle is lost. Parthias - you will take the left wing ahead. Sweep wide left then move inwards, squeezing the rebels in towards my center. I'll continue my advance, maneuvering the rebel's main body into Mundus' sword.

"And you Valentinian…"

Here Belisarius' sputtered a moment, stricken with a cough that sprayed blood onto his sleeve. Brushing away Parthias' concern, the General continued.

"…you Valentinian are going to rescue Basil with fifty of my best, that's all I can spare but it will be enough. It has to be enough."

I tried to speak but Belisarius' outstretched hand stopped me.

"These are my orders. To Basil's side. If the Captain fails to hold the Western Gate the rebels will disappear into the city and we'll have come this far for nothing. Justinian will fall."

Here Belisarius pressed his hand over my heart and in a barely audible voice he whispered.

"Go now. Our lives come to this. We triumph or we die."

With that Belisarius turned his back on me and commanded Parthias to begin his forward sweep.

◆ ◆ ◆

There was no more hesitating as I looked towards the Western Gate. The passage that Basil guarded was besieged by so many that all I could see were the very tips of the defenders' swords as they rose and fell. Halfway down the Hippodrome floor, in the midst of the barely controlled mayhem of his troops, I looked left one last time and saw Belisarius, with blood seeping through his tunic, swinging his sword, oblivious to the pain.

It was time for me to move. Calling to the right wing, I set off in a sprint with the sound of my own heart filling my ears. As the distance closed I thought of my father on my last day in Volerus, as we surveyed the contents of Scipio's chest.

'He lies in you boy, he lies in you.'

With Claudius' voice still ringing, I bore into the back of Actius' men at full speed, catching them by surprise. Penetrating five deep, carried by momentum, I fought away the hands that tried to pull me down. None of it felt real, my body moved more viciously than I thought possible and far away the boy I had been watched the fight unfold. Three fell, then eight and twelve as my troops entered the battle, clearing a path through the throng.

Wait for me Basil, wait for me.

Blind to the reinforcements, Basil stepped into the collapsing gap behind his warriors to give them the fire they would need.

And yet, what he would need no one could provide. For at that moment a monster broke free of the crowd and with two quick bounds he crashed through Basil's line.

Pleased with the brutality of battle, towering in the small space, Actius growled at the portly captain that stood between him and freedom.

"Out of my way old man, I have no issue with you — let me through."

Basil lifted his sword as if the world could wait, till its tip stood inches away from Actius' chest.

"But I have a problem with you, son of an ox. Defend yourself."

The blood that rushed to Actius' face made his cheeks pulse red as he drew one murderous breath. He didn't exhale and didn't speak but raised his own sword till it touched Basil's. Every ounce of his being focused on his adversary and when he saw Basil flinch, Actius didn't hesitate. He lunged forward with all his might.

Basil had executed this routine a thousand times or more, across the Empire, against foes large and small and had always emerged victorious. His trick was simple but deadly. *Let the attacker commit, let his momentum carry him forward.* And when the foolhardy attacker's point arrived at its intended destination Basil would no longer be there, but at his side, ready to strike the unprotected flank.

And so Basil began, feinting a half step with his left foot to draw Actius forward, then swinging his right foot backwards and around. Yet as Basil spun, his right heel caught in the mangled body of one of his own men underfoot, abruptly stopping his rotation and depositing him rudely in the dust.

A clutch of Actius' thugs battled me and I drove them back, slipping, dodging and bulling my forward.

'Justinian's whore. You'll die a traitor's death.'

My enemies wailed while I parried, pushed and craned my neck in search of Basil. Finally I found him, through the tangle of arms, past the bloodied torsos, just a flash of the Captain as he fell.

Actius stood there with his back to me. I had never seen such a man; he was more than twice Leo's size and his muscles snarled as he prepared to administer the final blow. Below him Basil twitched in the shadow of the Western Gate.

Compressing my body, I hurtled into Actius with all my might. The ensuing impact threw the giant forward, past Basil, through the arch into the dim corridor beyond while I landed with a heavy thud that knocked the wind from me.

For a moment there was no motion in this bubble, this infinitesimal space, filled with the noble Captain, the young novice and the titan. Mere inches away on the Hippodrome floor, the fight for the Empire raged.

Out of sight, around the corner, in the dark, the prone body of the giant stirred, shaking his head, throwing out his arms in a spasm.

Actius planted his hands on the ground and rose till his head brushed against the tunnel's ceiling. Deeper within the sounds of battle echoed and that way led to freedom. Back from whence he came lay his victim and the boy that dared confront him. There was a question of life and a question of honor that hung in the balance. So he turned away from the path of liberty, pressed himself against the wall, and edged his way again towards the corridor's mouth to finish what he had begun.

By that time I had regained consciousness and found Basil by my side. Hovering over the old soldier's head, I tried my best to soothe him as his breath rattled in the chest that ran red, over his tunic, spilling into the dirt beneath him.

'You fought brilliantly, Basil, friend of my friend. Stay with us and we'll carry this day - with Leo we'll toast to victory.'

Struggling to focus, pushing back the darkness that gripped, Basil looked into my face. I could tell that despite his agony he sought to comfort me with his eyes. And then, on the edge of consciousness, Basil saw the shape, something charcoal within the black and with the last shred of strength he screamed. No sound emerged and yet that was enough. That would make the difference.

When I saw him convulse I understood. Snatching the sword at my feet, I whipped about on my heel holding the blade flat, inches from the ground. The edge struck the charging Actius in the ankles and continued till there was nothing left to support the beast.

Actius fell with a blood-curdling scream that rushed beyond the battle, past Hypatius in his lonely box, past the gulls, to the very heavens above. With a swift cut across his throat I silenced him.

The Defenders had lost their man.

And as I returned to the side of the old soldier that had saved me, I realized at once that I too had lost. Basil, stout friend, fierce warrior, forever Roman, was dead.

◆ ◆ ◆

The Devil himself couldn't have had that carnage in mind. Drenched in blood, vibrating with screams, the Hippodrome filled with the dead and dying. With all entrances firmly blocked now after Basil's noble stand, the great humanity that had dared unmake an Emperor knew there was nothing left. There would be no dialog, no quarter offered, only battle to the death remained.

Lest they had doubted, the mob now knew that Justinian, the Emperor of Rome, would have them pay.
Though the Emperor's men called them traitors, the black shirts of Titus, the Greens, the Defenders, the simple opportunists and the true believers that had opposed Caesar were Romans first. As Romans they and theirs had been stoics since antiquity and stoics didn't beg for their lives. They could only die with a certain honor. And as Belisarius' knights moved against them, reducing the original thirty thousand to five thousand or less, this small consolation at least seemed certain to those that remained.
Yet it was not to be so.
For in the ultimate irony they themselves provided Belisarius with his most potent weapon - chaos. The crowd packed in the south end of the Hippodrome was so dense that most couldn't move to defend themselves as they compressed at the center. They could only struggle to breathe, the taller amongst them gasping for air above the heads of the unfortunates. The horror bloomed with the

waning day, as the panicked edges pressed in with ever increasing intensity on the mob's core.

The very young and weak were crushed by their brothers, their neighbors and friends. More dropped from the crushing weight of their brethren that final hour then fell at the soldiers' hands yet in the end it wouldn't matter.

They died just the same.

◆ ◆ ◆

Deep within the Hippodrome labyrinth, below the stadium seats, I had lost my mind. After stabilizing the Western Gate, I left forty-five of my fifty men in place and took the rest on a fool's mission.

Though Justinian's men dominated the battle the ultimate outcome hadn't been decided. Despite the carnage of the day, Hypatius remained in the Emperor's box and as long as he remained free the rebellion's heart would beat. So, madly, boldly, I decided that I'd be the one to take the Usurper into custody.

And so we dashed through the shadowy passages below the Kathisma. When we reached the back steps, we found the door that had been barred in the morning left carelessly open. We didn't stop to ponder our good fortune. Before a man could speak I was roaring upwards with the Huns in pursuit. We were driven by adrenalin, all of us.

No sound penetrated the Kathisma complex.

There was no carpet on the marble floors but our footfalls didn't echo, they were swallowed up in that heavy air, thick like fisherman's wool.

When I was out on the open battlefield I felt nerves but no trepidation. But I was struck with fear in the Kathisma - the fear that something terrible loomed ahead.

I put one foot in front of the other and the men with me did the same. The old marble Emperors, tucked in their niches, watched me climb the steps and their eyes were on my back. *Don't watch me you stone bastards, this is a thing of the flesh, of blood and bones.*

Sweet incense clung to me.

We reached the final landing and prepared to turn that last bend when Stilicho - the grizzled Hun half-breed with the Vandal name - pulled me back, around the corner, out of sight. He had been with Belisarius for years and when his burning eyes locked onto mine I felt the weight of those campaigns. We were on the verge of striking the decisive blow for Justinian; there was no time to lose.

'Stilicho, what?'

He pressed his bearded chin to the side of my head and growled.

"We should wait, trust me, I know, we should wait. We'll send a runner, call a few more lads for reinforcements, we have no idea what waits for us around that bend, behind that door. He's no ass and neither are we – with all due respect, I say that we should wait."

There was nothing I would have liked more. *'Leave it all to the men'*, the little boy in me pleaded. But there we were fifty paces away from the man that had brought Rome to her knees. We had all bled on the battlefield; thousands upon thousands had died during the Riots. And it was in our power to stop it all, to stop Hypatius before he slipped away. The civil war could end here, now.

I told Stilicho, Rome couldn't wait any longer. He told me that Belisarius put me in charge and that the decision was mine to make.

And so it was. And so I did.

There were no more questions from the men. Stilicho nodded silently at me then raised his finger and curled it, beckoning the other four forward. They swept ahead, sniffing the air, pouncing on the shadows, around the corner and out of sight.

Then a whisper called me forth.

The way to the Kathisma's inner chamber was clear.

I rounded the corner and saw the truth.

Three were dead.

The remaining two, including Stilicho, were on their knees, pinioned from behind with knives held at their throats. Those dirty beasts could only have taken my men through an ambush but how? How could it have happened without a sound? For a split second I stood there dumbfounded, in the open but still unseen. Stilicho must have known that I would be close behind and so he bellowed to save me.

"Valentinian. Run!"

Before the rebels could react, Stilicho thrust his head backwards into his captor's groin and the man went down. With quick hands Stilicho grabbed his head and dashed it against the floor, cracking his skull. On his feet in a flash and joined by his last colleague, Stilicho turned to face his enemies. There were four of them and then, with a flick of the wrist Stilicho launched his dagger into an attacker's throat and there were three. I was so gripped by his bravery that I couldn't bring myself to flee. Stilicho roared again.

"Run, bring help, go!"

Finally I understood that if there was any hope of saving him, and our mission, I had to escape.

The last thing I remember was the sight of the fist as it landed squarely between my eyes and then, nothing.

When I came to I had no idea how much time had passed but I guessed my location.

I was finally in the Kathisma's inner chamber, the throne room that floated high above the Hippodrome, close to Heaven. Three voices filled my head, muddled at first then clearer as my buzzing ears settled. There was no question that I was a captive and the longer they thought I was unconscious the better. So I kept my eyes pressed tight and listened to the men that had brought the Empire to her knees.

"This is all we get? Don't we deserve something, someone nobler, more worthy? For God's sake, have they forgotten who we are, have they forgotten whose blood we carry in our veins? I thought that he would have sent Belisarius or Mundus at the very least. But this is what we get, a boy who can't wipe his own ass and an honor guard of mixed breeds. This is a damned insult. Though I must admit, it was quite a delightful feeling when the little ferret went down with one punch. One punch!"

Someone laughed. The laugh didn't comfort.

"Pompeius. Tame your ego for a moment brother and let us at least try to think like rational men. Where from here? The Senate's thugs just slaughtered the Imperial troops that were sent to fetch us and that won't endear us to anyone."

My heart exploded. They were all dead, all of them. Dead because of my incompetence. Dead because of my arrogance. I wanted to shriek, to disappear into the ether but somehow I found the strength to keep my eyes closed.

A second man continued with a touch of madness in his voice.

"So, did they come to kill us or to negotiate our surrender? This is the most intractable of dilemmas and for the first time in my life I find myself guessing. Oh I'm lost, brother, I'm lost, all of those golden dreams lost, all the good we could have done squandered. But it's too late for regret now, far too late. Those dreams will never know the light of day. But so be it, we cannot regret, all we can do now is survive.

"So very well now, let us calculate. Let us consider the facts. It appears that we can't control the world and we can't control Rome. Barring a miracle we'll lose this battle and I don't think that God is inclined to favor us with a miracle now. So what do we have then? We have this one man here, we have one captive. He's certainly young but perhaps you're right Pompeius, perhaps he is their leader, a young man of importance. If so, then we might have a bargaining chip to use with Justinian. So brother, the young man shall live for now. But enough of that, we have more vital issues to ponder, wouldn't you say? It's a slaughter down there and not the one we intended. Yes, truly, we have decisions to make and quickly. So where from here, Pompeius? What now, Severus, man who knows all?"

Invisible Severus spoke - I remembered his name from Narses' spying in the Senate. This was one of the leaders of the Senate cabal that sought to topple Justinian. "Your Eminence, I propose that we take the direct approach and ask the boy what he knows. And there is no better time for confessions then the present, wouldn't you say?"

A pair of none too gentle hands plucked the sword from my scabbard before binding my hands behind my back with a rough leather cord. Then a foot slammed into my stomach, knocking the wind from me and jolting my eyes wide open.

I had no doubt that the face hovering above me belonged to Senator Severus. His mouth flickered with a smile and the corners of his eyes pulled outwards, narrowing his gaze like a hawk.

"Ah, very well then, let me be the first to welcome you to our little gathering."

He stooped and with his smooth hands he grabbed my tunic and jerked me to my feet. My head spun a moment, vibrating from the kick and from the Senator's obvious power. Seeing me still off balance he thrust me against the wall and stared at me with grim merriment. He drew his sword and waved the tip back and forth before me, a finger's length from my neck.

"And who might you be?" Severus hissed.

I looked deep within myself for dignity and strength and found fear. So I spoke with bravado, not bravery when I announced my name and mission, *'to request the surrender of Hypatius on behalf of the Emperor Justinian.'*

There were three men in the Kathisma with me, Severus and the royal brothers but I didn't remember which was which from my earlier glimpse of them in the Throne Room.

One stared at me with rabid eyes and another stood with his back to me. This latter man leaned over the balustrade and stared out over the field of battle. Silence fell after my introduction and he slowly turned, the scrape of his tread the only sound in the box. He didn't stop till he faced me, drawing me into his baleful eyes.

"Commander Valentinian Constans, please forgive us for your regrettable treatment. You came in peace and you were greeted like a villain and that was below us all. You also have my sincere apologies for the death of your comrades, I didn't order it and I didn't approve of it but what's done is done."

Then, taking a small step in my direction this man gave a short, elegant bow before continuing.

"I am Hypatius. With me is my brother, Pompeius, and the Senator Severus. Both have been kind enough to accompany me during this disconcerting time. I welcome you here, Valentinian Constans. Please tell me Justinian's wishes, I am here and I am listening."

Before I could respond, Severus' voice rang out from behind.

"Sad Hypatius, poor Hypatius, trust me when I say that you have much more to fear from me then you do from Justinian. So let us finally set aside our little fiction.

"You might stand on sacred ground, you might wear the diadem on your brow and the little people might salute you as Emperor but these things don't make you great. No physical trappings will exalt you and no powerful words will make you legitimate. There is only one thing in your life that shall do this for you Hypatius and it is not your blue blood. You would negotiate with Justinian's whelp but I say that this is not the time for negotiation – STAY."

In mid-sentence, Severus whipped the flat side of his sword backwards and across Pompeius' chest with a resounding crack. The royal brother crumpled to the ground, gasping for breath. Before he was struck, Pompeius had advanced to within a short step of Severus' back. Their honor was at stake and Pompeius was determined to preserve it, with force if necessary. Holding a short dagger in his hand he prepared to strike when the Senator struck first.

Like nothing had happened, Severus bent and plucked Pompeius' dagger from the ground.

Hypatius opened his mouth to speak but the Senator's glower stopped him.

I stayed in the exact same position where the Senator had left me, propped up against the wall, frozen in morbid fascination. We were on the verge of understanding the true nature of this plot.

Hypatius reached for his sword then and found nothing, realizing too late that he had not armed himself. Amongst us only Severus was armed.

The desperate situation was more desperate in fact but in the moment that Hypatius knew would define him forever he couldn't move, he couldn't speak. Like most men born noble, he must have always thought of himself as the center of the universe. But as he watched Severus expand before him, Hypatius looked like a stranger in his own skin, like a satellite and not the star.

Severus' hand floated in the air after hushing Hypatius until it slowly descended from high above until it stopped, pointing directly at me with the index finger extended. Then, in the Kathisma's odd silence, detached from the roar of death in the Hippodrome floor, Severus continued the speech that Pompeius had interrupted.

"Genius, from start to finish. The old Greeks invented tragedy but they have nothing on this Roman farce. Oh it's too rich, too good. Slow-witted Pompeius, you look confused poor man so for those of you that haven't followed the plot so far I'll give a brief review. In the first act, an Emperor was raised and the people stood mute. Then, a horse race appeared to bring life to a mob but in fact it was a mighty hand that stirred the pot. The mob thought that they raised a new Emperor but again it was the mighty hand that straightened the weak fool's spine. Of course the storm clouds must always threaten in these tragedies and so the old Emperor, the upstart with common blood sent an army into the field to kill his fellow Romans. He said he sought continuity but we all knew that he simply meant to save his own skin. But the old Emperor didn't realize that he fought something, someone, so sublime, so powerful that they began to transcend the earthly bonds. He fought the secret force behind it all. And here comes the best part Pompeius,

Hypatius, boy, are you listening? This is the part when the puppets realize that they are puppets - here they realize the truth of it all."

Severus joined Hypatius a moment by the balustrade where the royal nephew had retreated. Looking down on the battle whose tone had clearly changed, Severus rubbed his face as if he wished to change its character before continuing.

"Returning to the subject, Hypatius. I suspect that even now you haven't divined the truth so I'll deliver it to you in the small, simple words that you prefer. You are a *tool*. You are easily manipulated, your ego sated by craven flattery. Long ago I chose you as the wedge I would use to separate Justinian from his throne."

Hypatius' face ran as white as chalk and he grasped the front of his tunic. Those watery eyes now looked crazed as they flicked from Severus to his brother and back. Severus saw it all and saw nothing, he spoke to the roof, to the walls, to the sky beyond.

"You are the puppet of a puppet, Hypatius, and for you I have the utmost scorn. And Pompeius, you don't merit my scorn anymore than burrowing worms merit my affection. I knew your uncle Anastasius and let me tell you, his shadow had more substance than you."

Pompeius wrung his hands and groaned as if he would soon explode while Hypatius vibrated on his own. I felt pity for the brothers.

"Oh dear, I see shock on your faces. Did I offend you, did I wound you, did I breach the precious protocol? Well, my little mice, Severus is speaking his mind now and I suggest you shut up and listen. Hear me clearly. I am done with you but I am not done with this. Victory can still and will be mine."

I listened in awe as Severus revealed himself. Drunk with the promise of power, with rage, he raised his sword and stepped towards the center of the Kathisma.

There were three enemies before me and only one was armed. My mission had failed and there was no longer a question of capturing Hypatius. But I might still escape to report to Belisarius if I could make it through the lone door or over the balustrade. There were no other options.

As I contemplated escape, Severus moved closer to Pompeius and Pompeius squared his shoulders to the Senator's advance. That is when the door sounded with a small, sharp rap.

"Speak. SPEAK."

Severus rumbled then roared. The tension thickened. A small voice sounded from outside the door.

"I CAN'T HEAR YOU."

Severus was almost hysterical as he spoke through the door.

The brothers traded a furtive glance.

The same small voice piped through the door and the royal brothers chattered.

"It's a boy?"

"No, it's a woman's voice."

"That's not possible. What woman here, whose mother, sister, daughter here?"

"From Justinian, she said she comes from Justinian."

"Open, open and we'll see."

Severus took control. "Stand back all of you, a single move, a crossed eyebrow and I'll make certain that you die. Quiet now and we'll see what Justinian has to say. Oh yes the game is afoot now. So stand back, all of you and you and you in particular."

Severus lifted his sword and with the point touching my chest he pressed me backwards.

"I'm opening the door."

Severus drew the thick bolt and jerked it forward.

A sliver of the world beyond winked at me and it revealed the inexplicable, a flash of ebony hair and blue.

Perched on the threshold, prepared to slam the door shut on Justinian's emissary, Severus hissed.

"We can't very well negotiate, here my dear. Why don't you come here into the Kathisma dear? You'll be safe; you have nothing to fear from these fine men. After all, Royal Hypatius himself will guarantee your health and comfort."

"Sir, I would prefer it if you stepped into the corridor. Justinian clearly instructed me to remain outside if you don't mind," her silver voice rang out.

Severus shifted, leaning left then right as he set his feet wide. Bobbing and swaying I caught just the barest glimpse of the hallway but that was enough, I saw enough to know that Justinian's so-called *emissary* was in fact, Layla.

My heart pounded out against my ribs and the cord bit my wrists as Severus stepped into the maw, closer to Layla, obscuring my view. But just as quickly as he moved forward he leapt back and screamed like he had seen the devil himself.

"IMPETUOUS GIRL HOW DARE YOU?"

Severus snatched Layla by the hair and jerked her towards him. His other hand held Pompeius' dagger, and as she fell he placed the blade in her path.

With my hands tied behind me I lurched awkwardly, stumbled, then struggled upright, trying to reach Layla in time.

But I couldn't stop the dagger.

◆ ◆ ◆

Layla fell like a stone.
My love fell like a stone with blood streaking.
And that is when I saw the dark fury behind her.

Leo had swept past Layla before she hit the ground. The same
bloody tunic he wore that morning fluttered around him now but
it was all crimson, there was no more white, as he bore down on
Severus with nothing but his outstretched hands. He didn't truly
walk, he didn't run, all Leo could do with his broken body was to
fall with vengeance, with murder.

Severus had seen Leo hovering behind Layla when he first opened
the door and that had caused his outrage. Leo hid just around the
corner and using the doorframe for support he launched himself
into the Kathisma.
    After Severus stabbed her he cast the dagger aside and took his
sword in hand. He wound his sword arm tightly across his chest
and then uncoiled, sweeping the blade across Leo's path.
    In a split second Leo sized up the sword's arc then slipped with-
in its striking range, still falling.
    Shock registered on Severus' face. He saw his adversary up
close now and he recognized Leo as his former prisoner. The
Senator's bitterness welled up from deep within and he let out a
scream, flinging venom into the Kathisma's sweet perfume. But
Leo was deaf to it all, moving as swiftly as his battered body would
allow. Just a half step from Severus now he angled his right hand

like the head of an axe and swept it downwards, hitting Severus in the neck just beneath his ear.

The crack was sickening.

Leo completed his collapse, falling into my arms and we both tumbled to the floor. His chest rose and fell too fast but he didn't speak, he looked over me, past me, at Severus.

The Senator's neck snapped, his head fell forward and his body quickly followed. Gravity chose my other side to lay him down on his stomach with limbs asunder. But there was life in him yet and his fearsome eyes looked into mine. For a moment longer his fingers twitched, his torso convulsed and then finally, mercifully, death took him.

◆ ◆ ◆

Belisarius' attention was drawn by the chorus of voices from below the Kathisma. Mundus' stoic warriors broke their ranks, dashing about beneath the Emperor's box.

A corridor formed amongst the Imperial troops that had now taken complete control of the field. Only the bodies of the rebel dead, ranged from one end of the Hippodrome to the other, opposed them.

Belisarius' piercing eye found us, emerging from deep within the shadows. There was Leo Cantecuzen, leaning heavily on two young soldiers for support, barely limping his way across the killing field. There was Hypatius and Pompeius, bound together by a simple cord, their heads hanging low, their shoulders bowed. And there, at the rear, I cradled Layla's limp body in my arms.

The gulls called their sorrow.

As suddenly as it had begun, it had ended.

As the General led his battered troops from the floor, not a living body was left behind to tell the tale. All thirty thousand traitors had perished. The revolt was finished.

And my Layla, my Layla...

An Empire Reflects

"I WOULD RATHER BE by myself if you don't mind, just for a few moments. Zeno, would you stay with him?"

Zeno nodded quickly as he kept his scarecrow arm wrapped around Leo's broad shoulders, "gladly my dear, most gladly."

Despite Zeno's banter that day his heart wept for Leo as he held him close, attempting to still his friend's tremble with a tight, warm grasp. He had been in the capital for nearly a week now, ostensibly to enquire after me on my father's behalf but in truth he remained there for Leo. As he peered at Leo's pale profile he worried for him - I know he worried for us all.

Leo watched her back recede, longing to follow, longing to comfort but lacking the words. So there he stood, with the help of an old friend, on the edge of Saint Sebastian's cemetery, in the shadow of the Theodosian Wall, observing but not following Julia as she stopped in the midst of the yard and knelt before the crypt that held three ossuaries. Those three contained Leo's father, Leo's mother and their son, Mellius. She had buried them all.

"It has been more than a month my son, more than a month since I last saw you. More than a month since I could hold you close, caress you gently, tell you how much a mother loves her boy.

"Can it be that you left me? Can it be that I can never again look forward to you but only back? The thought haunts me, it crushes me. It is unbearable. It cannot be endured."

Her hair clung to her face, damp with tears as she clutched the marble laurel on the front of the tomb and held it for strength. There was nothing so cruel as the permanence of those letters, carved with conviction, adding punctuation to a death that required none. But just perhaps the mother did, she thought, she yet needed the reminder. The message was simple, composed with care by his father in the days when she could not open her eyes.

Mellius Cantecuzen Broseus. Young man in years, old in wisdom, unparalleled in goodness, much loved, most woefully mourned, lies here.

Julia pressed her fingers to her lips and then returned them to his stone.

"You left me too soon my son. Too soon, when I had so much yet to tell you, so much love left to give. What did you think that day, what possessed you to take such risk when you had so much for which to live. Didn't you think of me for just a moment? Didn't you think of a mother that lived only for you?

"I need your help to understand this thing, to make sense of this bleakness. That you should die on your father's chest, giving your life so that he might live is more than I can bear. You saved his life and there is nothing nobler. But you left me in a world defined by your absence.

"You left me with him.

"I wonder if perhaps somewhere within you knew, that you had divined something from the years of stories I told, from the cast of his brow when you met him, from what you saw in your mother's face. And I wonder, my son, what would you say to me now? How would you advise me today? What is your father to me and what can I be to him in the chasm you left behind. A chasm that can never be filled.

"And yet. And yet..."

◆ ◆ ◆

Across the city, deep within the Palace, Belisarius joined his hands in almost-prayer.

"A thousand battles, truly, I must have fought a thousand battles or more and I've taken more lives than I can count. But this is unique for me, these were Romans. I can't shake it Sire, it weighs on me fiercely."

Justinian paused in contemplation of the wall-spanning map that blanketed his private study. Inlaid with rubies, gold, emeralds and sapphires it captured the world he inherited from his uncle, the Emperor Justin, and in special relief the world that was Rome during the years of Augustus. He drank it in, lingering one last second before turning to Belisarius and beckoning him near.

"Approach General, please join me and sit. Your wounds must still give you pain, please be comfortable."

Belisarius approached as commanded and took the low bench with a visible wince.

"Belisarius of the *Flavii*, you more than anyone have saved my throne. More importantly, most importantly, you preserved our opportunity to do something truly great. You have given us a respite, a second chance that we mustn't forfeit. To that end, it is now time that we turn our focus to Restoration.

"Too long have we been removed from the ground that bore us. Too long have our ears missed the capricious rush of the Tiber. Too long have we missed our great ancestors who tamed the wilds, took civilization to the barbarians, and championed that noble construct of the citizen to the four corners of the earth.

"Has it been sixty years since we lost the Western Empire and the fair city of Rome herself? I say it has been centuries, millennia. Ah, my general and friend, we have been sorely tried and you have carried a lion's share of the burden these past weeks. But let me tell you what I see, what it is that I know.

"The ancient Romans brought light to the darkness. To be sure they did so with a firm hand. Through strong methods, wisdom and conviction our forebears gave the world long centuries of peace and prosperity. We dragged humanity from the swamps and forests. We placed them in warm homes, we brought them water from the mountains through our stout aqueducts, we brought them knowledge through our scholars, access to the Seven Wonders through our highways, art through our masters and equality through our laws. These things defined the Rome of our ancestors; these are the things for which we fight.

"Yet all around us the light begins to dim. Civilization cowers and retreats in the face of barbarians and petty tyrants, born of hellfire, bent on dismantling the earthly paradise our ancestors built.

"It's only a question of time. Darkness descends and the beauty of the Old World, the bequest of the Greeks, Romans, Persians and Egyptians is slowly eclipsed. But I cannot and will not let this happen. For as long as I have breath I'll fight for this, this ideal, this divine light.

"I don't belittle what you suffer Belisarius, far from it, my heart aches with yours that Romans perished at our hands. But there was no other way. This wasn't Rome's first civil war. Since the dawn of time there have been those that would create and those that would destroy. In your courageous act you struck a blow for those that would preserve a world where reason rules, where laws are made and respected, where beauty is elevated, where men are free.

"So cast off that weight, General, your service to Rome isn't over, it begins. Listen carefully and I shall tell you of a new horizon, a mission of mercy."

◆ ◆ ◆

Many miles away in the heart of Thrace, Claudius wiped his hands on a rough cloth and with a smile he couldn't control he opened the door, expecting someone, greeted by another.
Before him stood a strapping soldier of the Imperial guard, helmet held firmly under his arm.

"Claudius Constans?" the giant spoke and Claudius nodded his head in response. "Sir, I come to you with good tidings on behalf of General Belisarius."

Shrugging off his disappointment, Claudius beckoned the visitor inside. "Please, do come in, let me offer you something."

The messenger bowed his head and replied.

"Forgive me Sir but I must leave immediately with many more miles to cover before the day is done. The General sends you his warmest greetings and good tidings. He wishes you to begin the rigging for one hundred new warships to be completed within the year. I have an advance payment here with me. If you accept the General asks that you please begin work immediately."

With that the soldier reached into his saddlebag, strapped to the steed that Claudius noticed only now. From the bag he pulled a roll of parchment and a satchel of soft leather that he handed to Claudius. On the parchment in the Imperial flourish was the official commission. In the jingling satchel was a quantity of gold coins whose heft announced their importance. Claudius didn't count it but thrust it into his tunic.

"Is everything in order Sir? Do you accept the commission?"

My father looked up with a touch of bewilderment on his face.

"Why of course of course yes, all is in order and I accept. Please send my greetings to the General and tell him that I'll get these old bones moving immediately. Now are you certain that I can't offer you anything before you leave?"

The soldier had already sprung into the saddle and his warhorse chomped the bit as he bade Claudius farewell.

"Thank you sir but I'm off. I shall send your regards to the General – be well."

With a sharp whistle and a goad to his horse he was off, leaving Claudius on the doorstep.

◆ ◆ ◆

Back in Constantinople, we gathered in the Throne Room five weeks and five days after the revolt ended.

The Emperor smiled warmly at Belisarius, who stood foremost in the group. Theodora's eyes narrowed as she appraised the man that had saved the throne. If an undercurrent of tension existed at that moment Justinian gave it no heed as he spread his arms wide, cradling the assemblage in his grace. I stood in the back, where Mellius had stood by my side barely a month before.

The Emperor seemed to read my thoughts.

"We are pleased to see so many of those that accompanied us through the Riots. But there are many faces missing as well, many brave men who sacrificed their lives for us. We do not take this lightly. We miss those valiant souls."

Justinian bowed his head, inspiring all in the room to follow suit as we did, willingly, taking a moment to honor them.

"I regret that Severus was killed, I would have preferred to roast him myself. And yet, he was not alone, more must die. Amongst them Pompeius and Hypatius shall die first. There can be no redemption for the brothers, their crimes are too grave to consider clemency but for their families I feel compassion and so, they will be banished but they shall live. The same goes for Severus' family, they have suffered enough."

Whispers snaked through the room as Justinian raised his head and pulled in a mighty breath. His moment was nigh, the power gathered to him and he broke the rising murmurs.

"And so the past is now past and the dead are dead. I will not speak another word of yesterday. I have called you here today to plan the future of our Empire. Together we shall build a new Rome and that process begins now.

"First we will focus our efforts on Constantinople herself where this day you will see an army of masons swarming across the ruins of Constantine's Church of the Holy Wisdom. This is no simple operation to cauterize a wound. Rather, today you can see the first strokes of our campaign to rebuild a more majestic and lasting Constantinople than the one that they took from us. We begin with the heart, and we shall move outwards from there, giving her new organs, beautifying and strengthening her limbs and other defenses. The old Emperor Augustus said that when he claimed the throne his Rome was a city of bricks and that when he left it was a city of marble. I hope to accomplish a similar transformation for Constantinople, our *Nova Roma.*

"And yet, we cannot, we shall not forget the Old Rome. Some sixty years have passed since an Emperor ruled in the West. Some sixty years have passed since the Empire's birthplace fell into the hands of the barbarians and today I have given General Belisarius the task of returning Rome once again into the Imperial fold. The task will not be easy but we will not rest until we once again reign from the Tiber."

Every woman and man in that throne room took a sharp breath that moment, stunned, exhilarated by Caesar's words. I for one held by breath as he continued.

"That is it for now but I assure you that is not all. We have just survived a challenge that threatened to topple the Empire but know this. Before this Emperor leaves the throne, many years hence, he shall do so upon his death. Behind him he shall leave an Empire more worthy of the name. ROME."

PART V: EPILOGUE - THE LAST ROMAN

[I]t is well for one to administer the kingly office which belongs to him and not to make the concerns of others his own. Hence for you also, who have a kingdom, meddling in other's affairs is not just; and if you break the treaty and come against us, we shall oppose you with all our power...

Procopius of Caesarea quote Vandal King Gelimer's letter to Emperor Justinian

SAILING FOR HOME

THE SUN SPLASHED across the cobbled quay, blessing the Seven Hills, dancing on the Bosporus. It was a spectacular spring day, unlike any I had ever seen. But then nothing in our lives would ever be the same after the Riots, every taste was sharper, every breath richer. Even the gulls felt it, shaking off their winter lethargy, circling the Imperial caravans as they snaked towards the fleet that lay restlessly at anchor.

The vast majority of the troops had already boarded. The infantry and cavalry took their plum positions first, followed by the complex of retainers, medics, cooks, engineers and metal-smiths that kept an army in the field. All those that had been with Belisarius at the Battle of the Hippodrome were present along with many more raised for this expedition. Fifteen thousand men and five thousand horses settled into their ships for the first leg of the sea journey.

It was a far cry from the old Roman armies, when Caesars would lead a hundred thousand into the field, but the lack of troops didn't trouble Belisarius. As he told the Emperor during the year-long preparations, he didn't concern himself with sheer numbers but with the quality and flexibility of the troops under his command. Justinian had listened carefully, combing his Empire for the best his Imperial coffers could afford. The result of his efforts now packed the Imperial fleet from stem to stern, waiting for Belisarius to lead them into history.

The sun raced towards the middle of the sky and the sailors that would see the ships safely on their way were eager to depart. The Emperor and Patriarch were expected shortly. A benediction, a blessing, and the quest to restore the Empire of the West would begin.

Close to the flagship, Belisarius turned to me, his newly commissioned Centurion, and asked me to accompany his wife across the harbor.

"She wants to bid her sister farewell and you need to say your own goodbyes. When the Emperor arrives I'll need you by my side."

I saluted Belisarius, took Antonina's arm gently in mine, and together we made our way across the quay. Once we had plunged into the crowds I spotted Leo, Julia, my father and Zeno huddled together on the waterfront. It took some finesse to reach them but not too much, when the good Romans saw my companion they made haste to clear a path.

Normally I would have been irked by the show but on my last day in Constantinople I was grateful for her pace, she wasn't the only one interested in prolonging the moment. Constantinople would forever hold magic for me and I would miss it. This is where I became a man, where I played my small role in the fight to preserve Justinian's crown, where I had found love and where I had suffered loss. It wasn't easy to say goodbye.

◆ ◆ ◆

I had spent much of the last eighteen months meditating on those events, the Riots and the mystery of what happened in the Kathisma. With Leo's help, and his memories, I was finally able to reconstruct the picture of what happened in those final, fateful hours in the Hippodrome that saved Caesar's throne.

— 276 —

"War was my poison, not yours," Leo told me. "And I'd be damned before I let you face that on your own. So as soon as you left the Stables for the Hippodrome I started off. Physically, I knew what I could manage; I knew my limits. That left me with just one small obstacle and that was your Layla. Before I took my first step towards the door she was on top of me, barking in her way.

'Captain Cantecuzen, I know where you're going and you won't get there without me. With a word to the guards I'll make certain you don't get far.'

Leo accepted Layla's bargain because she did, in fact, have the authority to order him confined. They agreed that she would accompany him to the Kathisma entrance and no further.

"She was just…"

Leo explained it over and again and none of it mattered, I knew that he wouldn't have knowingly put Layla in harm's way. But good intentions wouldn't change anything now. The road to hell was paved with good intentions. So yes, Layla joined Leo on the mission to save me and the rest, the rest still haunted me.

According to Leo, he and Layla walked straight out of the Palace, unchallenged, because the Palace guard only cared about the people that entered that day. Anyone foolish enough to leave deserved their fate. So they ambled into the city's chaos with Leo leaning heavily on a cane, and her shoulder, to steady himself. When they reached the Hippodrome it was late in the battle and the mass of fighting men was concentrated far across the field. The only soul they found in the main entrance's innocuous shade was one of Belisarius' scouts. He told them that I had entered the Kathisma well over an hour before but hadn't exited.

Layla listened carefully, looked Leo bluntly in the face and told him that it was time to renegotiate.

'I won't be bound by little promises on this day of all days, the circumstances have changed.'

Leo didn't have the strength or time to return her to the Palace so he agreed. Together they scaled the Kathisma's back staircase and found the bodies of Stilicho and his valiant troops at the top. There was no immediate sign of '*the boy*' amidst the gore but with patience and a sharp eye, Leo found my footprints tracked in the blood. They lead to the Kathisma door and ended there.

"It was dangerous but I would protect her - I saw no imminent threat," Leo told me.

He had protected Emperors in his day and could certainly protect Layla. Standing before that daunting Kathisma barricade, Leo hatched his final plan. With Layla's help he would have a chance, a single chance to improvise a rescue.

So Layla struck the door.

The bolt ground open and she prepared to dash out of the way so that Leo, who clung to the wall for support, could catapult himself inside. The plan was rudimentary but reasonable and might just have succeeded if Leo hadn't positioned himself so close to the door.

As Severus approached Layla he saw Leo - too late to avoid the ambush but not too late to kill her for impudence. That would have been the beginning and end of the tragedy if it weren't for the scrap of metal.

I am speaking of course of Scipio's medallion. Layla had agreed to hold it for me during the battle and she hung it around her neck to keep it safe. That same scrap sat above her heart when Severus' blade pierced her tunic. And when the dagger's tip struck Scipio's ancient gold it glanced aside, across her chest, away from her heart.

For that, Layla Leonides survived the Kathisma siege, she lived. But she wouldn't remain in my world for long.

A month after the Riots, Layla and her father returned to Alexandria for a prolonged sabbatical. He claimed that his mother was dying but the reason was immaterial; the fact was that she was leaving me.

In her last month I saw her several times but she was always accompanied by her father. I told Leo that I wanted to steal her away. He smiled at me, his only smile in those terrible days, and he told me that if it were meant to be our time would come. I didn't think he could possibly understand.

We did sneak one solitary moment together little more than a week after the Riots. Leo's wounds needed attention and Layla volunteered to visit him at home. Leontius must have objected but he was so busy tending to the aftermath in the Palace he couldn't go himself. Whatever else he might have been, Leontius was truly committed to the lives and well being of his patients. So Layla visited us – I had not yet moved into the military barracks where I would spend most of the next year so I was also there.

She knocked and I raced downstairs to open the door, leaving Julia and Leo upstairs. My heart slammed into my ribs, I knew it was she before the door opened. That was truly the greatest moment in my life, not to be surpassed until you, my children, were born.

Layla threw herself into my arms and I twirled with her until we had left the earth behind. This time I kissed her and she buried her face in my shoulder. No word was said, nothing was needed, nothing, just time. Her heart said the same. It sounds preposterous but it is my truest truth, our hearts spoke. That is when I knew that she did truly love me as I loved her.

Julia called. She needed my help moving Leo. Layla and I ascended together. Leontius arrived moments later to check Leo's wounds or to check on me. Did I imagine his animosity? I think not. The reality is that two weeks from the day I watched Leontius and Layla board an Imperial grain ship bound for Alexandria. With that they were gone.

Three hundred and eighty two days later I stepped onto the Quay, finally ready for my own journey. Three hundred and eighty two days had passed since I last saw her and not a word, not a letter not a single line had she sent.

◆ ◆ ◆

My family is an odd lot. The Quay was littered with families that day but none looked quite like mine. There was handsome Julia, positively intimidating Leo, Zeno the Aristotle impersonator and my father, the Rope Maker. I was overjoyed to see them all but especially my father. Each reunion with him was the same, memorable and wholly inadequate.

He looked well, lean and alert as he scanned the crowd for me. When he spotted me, before anyone else, he stepped forward to greet me. I saw Julia hold Leo back so that my father might have his moment.

Claudius' arms were strong as his rope and when he wrapped them about me he wrung the breath from me. He smelled like his workshop, like home. I returned the embrace, trying not to imagine how few of these moments remained.

When my father finished squeezing he grabbed both my shoulders and examined me. I had become a handsome man, he said. My mother would have been so very proud, he said. And my tears came. Even his dry voice broke when he soothed me, reassuring me still.

"You are everything she could have hoped for, Valentinian. Everything. Simply promise me that you'll be safe. Return to me son because I'll be waiting for you."

All across the quay, officers took leave of their wives, mothers, fathers, children, not knowing if they would ever return.

"Papa."

A small boy next to me refused to release his father's fingers. His mother wept as she tried to gently pry him away.

"Papa."

The father's face expressed such profound love for his child, battling such exquisite pain. It sounds perverse but I envied his pain. For the first time in my life I thought I might like to be a father too.

"Julia, my sister I love you dearly."

Just a step away the two sisters embraced warmly, no longer separated by that extreme tension. How could such terrible events bring catharsis? Over a year later I was still surprised by the unmitigated good that emerged from the Riots.

"I could do nothing other than follow my husband to the ends of the earth, but it pains me to leave you. We need each other, you and I, we need each other and I hope that we aren't separated for long. And yet, we go in service of the Emperor and I go willingly, proudly."

Leo and Zeno approached my father and me. Leo extended his hand in greeting but a jumpy Zeno reached me first.

"My boy, I wish you would reconsider. You have just as much intellect in you as you have brawn, I daresay you have more. If you would only recuse yourself from this war, delicately as you know how, we could go on an adventure of our own. Of course Claudius you are invited to join us. First we'd visit Athens where my university friends would celebrate our arrival as if we were Plato himself. From there we would cross Persia in a style that only the King of

Kings knows, for many there remember me kindly. And then, per-haps we'd go to Alexandria, to the great library where there is so much to see. And then, and then..."

Zeno spoke about the future but he sounded like yesterday's man. I think he realized it because he stopped short. Putting on a brave face, wrapped his arms quickly about me, my father and Leo in turn and then he was gone, carried quickly on his spindly legs into the gathering throng. After all, he too had his horizons.

In Zeno's wake, Leo extended his hand once again and I responded in kind, grasping it firmly, testing Leo's grip, finding it strong as stone.

"Leo, I don't know if I ever told you, but to me you have always been..."

Leo placed his free hand flat on my chest.

"My boy, there's no need. Since the day I joined your household I considered you my son," and then, with a nod to my father, he added "my shared son." Leo's throat scratched and he searched for something more but that was the heart of it really, everything else was a detail.

"Boy, those horns announce the Emperor's arrival but there are a few last things you should know so listen to me very carefully. Keep your own counsel, Valentinian, embrace your comrades but maintain your distance. Mind your General but remember that he answers to an Emperor that no matter how benign, rules for an Empire, not for any single man. And finally, remember that there is no glory in battle, there is no glory in death. War is a regrettable necessity. Surviving with dignity, returning to comfort those for whom you fight, this is the hallmark of a man amongst men."

I struggled for words but none came, and when I finally found my tongue it was too late for there was Belisarius, stepping through the crowd.

The General presented himself with a salute that Leo returned with a sharper edge.

"Claudius Constans, an honor sir. You should be proud of your son. He has turned into a fine soldier who, I assure you, will not leave my side. And I thank you for your hard work on the rigging, we will think of you as we sail."

My father clasped the General's forearm in the ancient manner.

"General Belisarius, you honor me with the kindness you have shown my boy. But I will hold you to your promise, General, keep an eye on him. And the rigging, the rigging is my job for which you paid me my fee."

Belisarius smiled, he understood my father.

"Claudius, I will indeed keep an eye on him. That is precisely why I have made him my valet."

Needless to say that was the first I heard of this honor. The post of valet to a commanding Roman General was always filled by highly decorated, career officers. I was stunned. Fortunately I didn't have time to discuss the offer because the General had turned to Leo with a sharp salute.

"Commander Cantecuzen, it does my heart good to see you. If Justinian hadn't given you the Excubitors, I would have convinced you to join me." And then, as he caught sight of his wife speaking with Julia, he added, "but then, I suppose, that there does come a time in life when more important things than battle sway the heart. So be it, you are a good man Leo, and it has been my great pleasure to make your acquaintance this last year and some. I wish you happiness and peace for your deserve that and more. Now, if you will please excuse me, our Emperor approaches. Centurion Valentinian Constans, it's time for us to make our way to the flagship."

I threw my arms about Leo one final time and searched for solemn words. He would have none of my melodrama. Clapping me so roughly on my back that he forced a cough, Leo filled the silence.

"It is time for you, all is said and all is known. Now listen to your General and be gone."

Thrusting me away, Leo grasped Belisarius' arm, looked fiercely into his eyes, and bid him, "the blessings of the gods, old and new." Turning then before the General could respond Leo strode into the throng whose excitement had reached a fever pitch as the Emperor moved amongst them.

That left my father.

But before I could offer him the emotion I felt, before I could show him the depths of my sadness, he laid a rough, hard hand on my cheek.

"Just come home son, you can tell me everything when you come home."

◆ ◆ ◆

Justinian took the Empress Theodora by the hand and together they ascended the steps of the reviewing platform.

Ever conscious of the power in small gestures they remained standing in front of their elaborate thrones, facing their subjects as the platform below filled with those that mattered most.

The Patriarch took his place first, accompanied by two senior clerics. One waved a gold incense burner, spreading sweet musk through the harbor's salt air. The second sprinkled holy water as far as his frail arm would carry, intoning blessings as he went.

Belisarius followed directly, eschewing ceremony, with Mundus and me on his heels. We took our positions quietly, alongside the holy men. The men of God and the men of war touched shoulders and waited for the sign.

The Emperor and Empress sat then and when it was certain, the rest of us also sat on the low benches arranged at Justinian's feet. The Patriarch alone remained standing and after making the sign of the cross he turned, and kneeling before the Emperor he spoke in a voice that carried to the far edges of the crowd.

"Mighty Justinian, may God bless your endeavor, may Rome be returned to the fold and may we never forget that we are here only by his grace."

Justinian stood then, spreading his arms wide to encompass the citizens that crowded the quay before him and the warriors that crowded the ships behind him. Acknowledging us all he raised his arms further till they stretched before him, palms up, pointing off into the distance. And then, as the crowd's rumble cut to a whisper, the Emperor angled his chin ever so slightly and spoke a single word.

"ROME."

The multitude, prelates, warriors and citizens all raised their voices in unison, shouting their response with one interminable, mingled breath - "*ROME*".

Their shout did not flag and did not waiver.

It held its pitch, melding with the Patriarch's heavy incense, spreading out across the still Bosporus waters till it blended with the current. Their cry washed the stones, it scoured the sky and it drove the gulls higher in their orbit. It was a cry for restoration of what once was, a cry for deliverance.

Justinian raised his hands higher above his head and the crowd responded in kind, lifting their call more sweetly. The children of Rome spoke to him and Justinian, their Emperor, allowed his smile to spread unchecked. Closing his eyes then for what seemed an eternity he listened to them and the wild beat of his own heart.

It begins now. It begins...

◆ ◆ ◆

TO BE CONTINUED

Continue reading for an excerpt from

<u>**"AVENGING AFRICANUS", BOOK II**</u>

EXCERPT FROM VOL. II
"AVENGING AFRICANUS"

A dreadful rumor reaches us from the West. Rome is occupied. My voice chokes with sobs as I dictate these words. The city that has conquered the universe is now herself conquered...

- St. Jerome, Letter cxxvii

The Fourteenth Day Of June, 455CE

(86 Years Before Justinian's Reign)

"THE EMPEROR IS dead!"

Wretched night, choked with incense, scorched with fire. Within the City, Romans wept. It was the End of Days.

A task had been given to Marius, last of the Pincii, last to occupy the old palace on the hill, last of his clan to preside over the Senate. The last to care. A part of him thrilled that the rest had fled, that the honor was his. His voice rang distant and noble. The words issued spontaneous and true.

Words had always been his gift.

"Petronius Maximus has been murdered on the road to Ravenna. The Usurper is dead! May crows feast on his carcass."

Wails burst from a few senators and other luminaries that had sought shelter in the Fortress. There was no love lost for Petronius, but the death of an Emperor, even that of an usurper, brought tumult.

That night, as fires raged and the barbarians' numbers swelled, the Western Empire teetered on the edge of chaos. It was not spoken. The reality was too terrible to bear. But it was the end, all present knew it - their blood and the blood of their families would soon flow.

As the shriller edge of hysteria ran its course, the small group sought quiet, insufficient comfort in each other's presence. Their families had been friends for centuries - their ancestors' names littered the history books. And as they were together at the beginning so too would they greet the Apocalypse together.

So they muffled their tears and waited, listening to the ghastly din that rose from the Field of Mars below. What hope remained rested on the narrow shoulders of an old man from whom no more could be expected. No man could doubt that the frail octogenarian who intended to reason with the monsters was truly a man of God, a patriot, and certainly lunatic. Walking to the edge of the battlements, Marius looked down at the sea of fire and watched the Pope enter the barbarian camp.

Hell itself could not be so terrifying.

◆ ◆ ◆

"Is it not peculiar that the tomb of a man that fed our kind to the lions should provide us succor in our moment of peril?" The Pope spoke of the Emperor Hadrian's tomb that they had just left behind, the last secure place left in the City. Hadrian's antipathy to the Christians was well known but here too lay proof that not even Caesar could escape Christ in death.

"Yes your Holiness, it is your Holiness. But your Holiness, what will you tell them? How can you possibly influence them when we have no army, we have no sovereign and we have no gold to buy our safety?"

"Ignatius my child, I believe it best you stay here. The walk is a short one and I shall not traverse the ground alone, the Holy Spirit guides me and girds me. Hand me my cane now and stand clear."

Touching his silk clad foot to the granite floor of the Tomb's central keep, Pope Leo accepted the staff of hard ash that he preferred over the golden paraphernalia of his predecessor. He was no Emperor and did not pretend to be. He was the Bishop of Rome, the first amongst equals, and after Petronius' just murder, Leo was the most senior official left in the capital. So he would parlay with the beasts that were, after all, still the children of God.

"Open the gates please, I am ready."

"Your Excellency, let us send a small guard with you, you cannot be there defenseless."

"Open the door and step aside."

Dressed in white from head to toe with the single heavy gold crucifix draped from his thin neck, Pope Leo I stepped into the bloody glow of the watch-fires and crossed the open ground. On the other side of the Tomb lay the Tiber River. Beyond the Tiber lay the Wall. And behind the Wall cowered his flock of five hundred thousand Roman souls, waiting for Leo to deliver them.

A black shape, silhouetted in flames, stood on the edge of the Vandal camp. The shadow belonged to a man, armor-clad, massive, still. Though Leo could see nothing of his face he knew him to be Gaiseric, King of the Vandals and Alans, Arian heretic, scourge.

Behind him Leo heard the doors to the Fortress close as instructed.

"Bring a torch, quickly now." Grinding his leather boot into the dirt, King Gaiseric, the 'Spear King', son of Godigisel, brother of Gunderic, leader of the Hasdling Vandals, looked past the white priest to the marble and bronze barrel that hulked beside the river.

Gaiseric admired the man - Hadrian - that had led the Empire before it lost its way, a man that knew the use of power. Absolute power could only be understood viscerally. Acquired through

blood and betrayal. Maintained with wisdom, paranoia and cru-
elty. In short, the power so long sought was a curse once understood, too late. Yet, this exquisite thing that Gaiseric had carved
from dust, from blood, from desperation, that thing had no equal
on this earth. And the man, the god who built the mausoleum that
loomed above him most certainly understood that.

A tomb befitting a king.

His senses alive, on the cusp of a triumph that his father could
never have imagined, Gaiseric felt the dry heat of torches in the
dark space between pontiff and King.

"Bishop Leo, welcome to my camp."

"Peace be with you Gaiseric, rightful Kind of the Vandals and
Alans, recognized ruler of Carthage and the Roman lands of Libya,
vassal to the Roman Emperor. Peace be with you."

"Why does Caesar send a man of God to speak with a King?
Where is the Emperor, is he too feeble to meet me on the eve of
war?"

"King Gaiseric. I wish it were not so, and that this old man
was not the protector of this place. But the Emperor Valentinian
III was murdered months ago, and the murderer himself, the false
Emperor Petronius, died this day. That is why the People of Rome
have sent a humble cleric to speak with the Great King."

All of this was known to Gaiseric. His spies had followed
Petronius' flight. They had found the place where the coward was
felled on the Via Appenina, left to rot in the gutter. The spies said
most of the wealthy Romans had fled the City, leaving the simple
men to suffer alone. A part of Gaiseric felt sympathetic towards
those that cowered behind these walls, and for the relic that stood
unbowed before him. Yet that honest emotion would not deter him.

"Please sit, your Holiness, you must be tired."

"There will be time for my bones to rest before long - my days on this earth are counted. I shall stand, for what I have to say is short."

Even the old man is arrogant. It did not surprise. Nothing about them surprised. They were known. Gaiseric had spent a lifetime battling, menacing, admiring and negotiating with Romans, using every device at his disposal to ensure the survival of his race under the boot of the Roman war machine, the Roman law, the culture to which every tribe that came out of the North aspired.

"Very well Bishop, speak your piece for I desire to sleep well this night before I take possession of your Eternal City."

"King Gaiseric. Three years ago I stood before Attila, King of the Huns just as I stand before you now. And I said to him, as I say to you great King, please leave this sacred City and her people untouched. The mighty Lord that is the father to all creatures, great and small, watches over the City of Rome, center of the world. All that have menaced her have soon perished as Alaric, King of the Visigoths did shortly after he raised a hand against us. As Attila the Hun himself did, months after he led his army to these very gates. I shudder to think that this may happen to so great a king as yourself, mighty Gaiseric."

Gaiseric clutched his long blond beard that swallowed the torches' tendrils, and let loose a bellow. Legs stretched before him, he plucked his sword from the scabbard and stabbed it into the earth. Wrapping his hands around the hilt, he studied the Pope's pale face.

"Your concern is touching, holy Leo! Little did I know that I had such an admirer in the spiritual leader of the Romans. So let me put your concern to rest. I am eternal, Leo. These bones were set in Hell, my blood is ice, my heart is fire, and my teeth belong to a wolf, sharp as daggers to rend Roman meat from the bone. Now I will explain to you why I will not, cannot leave this place."

"Great King. I understand that you have incurred great expense to make this journey. We have little in the way of riches left, you know that. These last years have been a trying time for my people, but the Church can make a donation of gold to you."

"You are not listening to me Leo. Tomorrow I will lay siege to your city as is my right. Your Emperor Valentinian III promised the hand of his daughter to my son, Huneric. When Valentinian was murdered and she was married to another a sacred treaty between our peoples was broken. Even then I understood that this wasn't of Valentinian's doing, he was many things but he was noble and a man of his word. But when his widow, the Empress, sent me an urgent communication asking me to save her and the Western Empire from the clutches of Petronius it was my duty as the humble vassal that I am to respond to her cries for help. And so I have responded as you can see. The Vandal army is here to restore order and to insist that the treaty of Valentinian III be respected. My Huneric will marry the rightful Emperor's daughter."

"Thank you Great King but as I have told you, the usurper Petronius is no longer. Empress Eudoxia no longer needs your strong arm to vanquish her husband's killer and as you must know..."

"Pope Leo. I grow weary of dialog. Please return to your people and tell them to prepare for war, a war that will not end until I starve this city into submission and her gates are opened to my men after which I cannot promise what fate will befall your men, your women, your children. My warriors are great and true but they are men of course."

Leo closed his eyes and felt the fatigue deep within his bones. This path he had trod strung out before him, the delicate thread of his life, from the kitchen of his mother where a precocious child played underfoot, to apprenticeship at father's elbow, his rise within the clergy, the friendship with the young Emperor Valentinian

who made certain that the Bishop of Rome was truly primus in-
ter pares. And alongside the thread of his life he saw that of the
divinely inspired Roman civilization. Yet the thread that began
gold and strong, frayed and darkened over the years until the two
threads converged, here, in this place that had provided succor to
his people since the dawn of time, facing a monster determined to
extinguish the light.

And yet it was not too late, he would do what he could to spare
his children the worst of what would come.

"Good Gaiseric. Great Gaiseric. Benevolent Gaiseric. If we
were to open the gates to you, Great King, what then? If we did
not battle but invited you to enter in peace, alone..."

"I will enter with my army. Or it will be war."

"You will enter with your army, but in peace?"

"Of yes, assuredly, I shall enter with my army in peace."

"And you will guarantee the safety of the Romans? No rape,
no murder?"

A broad smile spread across King Gaiseric's face and beneath
the beard Leo was certain he could see the flash of the King's brilliantly white teeth, sharp as daggers...

For fourteen days and fourteen nights the army of ten thousand
Vandals plundered the City. What was left of the Imperial Treasury
was pilfered. Churches were stripped of silver and gold. Many
thousand statues were torn from their pedestals. Private homes
were ransacked. The touchstone of the city, the Temple of Jupiter
Capitolinus, lost its copper and gold roof that had cost Domitian
three hundred and eighty seven tons of gold to create. Even the
minor pagan temples that were maintained out of deference to
the past were emptied, including the Temple of Peace adjacent to
the Flavian Amphitheatre that had housed the storied and grand

Treasure taken from Herod's Temple in Jerusalem for the last four hundred years.

When they were satiated, when they could take nothing else, King Gaiseric loaded the Vandal ships of war at anchor in the Tiber with the City's riches. Gaiseric did what he could to minimize the murder of men and the violation of women and children - in that carnal sense the first sack of Rome by the Visigoth's under King Alaric had been more brutal. But the Vandal sack was more calculated, complete and irreversible.

As they prepared to leave, it was clear to the Left Behind that the City would never again be what it was. Not only did Gaiseric take what wealth the City had left, they took Rome's most prominent citizens as hostages, several senators, dozens of the most skilled craftsmen and engineers, as well as the Empress Licinia Eudoxia, Valentinian's widow, and her two daughters, Eudocia and Placidia.

On June 14th 455, the ships floated west to the sea, into history.

TO BE CONTINUED

In Volume II of the Legend of Africanus trilogy, Avenging Africanus and Volume III, Immortal Africanus available at:

www.amazon.com/author/matthewjstorm

The Author would be most grateful if you would take a moment and leave a brief review on Amazon or Goodreads.com.

BIBLIOGRAPHY

"Scipio Africanus, Greater than Napoleon"; B.H. Liddell Hart; March 2004; Da Capo Press

"Byzantium: The Early Centuries"; John Julius Norwich; March 1989; Knopf

"A Short History of Byzantium"; John Julius Norwich; December 1998, Vintage

"The Cambridge Companion to the Age of Justinian"; Michael Maas

"The Secret History"; Procopius; December 2007, Penguin Classics

"History of the Wars, Books I & II, The Persian Wars"; Procopius; May 2007; Cosimo Classics

"History of the Wars, Books III & IV, The Vandalic Wars"; Procopius; April 2007; BiblioBazaar

"History of the Wars, Books V & VI, The Gothic Wars"; Procopius; June 2007; Cosimo Classics

"Byzantium, The Empire of New Rome"; Cyril Mango

"Justinian, The Last Roman Emperor"; G.P. Baker

"The Age of Justinian, the Circumstances of Imperial Power": J.A.S Evans

"History of the Later Roman Empire"; JB Bury

M ATTHEW JORDAN STORM is the author of the Legend of
 Africanus trilogy available at www.amazon.com/author/
matthewjstorm (and also muses on related topics in his blog at mat-
thewjordanstorm.com).

Mr. Storm was born in New York City and was raised in a small
town in Connecticut. The Author is a history addict, raised in a
family of similarly inclined nuts. If he had more time and aptitude

he would have become an archaeologist or historian but given the constraints of work, fatherhood, marriage, gardening, etc., he poured his passion into writing historical fiction instead. For him it has always been about Rome, ever since he was a little boy. But the more he studied, and the more he traveled, the more fascinated he become with the history of the Empire when the darkness began to fall, and Caesar ruled from the Bosporus.

Made in the USA
Columbia, SC
16 April 2024

34481785R00200